Praise for *The Heroines*

"Quirky: adolescent angst meets metaphysics, screwball-comedy trysts with the underpinnings of reality. It's funny and tender; it's a chance to see Scarlett O'Hara and Emma Bovary off duty."

—Audrey Niffenegger, author of *The Time Traveler's Wife*

"A beguiling literary debut."

—*Good Housekeeping*

"A novel about being quite literally caught up in the world of literary fiction . . . a good yarn."

—*Chicago Sun-Times*

"This clever, charming debut is a must-read for literature lovers."

—*Booklist*

"Favorite offers a fun take on the impact literature can have on our lives."

—*Publishers Weekly*

"An interesting take on the impact of literature, a bit of fantasy, a hint of romance, and a coming-of-age story, [*The Heroines*] is a bookworm's dream come true that will appeal to both teens and adults."

—*Parkersburg News and Sentinel*

"Fact and fiction delightfully collide in this fast-paced read."

—*Redbook*

"Imaginative . . . plenty of fun."

—*Kirkus Reviews*

"Delightful."

—*Chicago Tribune*

"An intelligent understanding of literature [and] feminism . . . Favorite handles drastic plot twists impressively. . . . Funny and energetic."

—*Library Journal*

The Heroines

✣ A NOVEL ✣

EILEEN FAVORITE

Scribner

New York London Toronto Sydney

SCRIBNER
A Division of Simon & Schuster, Inc.
1230 Avenue of the Americas
New York, NY 10020

Copyright © 2008 by Eileen Favorite

First Scribner trade paperback edition February 2009

SCRIBNER and design are registered trademarks of
The Gale Group, Inc., used under license
by Simon & Schuster, Inc., the publisher of this work.

For information about special discounts for bulk purchases,
please contact Simon & Schuster Special Sales:
1-800-456-6798 or business@simonandschuster.com.

DESIGNED BY KYOKO WATANABE
Text set in Garamond 3

Manufactured in the United States of America

1   3   5   7   9   10   8   6   4   2

Library of Congress Control Number: 2007005170

ISBN-13: 978-1-4165-4810-2
ISBN-10: 1-4165-4810-6
ISBN-13: 978-1-4165-4811-9 (pbk)
ISBN-10: 1-4165-4811-4 (pbk)

For Martin and Lucille

Alas, if the heroine of one novel be not patronized by the heroine of another, from whom can she expect protection and regard?
—JANE AUSTEN, *Northanger Abbey*

It was undemocratic to compel characters to be uniformly good or bad or poor or rich. Each should be allowed a private life, self-determination, and a decent standard of living.
—FLANN O'BRIEN, *At Swim-Two-Birds*

Contents

Contents

Contents

PART II

The Unit

Contents

Contents

Contents

PART I

+

The Woods

CHAPTER I

✧ *The sorrows of delayed pubescence* ✧
Annoyance with Deirdre ✧ *Girlish fantasies* ✧
Appearance of the Villain ✧

I was so angry with Mother! I stormed down the prairie trail,
flip-flops slapping my heels. Walking the mown path through
the fifty-acre prairie was the only way to cool my head. Hell hath no
fury like a pissed-off thirteen-year-old girl, especially a late bloomer,
impatient for her body's transformation. I was pigtailed, knobby-
kneed, and flat-chested, thirteen, but physically more like ten.

Retreating to the woods was an act of rebellion. My mother had
forbidden me to go there at night, so I could hardly wait to get
through the prairie and reach the dark and leafy trails. The sun was
dropping behind the trees, and the cicadas rattled like electric
maracas. The prairie grasses and wildflowers reached my shoulders,
the flora so thick even someone as furious as I wouldn't dream of
walking through it. I stuck to the path. Out on the prairie, the temperature dropped by five degrees, but it was still muggy. The noise
from Route 41 sounded louder at night, cutting through the woods
and across the power lines. A far-off motorcycle gunned it, probably passing another car. The engine whined, built up steam, then
faded away. The sound of impatience. And escape. I could relate. An

M-80 boomed. You heard them less frequently as the July days marched past the Fourth, but then one would boom on the twentieth. Boom! Somebody out there just couldn't stop.

I couldn't stop either. The scent of clover, the *chicka-chick* of some odd bird. Mother had gone too far with Deirdre this time, and I couldn't stand it. I wished Deirdre would move on! Find some other bed-and-breakfast to colonize. Though *colonize* wouldn't have been my word at thirteen. Back then, I probably would have said, *Move your butt down the road, girlie!* Constant coverage of the Watergate trials and Deirdre were hard rivals for Mother's attention, which I craved in a classic pubescent way. I longed for motherly fussing precisely when my mother wouldn't give it; and I cringed when she touched my hair or asked how I was doing when I had a perfectly marvelous funk going. Her timing always seemed to be off.

But tonight Mother had gone too far. The weeping Irish girl had moaned so much that another boarder had complained, so Mother had given her the farthest room away from him: my room. My sanctuary with the dormer windows and peerless cross-breezes! And Mother hadn't even asked if I would mind. Even though three other rooms were empty, she volunteered my room, as if it were hers to give. I had spent the summer modifying the posters and pillows to my new tastes: my growing collection of Zeppelin albums, my purple beanbag chair. All bought with money from chores. Now I had to relinquish it to a pouty Irish girl who possessed everything I craved for myself: flowing blond hair, angelic skin, perfect curves. I would be stuck on a mat in the musty cupola with the dead horseflies and cobwebs. Unlike some boarders who came for a week or two, Deirdre hadn't specified her departure date. I could be trapped in the cupola for a month. I looked across the prairie at the fireflies flickering in the weeds. Maybe I'd camp in the woods.

Humidity blurred the peach half-moon. I usually took this walk earlier, but the weeping Deirdre had monopolized Mother, and I'd had to clean the whole kitchen myself. While I swept the remnants of our cook Gretta's potato salad and sauerbraten into the waste pail, Mother and Deirdre sipped ginger ale in the dining room, and Deirdre blathered about some boyfriend of hers who died. Gretta had the evening off, and Mother wasn't budging, so I had to rush to stack the plates and wipe clean the counters and sweep the great linoleum floor.

I swatted my arm and hurried through the woods toward the pond where a great blue heron I had named Horace lingered at sunset. I always tried to spot Horace before he detected me, but he took flight at the snap of a twig, unfolding his six-foot wingspan and gliding across the murky water. It was getting late. I had missed him tonight and it was no accident. It was Mother's fault. And Deirdre's too.

The residual buzz from a joint I'd smoked that afternoon with my neighbor Albie tilted my senses. Albert Gallagher was fifteen, a longtime nerd who'd recently morphed into a stoner. I wasn't a particularly capable joint smoker, and after a couple tokes, I noticed how the birds suddenly seemed to be having genuine conversations. I could deal with the whole alternate reality of the sound of the creek, but gawky and pimpled Albie was another story. He smiled at me too widely, his braces glinting, and I saw the chemistry-set dork of yesteryear. He had to be pretty desperate to hang out with me. I was not one of those thirteen-going-on-twenty-two type of girls. But I was grateful for his companionship in the summertime especially, and Mother hadn't really acknowledged that he wasn't the innocent boy he used to be. Her vigilance had waned precisely when it should have sharpened. She knew that Albie and I "took hikes" in the afternoons, but she had no clue about my nighttime excursions alone in the woods.

The woods at night had always been a forbidden zone, and up until a few months before, I'd always steered clear of them after dark. Mother never said precisely why I shouldn't go into them, and as my irritability with her increased, so did my desire to venture farther into the woods. I was growing beyond Mother's constant surveillance, and with every nightly walk through the woods that passed without incident, I became emboldened, venturing farther and farther into the dark.

A mosquito whined in my ear, and I swatted it, first calmly, then spastically. Between the black branches the sky was gray. I ran across a short extension bridge, making the chains and planks rattle like hell, then I flew into another small prairie. The sudden appearance of a Tudor mansion shifted everything. At this point in my daily stroll I always slowed down. I trailed my fingers along the flowers, suddenly elegant, suddenly cool. I pulled the rubber bands out of my hair and let my curly red hair hang. I imagined a handsome hero, half hidden by a velvet curtain, watching my pensive walk through the prairie and asking himself, *Who might that creature be?* I envisioned a future where every night I descended a spiral staircase, a butler handed me a champagne flute, and my dashing husband and I tangoed across the living room. Back then, I had no doubt that my life would have a happy ending.

After the second prairie, I wound up back in the dark woods. It was later, and therefore darker than I'd ever seen before. I turned onto a bridle path and heard something scamper through the fallen leaves. The cicadas' rattle grew louder, then suddenly stopped, as if warning me. A flame of fear blazed through my body; an animal, evil men, something was lurking and watching me from the dark corners of the woods. Two acorns thunked to the ground. Then I heard beating hooves behind me. I jumped off the path and pushed far into the brambles, swearing that I would never disobey my mother again. The scratchy, moist brush felt like a giant, thorny spider web, and mosquitoes immediately started to feast on my exposed skin. I turned back to look at the path.

I saw the silhouette of a man with billowing hair riding a horse at full gallop. Wood chips flew into the air behind him. In one hand he held the bridle, and in the other a flaming torch of such orange fire, I could scarcely believe it was earthly. I squeezed my eyes shut and pressed against a tree trunk, praying he wouldn't see me, and wondering if this was why Mother had warned me to avoid the woods at night.

"Where is she?" he roared.

The horse skidded to a halt, and he waved the torch into the trees, turning them from black to flickering gold. My fingers trembled, and it took every ounce of strength not to wet my pants. He held the torch high, next to his face, and I saw his muttonchop side-whiskers, his thick beard. He peered down his long, sharp nose, then tilted the torch so it shone in my face. I crossed my legs and hugged myself.

"Where is Deirdre?" he shouted.

It suddenly dawned on me that this girl I'd been fighting with and hating and wishing would go away was a genuine Heroine. Boring Deirdre was one of them; even Mother hadn't guessed. Never before had a man leapt from the pages of a book to recapture a Heroine. Deirdre was so depressed—crying all the time and monopolizing Mother's attention—she must have come from some awful romance. Only a cheap book would have binding too weak to hold back a stereotype like this guy. All of this flashed through my mind while my body trembled with terror. For, whatever the plot line, however base the literary merit, this guy and his torch were close enough to set the tree on fire.

CHAPTER 2

+ *My bastardy* + *The secrets of the Prairie*
Homestead + *I question the fate of Heroines* +
Mother-daughter tensions with a twist +

W here I was raised is the first, most important thing to know about me, more important than knowing why Deirdre angered me so, or that my name is Penny, which I despised (but grew to love). Where I grew up explains why I've had such a checkered career with both men and jobs. I grew up in an unreal place, a house not of horrors, but of magic, my mother's bed-and-breakfast in Prairie Bluff, Illinois. But before I recount that summer when my estrangement from Mother peaked, the summer of 1974, when the first U.S. president resigned from office, I must emphasize that my younger years were happy. I grew up in a large, lovely home with acres of land to roam, with kittens and gardens and a bedroom of my own with pale pink walls. Mother sent me to theater camps at Prairie College starting at an early age. Like any girl I believed my mother was powerful and beautiful. She was only eighteen when she had me, in 1961. My father, so I'd been told, was a football player from Lincoln Park High who died in a car accident on I-94 in 1964. He had never seen me, as my mother never told him I was his. They never married. Whenever I asked where my dad was, she always said, "In heaven," which I pictured in the usual way: clouds, harps, happiness.

As I was growing up, the house seemed more significant than my father's identity. My great-grandfather built it in the 1890s. He grew corn and soybeans, kept chickens and cows. At the turn of the century, an industrialist offered him a huge sum of money for the farmland, which he returned to prairie. He gave our family "strolling rights" into perpetuity. He built a large Arts and Crafts summer residence for his family. My great-grandfather kept the farmhouse as a summer home, and moved his family south to the city—Chicago—where he invested in residential real estate, snapping up apartment complexes and three flats on the south and west sides of the city. Eventually he bought back the Arts and Crafts summerhouse, which had fallen into disrepair after the industrialist died, as his family had no interest in the property. My great-grandmother soon restored it to its original grandeur.

As a girl, my mother, Anne-Marie, spent her summers in Prairie Bluff. Before she started to "show," Grandfather Entwhistle shipped her here from Lincoln Park to have the baby in seclusion. That was a year before the full thrust of black migration and white flight bottomed out the Chicago real estate market, rendering Grandfather nearly broke. My grandparents pressured Mother to give me up and had found a couple to adopt me, but once Mother held me she said she couldn't let me go. This was her first act of defiance against her own mother, who, I later learned, actually tried to forge her daughter's signature on the adoption papers. My grandfather caught Grandmother red-handed, paying off a secretary in the obstetrician's office.

When my grandfather finally accepted that his baby girl had chosen to raise her own, he let her stay in Prairie Bluff with me. With the Chicago housing market tanking, they couldn't afford the house's upkeep without additional income, so they decided to convert it into a bed-and-breakfast. They installed a front desk in the foyer complete with a bell and register. Mother liked the idea of running a B&B and she named it Prairie Homestead, which always had the ring of a lunatic asylum to me. And in some ways, it was. Though plenty of ordinary women lodged at our place while I was growing up, the Homestead seemed to have a special attraction for Heroines who needed a break from their story lines. Madame Bovary had dozed in the hammock for three weeks after Rodolphe abandoned her. Penelope had sipped our curried lentil soup while she waited for Odysseus. Daisy Buchanan took endless baths after running over Myrtle Wilson. My mother had always been a reader, hooked on *The Secret Garden* and *The Princess and the Pea* at the age of seven. She knew exactly how these women's stories would end, but she behaved as if she hadn't any idea. In the padlocked attic she'd hidden all her books on shelves with locked pine doors. One never knew who might show up and in what state. The last thing Mother wanted was for Anna Karenina to discover accidentally that she was bound to take her life on the railroad tracks.

When I was little I didn't always know who was or wasn't a Heroine. Sometimes a guest's lethargy, or constant weeping, or voracious appetite gave her away. My mother recognized the names of the Heroines immediately, but she never enlightened me until they had left. She was afraid I'd bungle and interfere with their destinies. But that summer after I turned thirteen, I wanted her to trust me. I wanted to stay up late with the Heroines, listening and nodding as my mother did, offering popcorn, never advice. I couldn't say that as a rule I preferred the Heroines to the regular visitors, but Mother did. She had a high threshold for their moods and self-absorption, and it seemed to me at thirteen that I was never granted such sway. Once again, with Deirdre, Mother had put a Heroine's needs before my own (though Mother didn't even realize at that point that Deirdre was a Heroine). I thought Mother and the Heroines knew some womanly secret, and I'd started stealing into the hot attic to paw through Mother's musty books. Up in the eaves, the dust motes swirling through the dollhouse replica of our house, I'd been getting an education.

"Why do so many of them wind up dead?" I once asked.

"We all wind up dead, honey," Mother said.

"I know. But couldn't their authors come up with better endings than having them poison themselves or throw themselves in front of trains?"

"It's just a way to create a dramatic ending," she said. "Some of these women were part of enormously long novels. There's got to be a payoff if you drag your reader through five, six hundred pages."

"But these women aren't real!"

"Penny—just go get my migraine medicine from my vanity. I feel one coming on."

I knew, as only a teenage girl does, how to rile my mother, so I harped on this point. She never could brook the argument that these characters weren't real. They nibbled chicken legs to the bone; they left strands of hair in the bathtub. When they breathed on the windows in wintertime, they left a fog on the glass. And then one day, they were gone.

Don't ask me to explain how these Heroines found their way to us (and God knows how they got their contemporary clothes). They never commented about our technology, and remained immersed in their narrative problems, living completely in their heads. The Heroines began to appear when Mother was a small girl, and they came only to the Homestead, never to her house in Lincoln Park. Though she has vague memories of beautiful women peeking over the bars of her crib, the one she remembers in detail (the first one she told me about) arrived when she was five.

She woke in the middle of the night; something had stirred in her room. As she rubbed the sleep from her eyes, she saw at the foot of her bed a young woman with hair that hung beyond the bedrail. Mother propped herself on her elbows and blinked. The girl was beautiful, her hair thick and flaxen. Mother's mouth fell open, and as her eyes adjusted, she saw something shimmering on the floor beneath her night-light. It was a river of hair, falling from the girl's shoulders to the floor, twisting and folding all around

Mother's bed, up the side of her nightstand, into her tiny baby-doll cradle. Worried that her doll was smothered, Mother jumped from the bed and dug beneath the silky hair to retrieve her hard-limbed DyDee Doll.

"She's okay." Mother patted the doll's back, and water trickled from the hole in her mouth. Mother licked the vinyl lips and extended her hand. "I'm Anne-Marie."

Rapunzel smiled and took Mother's hand, but tears welled in her eyes.

"What's wrong?" Mother asked.

"The weight of this hair, how it makes my head ache!"

"Lie down here and rest." Mother patted her pillow. As she rubbed Rapunzel's temples, she listened to the story of how a witch had locked the girl in a tower that had neither doors nor staircases, only a tiny window at the top. The phallic implications escaped Mother, of course, but she was astounded by such a fate. "And you can't go outside at all?"

Rapunzel shook her head. "But a handsome prince climbs the rope of my hair every day, after Mother Gothel has visited. He brings me some silken rope, and one day I'll weave a ladder and escape!"

"Is he a handsome prince?"

They stayed up whispering for another hour, but once Rapunzel drifted off to sleep, so did Mother. When she woke, Rapunzel was gone.

The next day at breakfast, Anne-Marie told her parents, Edith and Henry, about the nighttime visitor.

"That sounds like Rapunzel," her mother said.

"You met her?" Anne-Marie asked.

"She's a fairy-tale character from Germany. You must have dreamt it. Certainly we read the story together."

"I don't remember it."

"Sure," her father said. He folded the *Wall Street Journal* in two, and laid it beside his egg-streaked plate. "The witch finds out about the prince's visits, and she cuts off Rapunzel's hair and banishes her to the desert." He tipped his coffee mug and finished the last drops.

The housekeeper, Gretta, was from the Black Forest. She was young then, trim, with muscular calves and a high bosom. Hearing the tales of her native land, she wiped her hands on her apron and chimed in, "Then the witch gets the prince to climb up to the tower and scares the devil out of him."

Mother burst into tears. "Poor Rapunzel!"

"Now, Henry, Gretta, you've got her all worked up!" Grandmother pulled a handkerchief from her apron pocket and held it under Anne-Marie's nose. "Blow, please."

"Anne-Marie, dolly, don't cry." Henry pulled her onto his lap. "Didn't you read the whole story? The prince wanders the desert until he finds her. And then, you know what's really neat?"

Mother heaved a staggering sigh. "What?"

"They have twins! A boy and a girl! And then they live happily ever after."

"Are you sure?" she sniffed.

"We'll read it together after you help Gretta clear the table."

"We've obviously read it before!" Edith said. "How else could she have dreamt about her?"

"It was real!" Anne-Marie said, slamming her spoon in her oatmeal.

"Don't be fresh," her father said.

"One more word!" her mother said. "And I'll—"

Even at five, Anne-Marie knew not to cross her mother. So she piped down and kept quiet about Rapunzel. Later when Gretta found a twenty-foot strand of hair on the hardwood floor, they looped it around a spool and hid it in an attic chest. From then on, Gretta became Mother's confidante. Over the years, other Heroines visited her, and she cherished the easy conversation, the honesty, and always their timeless beauty, but she never told anyone but Gretta about them. She was afraid that if her mother found out, she'd scare the Heroines away, just as the evil witches, stepmothers, and queens always tried to thwart Snow White, Rose Red, and Sleeping Beauty.

Besides Gretta, I was the only person to whom Mother explained the Heroines. When I turned five, the same age as she was when Rapunzel arrived, she read me the story, then showed me the spool of hair, hidden in the attic. I stared at the long, glimmering strand with delight. At five, I could easily believe in the materialization of fantasy characters. Mother said that this was a big secret, and we had to make an oath to never tell anyone about it. She told me to pick my favorite book—*Goodnight Moon*—and we laid our hands on the cover and vowed never to tell a soul about the Heroines. That night I lay in bed, hoping the bunny from Margaret Wise Brown's book would visit me so we could bid the moon good night together. But Mother explained the next morning that you could never wish for a particular Heroine. They came of their own accord.

I don't know if Mother possessed supernatural powers that drew the Heroines to us, or if it was just odd luck. She didn't run around burning sage or conjuring literary ghosts; on the contrary, she was one of the most passive people I've known, and the weight of the Heroines' destinies oppressed her, perhaps as much as it did the authors themselves. Only her position was worse. She knew their destinies before they did. For weeks after a Heroine left, she'd worry about the Heroine's fate. Why her concern for them had begun to make me feel jilted is probably obvious, but I had no insight at thirteen. So to comfort myself, I'd say, "Mo-om [two syllables]. It's not like they're *re-al* [two syllables]."

But that night in the woods, fantasy became my terrifying reality, and deep down, I thought my capture by the Hero was payback for all my singsong shots at Mother.

CHAPTER 3

+ *Back to the present action in the woods* +

Escape attempt in the manner of a gymnast

+ *The wonders of bareback riding* +

The scent of a Villain +

"Step forward!" he yelled.

I moved away from the tree trunk, my feet sinking deep in the dried-up leaves and moist earth. The horse reared back and pawed the air at the sight of me, lit by the torch, in my orange terrycloth shorts and tank top, my pyramid of bushy red hair. I touched the kink above my ears, left when I pulled my pigtails out of the rubber bands. The glossy black horse had glowing eyes, and I smelled the funk of it, the sweat, the lather. The man pulled hard on the reins to calm the horse, then pointed an accusing finger at me.

"And why would you be rambling about the woods in your underclothes?" He had a thick Irish brogue and a baritone voice.

"These aren't underwear!"

"You'll rue the day, girl!"

He sounded so parental, I shouted, "You're not my father!"

"'Tis hardship in store for the lying woman who claims I am!"

"Deirdre said—" Here, I don't know what possessed me to say her name. Something vindictive, I guess, something like self-preservation or maybe just sheer confusion.

"So you *do* know the ill-fated Deirdre!" He laughed, the sort of haughty chortle only a man from what had to be a lowbrow novel would make. "Ha!" He even swept his cape across his chest.

"What do you want from me?"

"Silence!" He cracked a whip that he pulled out of nowhere, and I stumbled backward against the tree. However much I wished to protest his "reality," there was no denying the sound of that cracking whip, nor the fug of that frothing horse. My mother had taught me that the best way to defend myself physically was to use my voice, especially when I was widely outsized. But the sound of that leather strap cutting through the air was withering. Genuine fear finally descended on me. Living in the Homestead, I never was quite sure what was real, but not for a minute out in the woods with the stomping horse did I think I was dreaming, and I felt a sudden wave of sympathy for Deirdre.

"Tell me where she is!"

I glanced to my right at a split-rail fence. The thing to do was run. He'd need to get a good trot going to hop the fence, either backing up or turning full circle. With a sideways glance, I took off, tearing through the scattered leaves. I pressed my hands to the rail and pommel-horsed it like I'd practiced in gym. The leaves jumped around my ankles when I landed, and even in my flimsy flip-flops, I managed to snap a big twig. The horse whinnied, and I heard the commotion of its turning hooves as Conor tried to follow.

"Curses!" he cried.

I ran like a fiend down a narrow path, branches and leaves whipping my face; the threads of a cobweb got tangled in my hair and eyelashes. A spider scrambled down my back and I flailed and swatted my spine. I ran and ran, till the path broadened a bit. I heard the thump of hooves behind me, and I started to scream. Yet as I tore through the dark woods, I couldn't stop thinking, couldn't turn off my preteen critical faculty, couldn't stop asking, *What kind of a cardboard character yells, "Curses!"?*

The kind who's a savage horseman. He was gaining on me, cracking that whip. Overhead, oak trees arched, the night sky flashing between the leaves. My damned flip-flops were the worst shoes for running. Usually I switched to tennis shoes before my walk, but I'd been so mad at Deirdre and my mother, I'd rushed out without thinking. Deirdre had me hamstrung. A felled tree suddenly took shape, materialized before my eyes, transecting the path, a shade darker than the air itself. It was too thick to jump over, so I dove under it, felt the slap of tiny wild grapes against my cheek. I looked back. The man sliced the branches with his whip. I kept going, jumped another fallen trunk, then I heard the hooves clomping toward me. He jumped the second trunk and doubled his time just as I started to get winded. He was right beside me. I couldn't cut through the woods because a thick hedge had me trapped on the right. I ran and ran, hoping the hedge would end. The thump of the hooves and the heat off the horse overpowered my senses.

Suddenly I felt my head fly back. He had grabbed the back of my hair and he pulled me up. My scalp seethed with pain, and I started yelling and screaming, hating myself for disobeying Mother, hating her for being right about the dangers of the woods at night, as he lifted me off the soft path. Airborne, I kicked, but the next thing I knew I was lying sideways across the horse, and the man was carting me down the path like a bundle of wheat. Then, like some kind of samurai, he flipped me around, pulled me up by the waist, and sat me in front of him.

"Fuck!" I had to be covered in bruises.

"What class of curse would you be making there? There's no health in it!"

His wool tunic made my back itch, and he smelled like sweat and wood smoke. He rested his pointy chin on my head, holding me tight across the waist as we galloped through the woods.

CHAPTER 4

+ *Current action at the Homestead*
+ *More weeping from Deirdre leads to Mother's*
lightbulb moment + *A brief history of Mother's*
odd genius and feminist inclinations +

Weeks later, after everything had settled, Mother told me what had been happening back at the Homestead. I can easily imagine the scene. Mother tried to mollify Deirdre while keeping one eye on the TV, where Walter Cronkite discussed the Supreme Court's pending vote on whether Nixon had to release the rest of the White House tapes (which would incriminate him beyond doubt). For five days, while the nation awaited the vote, Deirdre had been crying over the death of Noisiu, a name Mother made Deirdre repeat several times: *Noy-shue.* We'd assumed that Irish people gave their kids Celtic names, just as Fawn, Summer, Sage, and Chastity had become popular in the late sixties here. After Mother ascertained that there were no further updates on the national saga, she led Deirdre up to her bedroom, so she wouldn't disturb Mr. Mazar, the boarder who'd complained about Deirdre's constant crying, and whose complaints precipitated her moving to my room, the farthest from his. Mother had the biggest room in the house, with a four-poster bed, sitting room, screened-in porch, and lovely bathroom with a marble sink. They settled into comfortable wicker chairs on the sunporch, and Mother poured a can of ginger ale into two ice-filled glasses.

Deirdre's sea-green eyes were finally free of tears, and she tossed a long blond tress over her shoulder. "Everything in my life changed the day I saw the raven drinking the calf's blood."

"Uh-huh," Mother said. She could truly be the Queen of Nonreaction. One could say such a thing to her, and she'd hardly blink an eye.

"I knew then that I wanted a man with hair as black as the raven, skin as white as the snow, cheeks as red as blood."

"I had an ideal man when I was your age too," Mother said. She felt, I'm sure, protective of Deirdre, who was no more than sixteen. "I wanted a boy with blond hair and blue eyes."

"Did you ever meet him?"

"Actually, he was quite the opposite . . ." Mother wasn't likely to go into the melodramatic details of my paternity.

"My vision came true! The son of Uisliu was exactly that! Dark-haired, fair-skinned, ruddy-cheeked. And now he's gone! Murdered by his own people! Ulstermen turned on the brave Ulsterman!"

Mother assumed that Deirdre's Noisiu had been involved in the IRA. Also, Deirdre's accent was wholly different than that of the southern Irish people who had previously stayed at the Homestead. When she'd arrived with a backpack and her hair bound by a red bandanna, we'd figured she was just another traveling student. Mother was careful in her assumptions, however. She didn't want to ask directly if Noisiu was IRA; mistaking sympathies in the northern Irish conflict would be like falling on a cactus: a prickly situation that would be hard to get out of. "Did Noisiu betray somebody?"

"They betrayed him! They pretended to welcome him back, when all the while they'd plotted his murder! They considered his love for me an act of betrayal!"

"You've been through a lot!" Mother patted Deirdre's arm, try-ing to make a logical deduction about the situation. It seemed that Deirdre's sympathies must lie with the British; Noisiu must be Catholic. Maybe Deirdre's father was high up in the provisional government, or a policeman. Had Noisiu been killed for falling in love with a Protestant? Was this a classic Protestant-Catholic romance? Star-crossed lovers of the Romeo and Juliet type? Sud-denly it dawned on Mother that Deirdre must be a Heroine. While Deirdre recited poetry about her exile from Noisiu, their lovemaking under dolmens, and fires across Erin, my mother sat with her hand on her cheek, mouth hanging open, trying to fig-ure out from which story Deirdre had come.

After Deirdre finished her ginger ale, Mother led her to my room. Now that she knew Deirdre was a Heroine, I'm sure she even tucked her in, watching her rosebud lips fall open as she drifted into sleep. Her profile made a cameo of the round blue pillow under her head. Without the bandanna and bell-bottoms, Deirdre could be a Heroine from any age. In fiction, beauty was run-of-the-mill. Beauty gave no clues. Beauty was too damn timeless.

Afterward, Mother crept up the creaky attic steps. She pulled the string to turn on the bare lightbulb and groped for the book-shelf keys, hidden on a broad crossbeam. As she blew the dust off the keys, she realized her hands were shaking. She hated not know-ing a Heroine's story. She unlocked her shelf of English and Irish literature. She reached immediately for *Ulysses*. If only Deirdre's name were Molly! She flipped through the pages, knowing deep down that Deirdre's story was too plot-driven to be Joycean. So she sat on the dusty floor, an overturned mousetrap a few feet from her sandaled feet, reading and reading. The bare bulb hardly illumi-nated all the pages. She scanned *Portrait of the Artist, Gulliver's Travels,* and cursed her lack of contemporary Irish lit. No matter that Mother was incredibly well read, she still chastised herself.

Her own mother had worn away her confidence with a relent-less perfectionism. *Stir the pot this way, Anne-Marie. You left the light on again. Chop the meat in the direction of the tendons, not like that. Iron the sheets! Your pleats are crooked. It will cost me hundreds to replace that vase.* Her nickname for Mother was Marmiton, which Mother learned only later meant kitchen gopher in French. Mother's only recourse was to retreat to her books, to laugh at her inadequacies, and to get the hell out of the house as fast as she could. Her father was torn between his haughty wife and rag-doll daughter. Mother's startling intelligence had everyone stumped, and I think her father dreamt of an Ivy League oasis for her. But then I came along and stirred up Mother's romantic notions of a Better Life for *Her* Daughter. My father must have possessed a more quotidian intelligence, with a dash of cunning. Mother may have been able to recite verbatim whole pages of *Finnegan's Wake,* but while she had her nose in books that night, I was in the thick of the action.

CHAPTER 5

✢ *Further horseback travels* ✢
The Villain's identity revealed ✢ *An allusion*
to ear-grabbing and druidical prophecy
✢ *I hatch a mediocre scheme* ✢

Another M-80 boomed, and the horse took off as if nobody sat on its back. Branches battered our faces. The man pulled the reins and they dug into my upper arms. The rough motion almost jolted me off the horse's back, and I gripped the mane tight. He and Deirdre had to be from an old story, before the invention of the saddle. The threat of snapping branches scared me so much I closed my eyes, let my body fall in with the horse's gallop. Finally, the horse started to slow, the man's chest moved away from my back, and the tug of the reins slackened. I opened my eyes. The horse headed toward Horace's pond; the bird must have taken flight ages ago.

The man stopped the horse and dismounted. He held his hand out for me, but I glared at him and slid my foot over the horse's side. I pedaled my feet, trying to gauge how far the drop was, but then his hands were on my hips, and he lowered me gently. Having never felt the press of a fatherly hug, I didn't know what to make of him. Before I could figure it out, he gripped my wrist and held on tight. He patted the horse's rump and sent it off to the water. Holding the torch next to his face, he examined me, still cuffing my wrist. He peered into my eyes, and I gave him the once-over back. He wore a burgundy tunic under his cape, which was fastened with a gold brooch at the throat. I wondered why he wore period clothes, when none of the Heroines ever did, and how had he brought the horse with him? Physically, he was stocky, thick in the calves and arms, but not overly tall. From the slight wrinkles around his eyes, I guessed he was around Mother's age, in his early thirties. He had thick, dirty blond hair, but by the torchlight I couldn't determine his eye color. His beard was well combed and his mustache trimmed. I hated him for pulling my hair; my scalp still stung, but that trick he did to get me on the horse was cool, and I dug his strappy sandals. But I couldn't let on. He wasn't hissing and vowing to eat my heart out, but still, I couldn't go soft.

"What kind of Villain are you?" I asked.

"Villain! Ha!" He let go of my wrist and pulled an enormous sword from his belt. "I am Conor, King of Ulster! Lord of the Red Branch Knights! Leader of the Men of Erin! Master of the Red Branch, the Twinkling Hoard, the Ruddy Branch."

His name didn't sound familiar, but I wasn't too expert in Irish lit. I'd read only a couple of stories in *Dubliners,* and at twelve I hadn't really understood them. If I had thought for a minute that Deirdre was a Heroine, I might have skimmed Mother's books days ago. We'd missed the obvious cues because her name didn't ring any bells. "How much ransom are you going to ask for?"

"There's no fear for you! A ransom!" Then he laughed that big, phony, lowbrow novel chortle. A girl couldn't help being offended. "I wouldn't ask for more than a mewling calf!"

"My grandfather's got *some* money left!"

"I'm not interested in you, you—you are a mere irritation, a fly I could swat, a maggot"—he dug his heel into the ground—

"I could squash. I am a man of honor, not a kidnapper. I only need you to help me reach my wife!"

"Deirdre's your wife?" I gave him a good, adolescent scowl. "She's only sixteen. You're old enough to be her dad!"

"Bound to me, she is. I spared her life. My men would have torn her from the womb of Fedlimid's wife and killed her at birth! It was I who said, 'Such beauty will not be destroyed!'"

"She was cursed at birth?"

"In the womb! She howled from the hollow of her mother. 'A weird uproar at the waist!' as Fedlimid said. Cathbad foretold that a woman with twisted yellow tresses and green-irised eyes of beauty would be born. High queens would ache with envy at the sight of her pure perfect body. And he said, 'Much damage, Derdriu, will follow your high fame and fair visage. Ulster in your time tormented.' My men wanted her killed, but I offered my protection, hid her high in the mountains, to spare the hard men of Ulster from carnage. But she defied me! Running off with the son of Uisliu. Harsh deeds were done in Erin on her account!"

I wondered what he meant by harsh deeds, but I was too afraid to ask. "So you want to rescue her from . . . ?"

"From herself!" He lunged and pointed the sword in the air. "And to rescue Ulster itself!"

"Why won't she come back to you on her own?"

He ignored my question and lifted the sword higher into the trees. "I could give her golden goblets, cups, and drinking horns, houses paneled with red yew, copper screens with golden birds, apples of gold. I could protect her with javelins and shields and swords, three times thirty warriors—"

"Why wouldn't she want all that?"

"This Deirdre is a stubborn child. Sure she doesn't know what's good for her."

I didn't like the sound of that. Sure, Conor was mighty robust, but he seemed a little too cocksure of what was his. My mother had warned me to beware of men who referred to women as children. She was a "libber," as they said back then, a feminist who, despite her own passivity, believed in equality between men and women. I had assimilated those ideas through her breast milk, but I had enough common sense not to try to enlighten Conor. Pretending to go along with him was my only hope to escape him.

"She *is* stubborn," I said. "She's always yammering on about true love and some guy that got murdered."

"Noisiu was doomed the moment she grabbed his ears!"

I let that cryptic allusion fly. "Why do you need me?"

He lifted his chin and sniffed the air. His wide nostrils flared and his eyes narrowed like a cat's. "There is a druidical spell on that field. Somebody has conjured a shield."

"Really?" That could be why he still wore his period clothes. "You think I can get you through the prairie?"

"With your ginger hair, I thought a shape-shifter you might be. But since you couldn't take flight to escape me, I saw that you had no power. But you must do something to lure Deirdre back into these woods."

Imagine me, luring a Heroine into the forbidden woods. Over Mother's dead body! "Deirdre won't listen to me."

"You must make her." The horse wandered farther into the trees, and Conor stepped over a fallen trunk and led it back to us. The horse rubbed its forehead against Conor's chest and he pushed it gently away. The horse pushed back, and Conor gave in, lovingly stroking its long nose. "Together—you and I—we can save her."

The movement of his hand along the horse's nose stirred me. He was so different from the clumsy boys and dull fathers I knew in the suburbs: more earthy, more confident and commanding. More sexy. "I don't know."

"Better for her to come with me than to be captured by the Red Branch Knights. They won't spare her."

"Why can't you just come to the house?"

"That field—prairie, as you call it—sure there's magic there. Deirdre must have put a druidical spell on it. I can't pass it."

I didn't know what to think or believe. Conor seemed valiant, but most of the Heroines ended up with us precisely because of bad men. Maybe escaping Conor had been Deirdre's heroic moment. But all the Heroines returned to their stories in the end, of their own mysterious accord. Mother believed the best strategy was to play dumb, to provide tea and sympathy and clean linens. Conor's presence annihilated Mother's strategy. No one else had ever followed a Heroine into our lives. And would my encounter affect Deirdre's fate? I didn't know anything about this story, so I didn't know how to play it. Possible plot lines twisted in my mind, and it struck me suddenly that the key to this scene was figuring how to get myself out of it. Exit stage left, quickly and with as little drama as possible. I looked at the pond, considered swimming across it, but imagined swallowing the scum and getting tangled in slimy seaweed. I was a weak swimmer in a regular pool, worthless with that kind of drag. To reach it I'd have to jump a log, and Conor would have me by the ankle in no time. Plus, it was entirely the opposite direction of home. For a minute, I wished Horace would swoop down and fly away with me on his back. Then I got real. A selfish twinge snaked up my spine. Just because Mother sacrificed herself and me for the Heroines, it didn't mean I had to. With Deirdre gone, I'd get my room back. And my mother.

"I know. I'll tell her I want to collect mint or cresses with her from along the water. She keeps talking about gathering herbs."

"Spells, no doubt. But a woman such as Deirdre has had servants to tend to such matters. She'll expect that you'll collect them yourself."

"I'll play dumb. Like I don't know a weed from an herb."

"There's sense in that. You've a clever head, have you not?"

I fought a smile. I didn't want him to think I was pleased by his compliments. I didn't want to feel anything for him at all, though I felt closer to him than I did to Deirdre, and attracted in a way I didn't wholly understand. In three years only one Heroine, Franny, had taken me seriously; the rest treated me like a nonentity. But Conor needed me, and I needed him. We had the same aim: getting Deirdre out of the Homestead. I saw myself running through the prairie, opening the door to my house, climbing the stairs to my bedroom, hiding beneath my pink satin duvet, reunited with all my things. This plan would work in two ways: I'd get what I'd want, and he wouldn't hurt me if I helped him. My mother had impressed one thing upon me: never meddle in the Heroines' lives. But where had it gotten me? I was marginalized either way. I had to fend for myself.

CHAPTER 6

+ Emma Bovary's quandary + Mother's
attempts at neutrality + My espionage
and bold revelation + The slap +

The trouble simmering between Mother and me had boiled over months before when Emma Bovary arrived. I found her novel five minutes after she registered—I didn't have to scour the shelves—there she was in gold leaf on the navy-blue spine: *Madame Bovary*. It was spring break, April, so I was free to keep whatever hours I chose, to lie on a mattress in the attic and read and doze all day. The rain pounded and dripped down the windows while I read, kept company by a half dozen box fans, the dollhouse replica of the house, three antique trunks, and the occasional scamper of a mouse across the floorboards.

I read to discover why Madame Bovary needed us, yet I soon became engrossed in the plot. I adored learning about the customs of the French country folk, the descriptions of hills and fields, the little towns, the ritualized, careful courtship of Charles Bovary and Emma. Their wedding feast delighted me, and I dreamt that I would one day have a country wedding where the guests processed through an open field following a fiddler. But did I understand Emma's character—the soul fed on romance novels, the convent girl who fasted with pleasure, who mourned her mother's death with a delicious sadness she deemed "inaccessible to mediocre spirits"? Emma drew deep and somewhat perverse pleasure from her pain, cultivated terrific funks that I didn't yet recognize as similar to my own teenage disposition. Everything she experienced seemed fathomable. I didn't judge this Heroine, as I took Flaubert's word as gospel. It seemed perfectly reasonable to me that women who made bad marriages lived to regret them.

Charles revered her delicate hands, her dark hair, her pale complexion. He adored her drawing skills, her piano playing, her ability to run a household. But she quickly grew bored with him. He lacked finer sensibilities. When she botched a piano sonata, he told her she played beautifully. He backed off when she was in a foul mood, rather than diving in to explore it. When she fell into a depression, the quintessential nineteenth-century antidote was prescribed—a change of scenery! When they arrived in the slightly bigger town of Yonville, Emma easily attracted Monsieur Léon Dupuis. He shared her love of the arts, especially literature. This interchange about reading killed me:

> "The hours go by without my knowing it. Sitting there I'm wandering in countries I can see every detail of—I'm playing a role in the story I'm reading. I actually feel I'm the characters—I live and breathe them."
>
> "I know!" she said. "I feel the same!"

When the naïve Léon realized his love could never be consummated, believing that Emma was happily married to Charles, he fled Yonville for Paris. Bereft, Emma suffered dizzy spells and tried to cope with the loss. She took Italian, changed her hairstyle, went on shopping sprees, chugged brandy. I loved when Charles's mother showed up and blamed Emma's depression on novels and banned them from the house. She went to the library and canceled Emma's subscription and warned the librarian that she would call the police if he "persisted in spreading his poison." The only thing that cured her latest malaise was the arrival of Rodolphe Boulanger, who immediately decided to seduce Dr. Bovary's beautiful wife. After a lathered horseback ride, he took her in the grass. After that, they had weekly trysts in her arbor; she snuck to his château for liaisons; they engaged in a heated letter exchange; they swapped locks of hair. They planned to run off together.

The problem was, Emma couldn't keep from going overboard, and Rodolphe decided to ditch her. She revered love and romance to a degree that made her lovers bristle. She was impulsive (showed up uninvited to Boulanger's château), reckless (walked boldly arm in arm with a lover in the streets of Rouen), and dramatic (sobbed uncontrollably when a lover was late for a date). As a wealthy woman, Madame Bovary could easily pawn her child off on the nurse or maid; she took erratic interest in her household responsibilities. She couldn't escape the feeling that there was something more out there. That something had to be a man.

I was versed enough in the language of feminism to get that much. At thirteen, I found Emma absolutely reasonable. (I'd had the same experience reading *Catcher in the Rye* at ten. I didn't get that Holden was heading toward a nervous breakdown at all. I thought he was hospitalized because he caught a cold or pneumonia from standing in the rain watching Phoebe ride the carousel.) Flights of fancy, delusions, moody rages—those were the everyday symptoms of adolescence. I figured the month-long swoons and fevers had something to do with the limits of medicine.

When I woke up with my thumb in the middle of the book, the dawn light pink in the window, I was frustrated. I couldn't stand the thought of another day passing without my knowing Emma's fate. I jumped ahead and read the last few chapters in horror. She'd run the family into irreparable debt thanks to the conniving Monsieur Lheureux (Mr. Happy!), a local merchant who exploited Madame's weakness for fine clothes and furniture. Worst of all, this woman sleeping below me, this woman who drank pots of Constant Comment tea, was headed for the arsenic.

Her grisly death stunned me: the vomiting, the convulsions, the nosebleeds. I never expected this ending. In her coffin, she was dressed in her wedding gown (Charles insisted), and black liquid poured from her mouth. They had to cover up the suicide, pretend it was an accident, so she could be buried in a Christian grave. For the first time, I felt genuine horror for a Heroine's fate. I could not understand why Mother didn't intervene. I didn't understand the complexity of Emma's mental troubles, and her debts seemed insurmountable. But maybe she had come to the Homestead before the real problems began. Maybe there was a chance to save her, to keep her from getting together with Léon, to warn her about M. Lheureux. I had to do something.

That night after dinner, Mother and Emma retired to the living room, and I said good night and went upstairs. Halfway up, I stopped, my hand on the velvet striped wallpaper. I couldn't hear much, but the name Rodolphe was pronounced with a perfect and loving accent. I tiptoed back down the steps and crossed the foyer, passing the front desk. I peeked around the wall.

They sat with their backs to me, watching the fire. Mother was curled up on the sofa; Emma sat in the wingback chair. I crouched, then crawled across the hardwood floor, hiding behind the sofa. Through the couch upholstery, I heard Mother crunching popcorn.

"He is so attentive and refined," Emma said.

"Uh-hum," Mother said.

"Perhaps he was worried about ruining my life. He couldn't bear to watch someone in my position take a fall."

I closed one eye, nodding my head. So she'd arrived at the Homestead just after Rodolphe ditched their plan to run off together.

"Maybe," Mother said.

"But didn't he realize that I was done with all that? I don't care about society anymore." She held her head in her hands and pulled on her long, black curls. "Do you think he'll return?"

"Oh, I wouldn't know. More popcorn?" Mother held out the bowl to Emma, who waved it away. Like most Heroines, she had little appetite.

"How could he abandon the promise of a life of love? Of passion!"

"Try not to worry too much right now. It's good to distract yourself."

"I'm driven to distraction, thinking of Rodolphe. Why did he leave? To bury his note in a basket of apricots! I'll never eat another!"

My toes ached from squatting. I was getting worried; Emma had fallen into a forty-three-day swoon after Rodolphe left. Were we in for a month and a half of this?

"I told him I'd do anything for him. I called him my king, my idol. I said I was his slave, his concubine—"

"Maybe he had some thinking to do," Mother said.

"About what? What do you think he might be thinking?"

"I have no idea what Rodolphe is thinking."

I nearly tipped over. Of course she knew what Rodolphe was thinking. There was an omniscient narrator. We readers had access to everybody's thoughts. Rodolphe was dumping Emma. It was right there in Chapter 12. He was bored with her love-slave routine. Even Charles Bovary had called Rodolphe "a bit of a playboy." But oh, that moment when she saw his carriage crossing the village square, escaping her. She keeled right over.

"But try to imagine," Emma said, "you are like him. Having left a person like me. What would you be thinking?"

"I might be lonely."

"Honestly? Do you think he misses me?"

"I really can't speak for Rodolphe . . ."

"I can!" I leapt up from behind the couch. "Rodolphe's not coming back! You have to forget him!"

Madame's mouth hung open, her skin pale and eyes wide. I could tell that her horror was twofold. It wasn't simply what I'd said, but that someone my age had said something at all. In her world, children kept their mouths shut. She held her throat; she looked as if she might be headed for another swoon.

"Penelope Anne!" Mother jumped off the couch, knocking the popcorn to the floor. "What on earth?" Already her hand was raised. She turned and knelt on the couch, leaning over the back of it.

"Get over Rodolphe!" I yelled. "He's just using—"

Mother swung back and slapped my face. Hard. I staggered backward. Then she jumped over the couch, covered my mouth with her hand, and pushed me out of the room. Tears sprang to my eyes. Never in my life had she raised a hand to me; I never once had a stinging cheek. I backed into the hallway. I'd never seen her so angry, her nostrils flaring, her eyes narrowed to slits.

"Don't you ever—" She pressed her hand harder against my mouth, and I stuck out my tongue and licked her salty palm, tasted popcorn. She yanked her hand away, recoiling. "Penny, my God!"

"You hit me!" I hissed.

"Don't you ever butt in—"

"I can't just sit there and let her ruin her life!" We were fighting in a whisper.

"You have to."

"Why? Because that's what *you* do?"

"Because it's not our place to change things."

I turned away and tried to start up the stairs, but she caught my arm.

"It's dangerous!" she said.

"It's dangerous to do nothing." I yanked my arm from her hand and made a gun of my index finger and thumb. I pointed it at my forehead. "You want her to wind up dead?"

"It's not my job to fix her life. Her fate is sealed."

"That's just an excuse. You could do something."

"You think it's easy for me to hold back? I feel so much for them."

"Yeah, the Heroines get all the sympathy, and I just get slapped."

Mother covered her face with her hands. She shook her head and slumped against the wall, dragging her hands down her face, pulling her skin so she looked almost ghoulish. She slowly slid down the wall into a crouch. "This isn't working anymore. You're getting too old . . . you're . . ."

"I'm what?" I started to sob then, a crooning wail right from my gut. All the pent-up confusion and rage I felt over no longer being her little girl overwhelmed me. "What's so wrong with me?"

That was the moment when I wanted her to say, *There's nothing wrong with you.* Instead, she let the tears roll to her chin without wiping them away. She looked up at the ceiling, avoiding my eyes. "Everything now. Everything is wrong."

CHAPTER 7

+ *My affection for Conor grows* +
The pleasures of deception + *My jealous*
nature + *Male rage* + *Escape* +

The woods smelled different to me that night—the ground more wet, the trees sharp and fragrant. Nighthawks shrieked and bats fluttered in the trees. Conor let me hold the reins. Our bodies moved in sync with the galloping horse. His hands rested loosely on my hips when we sped up, dropped to his thighs when we slowed down. He had relaxed since I'd dreamt up the half-baked scheme of tricking Deirdre to come into the woods. We were in cahoots, though my complicity was a lie. I got a sharp thrill from fooling a man like him. I would relish lording this over Mother. I had to meddle in a Heroine's fate this time! She couldn't slap me out of it. I really believed that I was an agent, that I would discover Deirdre's story and save her from her fate. I didn't have to inherit Mother's passivity.

"Deirdre's always moping around!" I yelled over my shoulder. "She needs to snap out of it." I was so judgmental at that age; I actually thought I knew better than adults, probably because the complexity of their problems eluded me. Deirdre was only a few years older, but I was a baby compared to her. I was thrilled by the

mere feel of Conor's chin sliding across my head. As I bad-mouthed
Deirdre, he shook his head as if she were a naughty child. I imagined him spanking her, felt a perplexing flash of arousal. I ducked
as we went under a railroad trestle, where a ragged cyclone fence
hung from the embankment.

For a minute I considered not turning Deirdre over to him.
Maybe he would take me away to his castle. In truth, I envied
Deirdre, with her waist-long blond curls, her cheeks of perpetual
blush. Men transcended time and space to capture her. Her curves
seemed to mock my planes, and I winced to think of how only last
week I'd balled up Kleenex and stuffed my bikini top to see how I
might look with breasts. My kinky red hair and head-to-toe freck-
les would have made me the child star of baloney commercials. I
wasn't ugly, but I had the look people loved because it was so
uniquely unthreatening; they pointed and smiled, secretly thank-
ing their stars for their tans and shimmering straight locks.

We broke from the bridle path and quickly approached the
prairie. The horse skidded to a halt before we could cross. My head
and chest fell over its neck, my fingers tangled in its mane. The
horse reared up as if an invisible brick wall had suddenly risen in
the path, though there was nothing but heavy air, then it dropped
back down and turned a circle. Conor leapt off its back in a split
second, and I followed, kicking my left leg over the side, and
shimmying down before he could help me.

Conor paced in front of the prairie path entrance, shouting and
cursing. With both hands, he angrily plunged his sword into the
dirt, kicking up dust and clumps of dirt. He pulled out the sword
with both hands and plunged it in again and again, as if he were
stabbing the life out of someone. His hair flew about wildly and
sweat flew from his face.

"The High King is the only man powerful enough to defeat the
druid's prophecy against Deirdre. Yet this shield has me stuck!"

I was stunned. He yanked the sword out of the ground and
angrily pointed at the prairie, the muddy sword flying back and

forth. My attraction to him changed into a burning feeling in my stomach. I'd never witnessed such fierce and sudden male rage. I wrapped my arms around my skinny ribs and cowered, my legs beginning to tremble.

"Deirdre cried out while still in her mother's womb. Everyone heard it! Cathbad foretold that she would be the most beautiful woman in Erin and that she would bring death and destruction to many an Ulsterman. Only I, Conchobor MacNessa, son of Nex, the daughter of Eochaid Salbuide of the yellow heel, foster son of Cathbad, King of Ulster, can keep her from destroying herself and Erin."

My fear of him made his lineage sound like gibberish. Deirdre was no physical match for Conor, nor was I. Duty bound me to the Heroines, even when they stirred envy and resentment in my childish heart, a heart that nonetheless possessed a sharp sense of justice. I looked down at my chest, weary of my mediocrity, my body's refusal to transform into curves like Deirdre's. My thin legs and bony arms made me feel weak. There would be no defeating this man physically. I had to take a different tack. So though my mind screamed *Run!,* I kept my cool and assumed the demeanor of a lowly servant, bowing my head and delivering with great humility this versatile cliché: "At your will, sire."

"Bring her to me!" he roared. He rested his hand on his scabbard and cleared his throat. His voice too had a depth that could only be described as regal: both commanding and gentlemanly. He must have sensed my fear, because he lowered his voice when he said, "I'll be waiting here."

"I'll bring her in the morning." I struggled not to look him in the eye; lying to him wasn't easy for me. However much I was drawn to Conor, some instinct told me to beware. He was muscular and smelled great, but I couldn't let that make me forget that he was a hunter of women. I had to get away from him, out of the woods and back into the thick, weedy sanctuary of the fragrant prairie.

"Excellent. Till the morning!" he said.

"Do you need food?"

"I can manage." He pouted modestly, shrugging his shoulders and looking around. "I've slaughtered many a wild boar."

I bowed again, and refrained from telling him he'd have better luck finding a buck. "Okay."

I turned and ran, soft wood chips crunching beneath my flip-flops. I didn't want to enter the prairie from that spot, right in front of Conor, as I worried it would irritate him, so I took a side path. Something darted into the rustling leaves, and I briefly thought Conor was following me, but that was unlikely. Up ahead I saw the outline of a wooden signpost with six arrows, an old guide for wagon trails. I'd passed it a thousand times, knew to follow the arrow pointing to Chicago to reach the prairie. The trees waved above me, darker than the sky. The sound of my footsteps threw me off, and I thought I heard another horse coming down the path at me. Maybe it was Conor's men, so I ran harder, my eyes wide and dry with fright. I was afraid to look back, afraid not to, and as the trees cleared and opened into the prairie, I dared to look over my shoulder. Conor was gone.

I burst into the prairie. It seemed like daylight compared to the woods; nothing blocked my view of the stars. Fireflies flickered among the weeds, quiet and golden. The hazy half-moon had dropped behind the power lines. The sweet, peppery scent of wildflowers overwhelmed me like a potion. I ran through the swampy dip beside the natural spring, swatting mosquitoes as I went. My knees were bleeding and blisters webbed the space between my big and second toes, but I didn't care. The cool prairie was alive with crickets. This was a true taste of freedom. Suddenly I saw our windows, glowing pinkish orange. I was nearly there. The haze of Conor's charm was clearing quickly, and it dawned on me that this man could have done anything to me, could have killed me. I had been abducted. This night went beyond anything Mother had ever experienced with the Heroines. I had either encountered a Hero or I'd galloped through the dark woods with a genuine Villain.

CHAPTER 8

✦ *My prodigal return* ✦ *An exhausted sleep* ✦
The towering Officer Marone ✦ *Mother's*
betrayal ✦ *Her First Pelvic Exam* ✦
I'm taken for a crazy girl ✦

I slammed the door behind me and pressed against the oak panels, breathless. Mother came tearing out of the living room, her long auburn hair flying behind her in wavy kinks.

"Penny! Where on earth have you been?"

I struggled to catch my breath, blinking at the bright overhead light, not quite believing that I was staring into the opaque pink glass with a scalloped edge. Woozy, I squinted at my blistered feet, toes gripping the rubber flip-flops, stunned to find them planted on the checkerboard ceramic tiles of my home. I had the strange feeling that I was entering a house completely known and completely unfamiliar. The rumpled elegance of the Prairie Homestead, with its faded velvet settees and ragged Persian rugs, seemed like a movie set. Something had transpired in the woods, and I was not the same girl, and this would never, in my mind, be the same house for me again.

"Look at you!" Mother cried.

I ran to the hall tree and gazed in the small oval mirror. My hair was wider than the glass, and razor-thin slashes crossed my cheeks and forehead. Everything about me looked wild: my eyes, my panting mouth, my sweaty, freckled forehead. The grandfather clock chimed the quarter hour. It was after midnight.

"I've been worried sick!" Mother said. "Where have you been?"

My mother's interrogation seemed like a parody of an exchange any mother and daughter would have over a broken curfew. I almost laughed.

"You were in the woods, weren't you? How many times have I told you to stay out of the woods after dark?"

"I'm not seven years old!" I snapped. "I go to the woods all the time."

"You what?"

My big mouth had done me in again. Admitting that I wandered the woods was not a smart tactic. Even if minutes before I had vowed never to return to the woods, I couldn't let pass any opportunity to challenge Mother's authority. My fragile young ego didn't want to admit that she'd been right about it. To save further browbeating, I started to cry. "It's not my fault! This man—"

"What man? Your face is all scratched, and oh, my God!" She pointed at my legs.

I looked down. Two purple bruises had blossomed on my inner thighs from squeezing the flanks of the horse. They looked like perfectly oval plums.

"What did this man do to you?"

"He pulled me on his horse—"

"Sweet Lord." Suddenly her anger evaporated, replaced by horror. "Oh, my darling. Lie down on the couch. You need to rest, to stop thinking—the police are on the way."

"You called the cops?"

"Come lie down." She held my hand and led me to the living room couch. I walked with my eyes half closed, pressing my hand to my chest, hoping that would help my heartbeat to slow. The sound was turned down on the television, but a picture of G. Gordon Liddy with his fat black mustache dominated the screen. Mother had told me he was the mastermind of the Watergate break-in. I lifted my hand to point at him, but Mother stopped me, put a pillow under my head, and peeled the flip-flops off my feet, the plastic sticking between my raw toes. I wanted to explain everything, but I was suddenly so tired, and I enjoyed her touch so much I didn't want to ruin it with words that might be misconstrued. She stretched out my legs and laid an afghan across my chest, which moved up and down more and more slowly. Mother's touch was utterly soothing. I hadn't let her come this close to me since Madame Bovary had left. The velvety cushions felt wonderful, and fatigue fell on me; my legs felt heavy and leaden. I closed my eyes and a little while later felt a warm cloth on my forehead. Mother gently washed my face.

"That feels good," I said.

"Shh. Rest now."

Her voice lulled me to sleep, the warm soothing tone she used when I was a child. I hadn't known how much I missed it.

I woke to the sound of a hissing walkie-talkie and gruff voices in the hallway. The back of my neck was killing me. I blinked, wondering why I wasn't in my bed. Then everything came back to me. My head thrown back as he'd pulled my hair. The flash of fire in his torch. The thrum of the horse beneath us. My high-speed escape through the prairie. I pushed the afghan off and propped myself on my elbows to listen.

"My men are combing the woods, but we need to ask her a few questions."

Combing the woods? I sat up and plunked my feet on the floor. Could the cops possibly apprehend Conor? Would they even see him? We kept the Heroines a secret from all outsiders. Hell, in Mother's mind, *I* was an outsider. But if the cops brought him in, what would happen to Conor? And what damage might he do to them with that hundred-pound sword of his? Did Conor even exist? I touched my legs; the bruises were real, the scratches too, and the memory of his holding me on the horse sent streams of warm feelings through my legs. For an instant I hoped they'd bring him in. But that was crazy, and I felt ashamed and confused. I wasn't supposed to have liked a brutal man like that, was I? I wasn't supposed to have found him handsome.

"I want her to rest!" Mother barked. I rarely heard her sound so forceful.

"But if we're going to catch this guy, we need a description."

I crawled back under the covers and squeezed my eyes shut. I was in it deep. What could I tell the cops? That a fictitious character had yanked me up to his horse? I needed to ask Deirdre if Conor was a Villain, but getting up the stairs without their noticing was impossible. If only I hadn't passed out so quickly, I could have told Mother to call off the cops.

"Did she give you a description?" the cop asked.

"She was delirious. In shock. She said something about a horse."

"That'll help." His voice became clipped and deep. "Flannery, read me?"

The walkie-talkie hissed "Roger."

"Suspect on horseback."

"Roger that. Found some hoofprints."

My stomach dropped when he said that. Hoofprints proved that it had really happened. Then again, the prints could have been made by another rider earlier in the day. This was a horsey town.

"Miss Entwhistle, you're going to have to bring her down to the hospital. To verify that nothing happened."

"Does it have to be tonight?"

"The sooner, the better. They'll need a fresh sample."

I had no idea what *fresh sample* meant, and I certainly didn't need a doctor for a few cuts and bruises, but they had lowered their voices, and I couldn't hear anything else. I needed to get upstairs to talk to Deirdre. But what would I say to her? We had never initiated a discussion with a Heroine about her circumstances. Mother had pacified Emma Bovary with little trouble after my outburst. Emma had been too steeped in her sorrow to worry about anything I'd said. Mother had slapped tactfulness so deeply into my skull that I imagined the truth would make a Heroine melt like the Wicked Witch of the West when doused with water. I couldn't flat-out ask Deirdre if Conor was a bad guy. And if I was going to lure her to the woods, I couldn't tell her he was there. I had no clue what book Deirdre came from, so it wasn't as if I could reveal her lucky or unlucky fate. This was another league of Heroine. Mother and I were as in the dark about her fate as she was.

Mother came into the room with a tall, broad-shouldered cop in high-riding, polyester pants. He stood a full foot higher than Mother, and he had short, dirty blond hair and a dishwater-blond mustache that was as thick as my grandfather's shaving brush.

"Honey?" Mother switched on a standing lamp and a cone of light fell on me. I squinted and tugged the quilt up over my mouth.

Mother pulled up a caned side chair for the cop, then she sat down in the rocker and scooted closer to the couch. "Officer Marone would like to ask you a few questions."

I looked up at him. He smelled like tobacco, and his towering height struck fear in me. A hard pack of cigarettes nested in his breast pocket, and I could read the word *Marlboro* through the thin blue fabric. Aviator sunglasses hung from the other pocket. He wedged his large self into the chair and leaned his elbows into his thighs, staring at me with intense curiosity.

I looked away from him, toward Mother's puffy, tearful eyes. "I need to talk to Deirdre," I said.

"We have to take a quick little trip to the hospital first, okay? Just to make sure you're all right," she said.

"Who's Deirdre?" the cop asked. A pair of handcuffs rested on his leg, dangling from a clip on his belt. The silver star on his breast pocket read "Prairie Bluff." Everything was becoming so official! I eyed the gun in his leather holster. Even the Illinois flag patch on his sleeve intimidated me.

"A boarder. But she has nothing to do with this," Mother said. She widened her eyes to warn me against mentioning Deirdre again. I realized then that she had figured out that Deirdre was a Heroine. It angered me, how she wanted to protect Deirdre, and how she wouldn't listen to my story.

"Miss, have you seen this man before?"

"Never."

"What color was his hair?"

"Blondish brown, I guess."

"Did he have any distinguishing marks?"

"He had a beard. And long hair."

"Damned hippie," the cop said.

"Did he look like a hippie, Penny?" Mother asked.

This was going in the wrong direction. I didn't want them to catch Conor, even though I doubted they could. But if he did appear, he'd probably slice off their heads with one blow. I remembered him slashing and stabbing the earth in his rage. Would Mother and I be somehow responsible for a cop-killing? I had to get them to stop searching. The wilder my story, the sooner they'd call off the search. "He was a Celtic king! Come back to look for his lost wife."

"A king?" Marone's eyebrows came together.

"Don't make up stories," Mother said.

"I'm not. Ask Deirdre. She'll tell—"

"Officer Marone, please." Mother looked up at the cop with a soulful stare. She was using her big eyes to derail my outing of Deirdre. I knew it was bad, if Mother was turning on the charm for a cop. "This isn't going anywhere."

The cop was not immune to Mother's beauty. "Okay," he said. "That's enough for now, Penny."

* * *

Mother and I sat in the back of Marone's squad car, the lights flashing without the siren as he sped through the empty Prairie Bluff streets. The faux gas lamps shone with a meager yellow light. I was too worried to speak to Mother, and the harsh and raspy voice of the dispatcher spewing code numbers and addresses from his radio silenced us both. Everything felt recognizable, but in a TV way: the grating between us and him, the back doors that wouldn't open. I stared out the window, watching the houses get smaller, from Tudor mansions to split-levels to ranches; the gas lamps changed to ordinary streetlights. When we pulled into the Northbluff Hospital, I felt as if I were entering a movie set: the squares of lit windows, the staff milling about in the parking lot, the boxy ambulance with the doors flung open. Marone let us out of the backseat, then said he'd go and talk to the admitting desk for us. Mother and I followed him in.

The corridor and waiting room were crawling with people. Two little boys ran circles around a pregnant white woman. When I sat down in a vinyl chair, one of them cocked an eyebrow and said, "You don't look sick." A woman with pudgy arms and swollen ankles wept in her husband's arms. He patted her back and said, "We'll find a way."

Behind a curtain, a woman screamed, "I just want this needle out of my hand!"

A nurse charged in and yelled, "We have a life-threatening situation here! I'll have him talk to you when the life-threatening situation is settled!"

But the woman wouldn't let up. "I want this needle out of my hand right now!"

A Boy Scout hobbled around on crutches, his purple and swollen foot tucked behind him. A baby squalled in his mother's arms. A man held his stomach and stared up at a bombed Vietnamese village on a corner television. Mother shook her head at the screen, tapping her foot. I scanned the room for Marone. He stood at the front desk, talking to a man in a doctor's coat. Pushing huge silver-rimmed glasses up his nose, he laughed and patted Marone on the back. He gestured to a box of Dunkin' Donuts, but Marone shook his head. They both turned and looked at me, and I dropped my head.

A few minutes later, a nurse with a single gray braid called my name and led us into a private examination room. Mother sat down with a clipboard and started to fill out papers the nurse gave her. The nurse had me pee in a cup in an adjacent bathroom. I thought they would put iodine on my cuts, make me say ah! and send me along with an aspirin. Instead, the nurse wrapped a tube around my forearm and told me to pump my fist.

"Gonna draw some blood."

I squeezed my eyes shut as she stuck the needle in the crook of my arm. It was only a pinch, but I still couldn't look. She handed me a cotton ball and told me to press the spot. As I sat on a stool, she swung up two foot pedals from under the bed and tossed a gown to me.

"Put this on, honey."

I pulled the gown over my head, slipped my tank top off my shoulders, and stepped out of my shorts just as the gown dropped around my hips. The shy girl's disrobing style.

The nurse draped a sheet across the end of the bed and patted it. "Have a seat, Penny. The doctor will be here in a moment." She pushed open the door and stepped out of the room.

Mother and I sat there quietly, the air conditioner humming. Somebody knocked on the door, and the man I'd seen in the hallway breezed into the room, the flaps of his coat blown back, a cloud of musky cologne in his wake. He pulled on his Fu Manchu mustache and extended a clammy hand.

"Penny. Dr. Keller."

I shook his hand quickly, and he turned to Mother. "Ms. Entwhistle? Dr. William Keller."

His use of "Ms." was well calculated, and Mother visibly relaxed, her shoulders dropping down from her ears.

"Can I call you Anne-Marie?"

Mother shrugged. "Sure."

"Great, Anne-Marie, I just need to ask Penny a few questions, and then we can see what's what." His voice was smooth and friendly, but with the smarmy warmth of a car salesman. He picked up his clipboard again and smiled big at me, showcasing his oversized yellow teeth. One front tooth protruded farther than the other, like a battered picket fence. "Now, Penny, do you know what year it is?"

"It's 1974."

"Do you know where you are?"

"At the hospital."

On and on went the battery of questions. Then he asked, "Do you know who the president is?"

"Unfortunately."

He pointed a finger at me and snapped his fingers, winking like a talk show host. "Good one, kiddo!" He checked some boxes on his clipboard. "That's great. Mental status seems fine at the moment. Now, here's the nurse. She'll be giving you a little examination, and then you and I will continue our chat!"

The nurse set down a plastic tray that held a pile of large Q-tips, a box of rubber gloves, a tube of something. Even though she was probably only in her mid-twenties, the circles under her eyes and the heavy way she moved made her seem much older. "Okay, Penny, I need you to lie back on the bed. There you go. Now put your feet in the stirrups, and scooch to the end of the bed." She turned to Mother. "Ma'am, perhaps you should wait in the hall?"

"I'm not going anywhere!"

"Is this Penny's first time?"

"She's thirteen!"

"My first time what?"

"Honey." Mother loosened her grip on my arm. "The nurse needs to examine you . . . inside."

"Up my—?"

"Vagina." Mother bit her index finger, nodding her head. She'd always insisted on using real anatomical words and not euphemisms.

"Why?" Then it dawned on me. They thought I'd been raped. "Nobody. Did. That."

"I'm sure you're right, but we have to confirm it."

"It's a simple procedure, miss. Be over in no time." The nurse moved to the foot of the bed and palmed the stirrups from behind, giving each an encouraging pat. "Just put your feet in here."

"Nurse. Will you please give me a moment alone with my daughter?"

"Yes, ma'am," she said. "But we're packed to the gills tonight."

As soon as she crossed the threshold, I started to whine. "Why won't you believe me?"

"I do believe you. I want to believe you more than anything. But there's only one way to satisfy the police. They have to know what sort of predator they're looking for." She handed me a tissue.

"It's Deirdre's husband. She ran away from him, and now he's come to get her back. Just tell them that."

"You know I can't tell them that," Mother said.

"Why not?" I challenged. "Why do we have to keep hiding the Heroines? Why do their needs always come first?"

"Don't be so dramatic. They don't always come first. Anyway, how can we tell the police about Deirdre when she isn't . . ." Mother closed her eyes. "Isn't real." Her face buckled when she said that; it looked as if she wanted to devour her own lips.

"You know she is!" I cried.

"But nobody will believe us. They'll think we're nuts. And we don't know what might happen to Deirdre. Others could interfere. Oh, Penny! I've explained this a million times." Mother wrapped her arms around me, but I pushed her away. I couldn't believe she was denying a Heroine's existence! She, who defended them at any cost, was now a cowardly Peter. I half expected a cock to crow. I didn't believe she was trying to protect me. She was protecting Deirdre, the Homestead, all the past and future Heroines. She was protecting herself. Everybody but me. I truly felt like a lunatic. I didn't want to listen to Mother's logic. All she was doing was choosing the Heroines over me. I harped on one point. "If Deirdre isn't real, then who's that blonde upstairs in my room?"

"You know what I mean. Nobody's going to believe it. And if you keep talking about it, they'll think there's really something wrong with you."

"I'm not the one with a problem! Why did you even call the cops?"

"I was worried sick! You were gone for hours and—"

"I wish you'd just gone to bed." I balled up the Kleenex and threw it at her face, but it struck her shoulder, and she bent to pick it up.

The nurse knocked at the door and poked in her head, pointing at her watch. "Ma'am, I really need to get this done. The police need the report."

Mother nodded, and helped me to get situated in the stirrups, which were cold against the pads of my feet. I wasn't used to spreading my knees, and they instinctively knocked together. The nurse put on a rubber glove and squirted gel on her hands and came toward me. "Now, you'll feel a little discomfort, Penny. But the more you relax, the faster it will be over. First I'll put this speculum in."

I didn't know how to relax. She pressed my knees apart and guided something cold inside me; it felt like the top of a metal baseball bat was going up me. I looked at Mother, and she squeezed my hand, as my tears welled. If this was what girls had to go through, I never wanted to grow up.

"Now, I'm just going to put this swab in. Hang in there, Penny, you're doing great. It'll be like a little pinch."

It felt more like being pierced by a needle. "Ouch!" I cried.

"Relax!" the nurse urged. "We're almost there."

"Honey, breathe in through your nose and out through your mouth," Mother said.

I sniffed and snorted, but then I felt the baseball bat pull out of me in three distinct tugs. The nurse raised her head. "Hymen's intact."

"Thank God!" Mother blew air out of her mouth, then hugged me, but I stiffened, drawing my arms in closer to myself.

The nurse tugged the fingertips of her glove, then pulled it over her hand. She stepped on the foot pedal of a garbage can and dropped something inside. "I'll tell Dr. Keller you're ready to see him."

I sat up and squeezed my legs together. Mother tried to smooth my hair, but I ducked. Dr. Keller whisked into the room, jazz-tapping his clipboard with a four-color Bic pen.

"All right, all right. Penelope Entwhistle. Lovely name. Musical." He hummed a corny melody. "Now, according to the police report, you encountered a man in the woods, is that right? Officer Marone said something about a man on horseback . . ."

I looked at Mother. She shook her head almost undetectably, but Keller caught it. "Anna-Maria, perhaps it's best if I speak with Penny alone, don't you think?"

"I won't—"

"Of course you won't." He wrapped an arm around her shoulder. "But still, it's a little better if we make this a tête-à-tête. Volition effect, you see? It's when the patient tells the doctor what they think the parent wants to hear, instead of telling the truth. Messes up"—he waved his hands fussily, as if he were shaking drops of water from his fingertips—"the whole diagnostic procedure. You understand." He led her to the door, and I thought he might pat her on the ass. "Go get yourself some coffee. I bought some donuts for the staff. Help yourself. I'll send the nurse for you the minute we're finished in here."

I suddenly felt exhausted. The deflowering-by-speculum had depleted what sparse reserves I had. Outwitting a smooth psychiatrist was outside my range. So instead I just went silent, shrugged, and said, "I don't know" or "No" to his myriad questions. Had I seen the man before? Had I ever had a blackout? Did the man speak? Had I heard voices before? Where was my father? I had no idea what his questions were driving at. But I must have said enough to fit some profile as a paranoid schizophrenic.

He took another tack with Mother.

CHAPTER 9

Further back story +
A mid-twentieth-century Heroine's
philosophical crisis + *Mother tries to*
indoctrinate Franny + *Franny afoot* +

Mother had little experience with the psychiatric world. Her parents subscribed to the "unexamined life *is* worth living" philosophy. When Mother got pregnant, they would never have allowed her to discuss her private problems with a psychiatrist. At that time, only complete neurotics and lunatics needed psychiatric help. The Entwhistles were above that sort of thing, though Mother later told me she wished she'd received some psychological support during her pregnancy. Ever the autodidact, and disparaging her parents' approach, she'd read profusely in the pop psychology of the day when she had to figure out how to raise me. Thanks to Dr. Benjamin Spock, I was cuddled whenever I cried, toilet-trained with patience, encouraged to become an "individual." With the Heroines, however, Mother stuck to the bromides of their own eras; she treated the Heroines' nervous breakdowns with bed rest and broth.

The most contemporary "unhinged" Heroine who'd visited was

Franny Glass, Salinger's depressed waif who'd taken to the couch with *The Way of the Pilgrim,* a book about a pilgrim who'd learned to pray incessantly. Mother, like any literate girl of the fifties, had read every letter of Salinger's work. She was delighted to see Franny at the Homestead, who'd arrived in 1972 when I was eleven. Mother relished the fact that Franny wasn't in a romantic funk, pining for some man, but instead in the midst of a philosophical crisis. She didn't see Franny's problems as psychological, but sociological. The feminist in Mother was troubled by Franny, who had remained passive, prostrate on the couch, while Zooey tried to bully her into sanity. Franny never took any decisive action. In Salinger's other book, *Raise High the Roof Beam, Carpenters,* Franny recounts a tale of her flying around the living room. She remained "otherized, objectified," obviously an adored child who'd morphed into a problematic woman. What really struck Mother was that Franny's story had no ending. She never got out of the cluttered Glass family's Upper West Side apartment. At the Homestead, Franny was full of invectives for Zooey, so it appeared that rather than arriving in the middle of her narrative, she'd arrived at the *end* of it.

I had read the Salinger classics with nominal comprehension the summer before Franny showed up (*Seymour: An Introduction* had especially bored me). I didn't really understand what she was depressed about, and I enjoyed the beginning best, when she and Lane went to the restaurant to eat escargots and he weirdly sniffed her raccoon coat. It all seemed oddly sophisticated.

Mother was more forceful with Franny than she'd ever been with other Heroines. Maybe it was the newly minted copies of *Ms.* scattered around the living room, maybe it was Franny's age, or the lack of resolution in Franny's story. But something about Franny's situation surmounted Mother's usual wall of restraint, and for the first time I saw her try to persuade a Heroine to reexamine her situation.

"You can't let your brothers do your thinking for you!" Mother said. "Don't be a prop for their egos."

We were sitting in the living room after lunch, Franny curled up on the couch, Mother in an armchair, and I stretched out on the window seat, pretending to read. Mother had me well trained to pipe down back then, and the Heroines' drone usually sent me into a post-repast snooze. But Franny was different somehow. Modern. I liked her black pixie haircut, her slight New York accent. She had striking Irish-Jewish features, fair skin, blue eyes, thick hair.

"They're brilliant people, why shouldn't they guide me?" Franny said.

"We women have to find our own power!"

"Power's an illusion. Often power and wisdom are revealed through the most lowly—the poor, the children."

"Exactly the people the patriarchy seeks to silence!"

Franny sank back into the couch, and I noticed her fine lips moving. She was trying to pray without ceasing, and she clutched the book she'd brought with her, *The Way of the Pilgrim.* I'd never seen a Heroine bring an object with her, which tells you just how much she was clinging to that book. I squinted to see her mouth the words, "Lord Jesus Christ, have mercy on me." We weren't religious, Mother and I, so I had an atheist's fascination for the devout. The prayer, according to *Zooey,* in its full recitation was, "Lord Jesus Christ, have mercy on me, a miserable sinner," but Franny had dropped the last part. Her praying was like a nervous tic, a Tourette's that kicked in when she wished to drown out Mother. I tried it myself, *Lord Jesus, have mercy on me.* I liked the idea of setting my experience to this refrain, imagined standing on the field with my lacrosse stick, hurling a ball into the goal and chanting, *Have mercy on me.* It was like apologizing to the other team for scoring.

Franny lifted up on an elbow, suddenly inspired, perhaps by her mantra. "I mean, what's important is to lead a simple life," she said. "We're too busy complicating things, with the trappings of conventional life." She gestured to the room, and I took in the faded Persian rugs, Grandma's old fringed velvet couches, the standing lamps, the magazines. "By just saying this prayer, over and over, you come to know God."

"The ultimate patriarch. The guy with a beard and a staff."

That sounded cool to me. A force. I nodded my head, and though I didn't say anything, Franny glanced in my direction and we locked eyes for a second.

"You just have so much going for you, Franny," Mother said. "So much strength and intelligence. I'd hate to see that thwarted."

Franny resumed the quiet mumbling and pressed the book under the pillow. Mother was giving one of her live-up-to-your-potential speeches, which I usually received when I brought home any grade less than a B. I found it mildly amusing to watch Franny zoning out the same way, and I started to softly say the prayer. Franny's mysticism appealed to my imagination far more than Mother's feminism. But mostly, the whole conversation made me uncomfortable, a little embarrassed by my mother, and I wanted to help Franny escape. An idea came to me. "Hey, Franny, do you still want me to show you the path into the woods?" I asked.

Franny sat up, relieved to have an exit strategy. "Oh, yes!"

I looked toward Mother and said, "I wanted to show her the path. So she wouldn't get lost when she's on her own."

"Oh, all right." Mother shrugged and started to straighten the copies of *Ms.* she'd strategically placed on the coffee table to tempt Franny. "Don't go too far. It's getting dark earlier. And put some Off! on. The bugs are murder out there. Be back in time to help Gretta with supper."

As Franny and I walked through the prairie, monarchs with their spread wings pulsed on the sunflowers. She threw her arms in the air and breathed in the spicy scent of weeds and wildflowers. "Thanks for inviting me out here, Penny. Your mother's a good lady, but I just can't bear another lecture!"

"Tell me about it."

Franny had hardly eaten since she'd arrived, and her eyes were swollen from so much crying. But the prairie worked a visible magic on her. Color returned to her pale cheeks, and her thin arms started to glow pink.

"How simple it would be to live out here! You must adore it, Penny."

"Wait'll I show you the pond!"

"Marvelous! I know it's absolutely too Thoreauvian of me, but I *do* think nature holds the answer, don't you?"

"Uh-huh," I said. Franny was the first Heroine who had paid attention to me, and I felt like I could be myself with her. "But what's the question?"

She burst into laughter. "Oh, Penny. You're so right."

We ran down the path and into the cool woods. The oaks arched over the path, a flickering canopy. Franny was easily winded, so I slowed down to let her catch her breath. "It's been ages since I've left the city. You have no idea how perfectly oppressive it is!"

"My grandparents live in the city," I said. "I hate going to their house."

"Why?"

"It's so fancy. And everything's white! The couches and the carpets. It's impossible to eat or move. My grandma practically chases me around with a dustpan, catching my crumbs."

"That's not really living." Franny sat down on a bench and ran her finger along the face of a parsnip plant. "I think that's what the question is. How do you live? How can anyone live a worthwhile life?"

"You have to be happy," I said.

"But what really makes anybody happy? Having a swanky apartment? A huge collection of cashmere sweaters and flannel skirts? Witty repartee in a martini bar? Or having your college team win the game? Is that as happy as anyone can expect to be?"

I had never really questioned whether or not I was happy, and the substance of Franny's list meant little in my eleven-year-old world. When you're a kid, happiness means having fun: parties, running around outside, sweets. But I could sense that Franny had another, mystical happiness in mind. "Does saying the prayer make you happy?"

She tucked her legs beneath her on the bench, and squeezed her hands between her knees. Staring into the trees, she looked penitent and shy. "More like content. At peace. Not laughing ha-ha happy, but relaxed, like I've moved out of this world." She turned her blue eyes on me. "What do *you* think of the prayer?"

"It seems like it would be kind of hard. To remember to say it all the time."

"You only have to work at it at first, then after you say it enough, it just becomes part of you."

"Like tying your shoelaces."

"Precisely. You do it without thinking. Your connection to God becomes automatic."

I sat down cross-legged on the bench beside her. "I don't think I believe in God."

"That's okay," she said.

"It just seems wrong, to pray for God to give you stuff. Then what happens when you don't get it? What does that say? It says God doesn't like you."

"There are a lot of different ideas about God out there. Not everyone believes in that kind of God either, one who intercedes for you. I think you're right too. That kind of God's pretty easy to disprove. If he doesn't intercede and give you what you want, then he either hates you or he doesn't exist at all."

"You said before that you thought God was a force."

"I guess I do. It's a feeling, and I swear, I can sense God in these woods, in these trees and plants, far more than I do in a temple or church. I mean, I haven't felt this marvelous in months, Penny! Just talking to you, being out here. Just think what it would be like to live here out in the woods. Build a little cabin, live off the land."

"You could fish! And grow vegetables," I said.

"Who needs the trappings of civilization? I'd need only my book, some blankets, a little cot. It's really the only way that the prayer could work. You have to simplify your whole life."

"But it's really cold in the winter. You'd have to keep a fire going, for sure."

"A great roaring fire!" Franny jumped to her feet. "C'mon. Let's look for the perfect spot!"

We spent the afternoon walking deep into the woods, as far as Albie and I had dared to go, and farther. This was before the village set aside certain acres for preservation, adding quaint bridges and cement benches with corporate plaques. There were no controlled burns, no deer-population control (other than lawless hunters), no cinder paths. The trails were overgrown, and we pushed through bramble and picked burrs from our clothes and hair. When we reached the edge of the woods and came to a prairie where the ground sloped and rose to a railroad track, the hot sunlight assaulted us. Along the gleaming tracks, four-foot thistles with their spiked purple heads waved in the breeze. The sunflowers reached riotous heights in the bright light along the tracks. Even the dragonflies looked bigger, more violet in their iridescence. Franny's cheeks were bright red, two drops of sweat in the space above her upper lip. Her damp bangs clung to her forehead.

"I feel like a kid again," she said.

I looked down at my Snow White watch, shocked to see that two hours had passed. I felt suddenly hungry and tired. I'd sweated off most of the mosquito repellent and had unknowingly scratched new bites till blood streamed from the crimson buttons.

"I have to go back," I said. "It's almost four. We'll just make dinner if we turn back now."

"I can't stop!" Franny said. "I can feel it. We're getting close to the spot."

"My mom'll be mad if I don't help Gretta with dinner."

"Is it that late already?"

I looked at my watch again. "It's twenty to four. I have to be back in time to set the table."

"I'm not the least bit hungry," Franny said.

"I'm kinda. Plus if I don't help Gretta, I'll be in big trouble. Tomorrow's the parade. My lacrosse team's marching."

"You can't miss the parade." Franny bit down on her thumb and looked with childish longing at the woods before us. The dark green foliage, the whiff of earth and dead leaves, promised a cool shelter. But she saw something more in there; she squinted, as if spying something undetectable to me. She'd become wild-looking, elfin, her pixie hair tangled with leaves, her fine limbs fluid beneath a cotton print dress. I suddenly got an eerie, feral feeling from her. Her dazzled blue eyes, the tang of her sweat. I was eleven. I didn't understand what I was dealing with, and I feared that Franny would just keep running till night had fallen, leaving us easy prey to whatever menace Mother said dwelled in the woods.

"Look," I said. "We can come back tomorrow morning. First thing."

Franny shook her head, a nervous shake that lifted one side of her twitching mouth. She pressed the cloth-bound, emerald book between her small breasts, then extended it, pointing toward the woods. "This just feels right, like the path, the way."

"I'll get in really big trouble. Maybe . . ." I wiped my forehead and shook drops of sweat from my hand. "Maybe you should go ahead without me. You'll be able to find your way back alone?"

"But I want you to enjoy the tranquil space with me!"

"I can't!" I yelled, my temper flaring.

"Oh!" Franny stepped back and started to mumble the prayer to herself. *Lord Jesus, have mercy on me.*

"I'm sorry," I said. I was as big a bully as Zooey and my mom.

"I'm sorry. I just thought you . . ." She pulled in her lips and set her bright eyes on me. "You're practically my best friend."

I felt flattered and oddly put off by this title. I was a little girl! When I didn't say anything, Franny said, "I understand. Your mother. You have to . . . answer. But are you sure you're okay alone? See, I hate to make you walk home without me, buddy, but I really feel on the verge of something."

"I'll be fine. Don't worry." My voice had softened, I was sorry to have been angry with the only grown-up Heroine who'd ever noticed me. "But promise you'll come back tonight. Mother says the woods are dangerous at night."

"Absolutely." Franny embraced me, and I felt the dampness of her dress, her bony ribs. I'd never actually *touched* a Heroine before, and she felt frail to me, skinny and short though I was. Her sharp sweat smelled like craziness itself, and even as I pulled away, she held the hug a second or two longer than I liked.

"You're the best," she whispered, squeezing my hands.

"See you later!" I ran up the embankment and back onto the tracks, relieved to get away from her. How quickly things had taken a weird turn. My instincts to retreat toward home were deeply ingrained, as was my fear of the woods. My growing suspicion that Franny was a little bit off unnerved me.

The tracks eventually curved back into the woods at the edge of our prairie, so I just had to follow them. I ran from crosstie to crosstie, gauging my stride to meet the dark brown, splintering planks. Sunlight glinted silver off the rails, slashing my eyes. I had a pretty good sense of direction, yet fear gripped me the whole way. Even in the daylight, I imagined scaring up a wolf or bear, animals that didn't even frequent our woods. I took my eyes off the crossties for a second, scanning the horizon. In the distance, a deer and fawn dashed across the tracks. My mouth fell open, my foot caught on a crosstie, and I fell face forward onto the track. My hands flew out, bracing my fall. Pointed chalky rocks scraped my knees and hands, and a sharp jolt in my kneecap made my head swoon. I shut my eyes, and when I reopened them, sunspots clouded my vision. I breathed deeply, trying to shake the dizziness. When the sunspots cleared, I saw myself, sprawled out on a railroad track in the hot sun, desperate. I'd made a big mistake. Leading Franny out into the woods had been a big mistake. I broke into a cold sweat.

I climbed off the tracks and went back into the woods, miraculously picking up a trail that still had the trace of our footprints. Thank God! Soon enough I smelled water, heard the croak of frogs, and felt a rush of relief. I was on the other side of the pond I visited daily, the cattails waving in the sun. I ran along the edge and picked up the trail back to the prairie. I was so relieved to be in familiar territory, yet I also realized that just as I had doubled back toward home, Franny had probably doubled her distance away from it.

I made it home by four-thirty, and caught my breath against the patio wall before opening the kitchen door. When I looked through the window I saw Mother shaking salt onto a big bowl of potato salad and Gretta stirring a pitcher of lemonade. Gretta was just past forty by then, still blond and smooth-skinned, with a comfortable roll of fat above her apron ties. I feared and loved her in a way that was completely opposite of what I felt for Mother. She essentially wore the pants in the family—keeping me in line, teaching me the proper ways to do housework. She was always bent to the task at hand; I never worried about her prying into my life. She dealt in tangibles: meat, drink, roasted root vegetables. She mostly ignored the Heroines, only occasionally stepping in when a wily one needed a firm hand. Franny had been like any other guest to her.

"Where's Franny?" Mother asked as I came in.

"She's not coming for dinner. She doesn't feel good."

"Doesn't feel *well*," Mother said. "Is she up in her room?"

I ran to the cabinets and opened the doors to twin stacks of plates. "Which plates, Gretta? Inside or out?"

"Outside," Gretta said. "Too hot in dining room. Wash those hands first, you."

I went to the sink and let the cool water run over my dusty arms first. My hands shook as I rubbed the soap between my palms. I wiped them on a dishtowel and went back to the cabinet, taking down a stack of miscellaneous china plates, oddballs Mother had collected at yard sales and thrift stores.

Gretta handed me a large cotton tablecloth with bright red strawberries. "Put this down first."

"We'll need to bring Franny a tray," Mother said.

"I'll bring it up later." I backed into the door.

"That's very nice, Penny," Mother said. "She seems to like you. I'll make dinner for two. Maybe she'll eat if you're with her."

After I'd set the table and the other boarders had gathered around the picnic table, Mother handed me a tray with two plates with chicken salad sandwiches on hard bread, potato salad, and grated beets. I was famished, so it wouldn't be hard to eat Franny's share. I climbed the stairs to her room, half hoping I'd push open the door and find her curled up on the window seat. But the room was empty, her white bedspread tucked in with tight Gretta-style corners. Sunlight filtered through the yellowed eyelet curtains. I put the tray on the nightstand and sat in an armchair. I ate my sandwich absentmindedly and stared at the edge of curling, flowered wallpaper in the corner of the room. I was really afraid now. If Franny got hurt out there or didn't come back, I wasn't sure what would happen. I was just young enough to care most about not getting in trouble. Mother would probably assume that Franny had returned to her story. I didn't think anything could change in her story, since she'd come to us at the end of her book. But I was deeply dismayed that the first Heroine who'd cared about me might meet a terrible fate. And it would all be my fault. I finished everything on my plate but the beets, and I glanced around the room feeling morose. Water spots stained the ceiling; the Persian rug was threadbare at the corners. Everything about the Homestead seemed worn out and old. I longed for multicolored shag, rainbow canopy beds, denim beanbags, the furnishings

I'd seen at Albie's house. I was young enough to believe that these trappings would prove I had a normal life.

Just as I picked up Franny's sandwich, somebody knocked on the door.

I shot out of the chair. "Franny?"

Mother poked her head in the room. "Isn't she here?"

I shook my head and looked down at the crusty bread in my hand. Mayonnaise squished along the edges.

"Where is she? Is she gone gone?"

"I think so," I mumbled.

Mother came in the room and sat down beside me; she wrapped an arm around my shoulder, and I started to cry. "You really cared for her."

I shrugged, sniffling and wiping the tears with the back of my hand. I longed to tell Mother the truth, to ask her to organize a search party. But I'd deliberately disobeyed her order not to go too deep in the woods. And her comforting arms felt so good. She kissed the top of my head. "I sometimes get too attached to them as well."

"It's not fair. Nobody else here even talks to me."

"She really took to you. I can see why. You're very compassionate."

I shook my head. "No, I'm not." I couldn't bear to be complimented, not when something really bad might happen to Franny.

"Let's go downstairs," Mother said. "There's ice cream."

I shrugged again, and Mother lifted the tray from the nightstand. She sighed as she glanced around the room, some trace element of Franny still lingering in the air.

"Mom?"

She looked back. "Yes?"

"What's so bad about the woods at night?"

"It's just—" She sat back down on the bed. "It's not the woods—the trees and plants. It's that sometimes bad people lurk there. And it's just not a good idea to go alone. You should always have somebody with you, that's all."

I didn't feel any closer to understanding. "Has a Heroine ever just run off?"

"Most of them hardly get out of bed." She looked at me with alarm. "Why? Do you think Franny ran away?"

"No! I left her up here."

"That would be unthinkable. Having Franny wandering around the woods."

"I said I left her up here!" I snapped.

"Then she's probably returned to her story." Mother patted my arm. "Don't get so upset. I know how hard it can be when they leave."

I'd begun to notice how few friends Mother had. She didn't socialize with anybody but the boarders and Gretta and me. Sometimes I was afraid that I'd wind up like her, friendless and isolated. Who did I have for friends? Just Albie, and we hung out only in the summer now that he was in high school. I wasn't one of the cool girls on the lacrosse team. The Heroines secret kept me from ever gaining deeper friendships. Most of the girls from the Academy boarded, so they had their own hierarchies and cliques, and the day school girls were the oddballs, so odd we never ever wanted to associate with each other. Even though Franny was older than I, I felt like we'd had a genuine connection. I couldn't believe that I'd actually let Franny get lost, leaving me alone again. "Franny was great."

"Yes, but I don't know if I got through to her. Usually I feel like the Heroines are doing a little better before they leave."

I hoped that Mother hadn't gotten through to Franny, but to deflect her suspicion, I said, "No, when we were out walking, she seemed better. More relaxed. Maybe she was just ready to go back."

"I hope so."

The next few days I roamed the woods, but a paralyzing, irrational fear kept me from going past the point where I'd left Franny at the railroad tracks. The leafy woods seemed haunted now. At night I hardly slept, hoping that every creak on the staircase was Franny coming back to the Homestead. I longed for her so. But we never saw her again. No other subsequent Heroine ever made me feel as special, and I think that's when my attitude toward the Heroines started to change. Franny's attention had spoiled me, or maybe just awakened me, and as I became twelve, and then thirteen, I lost my tolerance for the way the Heroines monopolized my mother and ignored me.

CHAPTER 10

✦ Con Man Keller ✦ Mother caves for all the rightish reasons ✦

After Dr. Keller finished with me, he brought Mother down to his office to make his hard sell. I learned of it later through Mother and by hearing similar accounts from mildly troubled girls who had wound up in the Unit. Keller's trick was to bring the mother (preferably a single mom) into his office, and leave her there stewing for about ten minutes. He lifted a stack of *Pediatric Psychiatry* journals from a chair and offered Mother a seat. The room was overfurnished, with crammed bookshelves, a dusty rubber plant, and a bronze sculpture shaped roughly like a vulva. Piles of psychology journals still in their plastic sheaths occupied an old velvet chaise longue, some vestige of earlier, more Freudian days. A 1973 calendar with a picture of a smiling woman and a giant Valium pill was tacked to the wall beneath framed diplomas.

"I'll be back momentarily," he said. "Just need to double-check about some insurance forms."

Mother's initial ease with Keller was dissipating more quickly than the trail of his French cologne. On his big oak desk, a mantel clock ticked like a metronome. It was one-thirty in the morning, but Keller was as fired up as a rooster at the crack of dawn. Mother was exhausted and intimidated. She stared up at the framed diplomas above his large desk: BA Yale, MD University of Chicago. His wiry hair and comical mustache reminded her of the son-in-law on *All in the Family,* but the Latin-scripted, gilded certificates proved that Keller had the weight of the Establishment behind him. Ivy League bachelor's degrees always stirred feelings of inferiority in Mother, having forsaken Vassar to give birth to me. Who could blame her for the occasional twinge of regret for making that choice? That old feeling of shame seeped in, I believe, and made her more vulnerable to Keller's schemes.

Dr. Keller bustled back into the room and sat down in his big leather chair. He tapped his pen on a stack of papers and lay them down. "Sorry to keep you waiting, Anne-Marie. Busy night!"

"That's fine, Doctor," Mother said. "I just am—"

"Wondering what's going on with your daughter." He leaned his elbows into the desk and smiled grimly. "Now, I don't want to alarm you. But I think what we're dealing with here is a schizophrenic episode."

"No, no! Penny might be a little *imaginative,* but she's hardly schizophrenic."

"I agree, it's rare for girls her age." He tapped his large teeth with the end of his pen. "But there are reported cases—and I have personally seen a number of them—of schizophrenia in children her age. It's rare, but we want to make sure. And the incidence is on the rise. Some scientists think it's linked to early drug use. Penny hasn't been using any drugs, has she?"

"Penny's not a druggie girl," Mother shot back, without thinking. Like most mothers, Mother was reluctant to have her child labeled, even if she had caught the whiff of weed on my clothes a few times. We'd actually had two harrowing conversations in her sunroom about it, and I'd promised not to smoke again. I wasn't really into drugs then; I sometimes just got tired of watching Albie smoke alone.

"We should have her blood test results in the next day or two. Just to be sure about that." He peered over his glasses at Mother.

"Now, even though Penny's initial agitation seems to have normalized, I would like to keep her for observation."

"Overnight in the ER?"

"No, we would move her over to the Unit."

"What's the Unit?"

"It's a safe place for adolescents who share some of Penny's troubles." He said this in a modulated singsong, tilting his bushy-haired head from side to side. "I think it's important for Penny to get a break from some of her current influences. She'd be very safe in the Unit. Nobody from outside could come close, you see. We don't know if we're dealing with a teenager or a grown man, but I'm convinced that Penny met somebody in those woods. If not, then her situation may be very grave indeed. On the schizo-affective front."

"I don't think it's her imagination," Mother said. Keller must have somehow sniffed out that Mother was worried about Conor getting close to me again. Locking me up would ensure that Conor would be unable to reach me, and that I couldn't go out looking for him.

"Then she's involved with somebody. Into something that's way over her head."

"Maybe so," Mother said. As long as she could talk me into not blabbing about Conor, she reasoned to herself, I'd probably be out of the hospital the next day. One night of observation meant one night of her not having to worry about my safety. She looked at the folds in the drapes and whispered, "I'm not sure."

"It's completely up to you, of course. But I assure you, we have very effective treatments these days. And the number one thing is Penny will be safe."

"Until—"

"Until we learn exactly what or whom she encountered in the woods."

"But can't I just keep her at home?"

"Certainly you could do that. Absolutely yes. But I ask you"—

he leaned in close and patted her arm—"do you honestly think that you can provide care on the level that we offer here?"

"I suppose not."

"And you have so much else on your plate." He jabbed her weak spots with the tip of his patriarchal spear. "A woman raising a teenager on her own."

"We do all right."

"Of course you do. But if Penny *is* delusional, better for her to have an episode here, where she's under wonderful care. Think of it as a nice safe break from the pressures of everyday life. So many of our patients find renewed energy and strength."

"You wouldn't keep her for more than one night!"

Keller scrunched up his mouth and closed one eye. "Ballpark—two, three nights. If that's what's called for. We do have to see how the tox screens go. And in the meantime, you could get some rest."

"You said those tests take only a day or two." Mother was doing the math. A few days would buy her time to deal with Deirdre, maybe do something to get rid of Conor.

"True. And if we can get Penny to speak honestly about her feelings, she'll be back home, lickety-split."

That was the rub. If I did start leveling with the doctors, I'd be in there forever. Mother knew she'd have to convince me to keep quiet about Conor. I may not have been schizo, but she figured I might be angry enough to sabotage myself just to get back at her.

"We have wonderful treatments for all kinds of conditions that afflict our young people today. Under so much pressure from peers, school, parents." Keller took Mother's silence to drive home the hard sell. "And if you don't, I'm afraid . . ."

"Afraid of what?"

"Well, you see, if we don't admit her, and she's in the ER, and even though you have quite excellent coverage, your insurance might not pay for it."

"They have to!" Mother said.

He *tsk*ed and shook a pen at her in a gentle, scolding manner.

"Not necessarily. Not if you take Penny home now. See, I hate to do this, but if you make that decision, I'll have to sign the order that says AMA." He lifted a pen and scribbled the letters in the air.

"AMA?"

"Against medical advice." This is where his routine really kicked in, his tone terribly earnest and apologetic. "I've seen it happen, Anne-Marie, to good people like yourself. And God, I hate to see it—but people lose their insurance for going AMA. I don't mean to scare you with this, but there could be severe consequences for Penny's insurability for the rest of her life."

"That's ridiculous!" Mother said.

"I know, I know. But see, if something happens later with Penny—even if it isn't immediately after, but down the line—if she has another episode which requires further treatment, the insurance can use the AMA as an excuse to cancel your coverage. They can say you were negligent. That you aggravated her existing problems by going against what the doctor recommended."

Mother sat up straight in the chair and tried to blink away the fatigue in her head. At times like these she wished she had a partner, boyfriend, husband, or even that Gretta were there. Gretta always understood what Mother was up against. Grandfather Entwhistle paid for our medical insurance, and if we lost it Grandmother would breathe fire. My grandparents were summering in Nice with some old friends, so there was no risk of their finding out right away that I'd been hospitalized. But if she lost the coverage, she'd have to sell the Homestead and find a full-time job. "I can't let that happen."

"No, you can't. AMA can have consequences, see, even for Penny's future employability."

"It can?" Mother saw a lifetime of obstacles stretching out before me. "You won't drug her, will you?"

"Oh, I doubt very much that will be necessary. We have wonderful group sessions, where the kids can open up with a highly trained therapist." He held open his hands and tilted his bushy head like an unconditionally loving grandfather to deliver the soft sell. "Remember how Penny was as a little girl? With that joyful affect? We can get her back to that state of bliss! I'm sure she wasn't always sullen and silent, was she?"

"No, she's always been charming, lovable."

"And don't you want that Penny back?"

What parent wouldn't want to see her disgruntled teenager returned to the sweet innocence of her childhood, to the days before her cynical and critical eyes turned mercilessly on the one who gave her life?

"Yes, I do want her back," Mother said.

"Then you just need to sign some forms. They'll be ready in the morning."

And that was that.

CHAPTER 11

*+ I wake up + Flash-forward: psychic
revelations + Tips from Florence + Fresh
betrayals from Mother + I'm committed +*

They moved me into the Unit that night. I awoke the next morning to the sound of curtain rings being flung back, and the sun stabbing my eyes. Groggy and dry-mouthed, I had no idea where I was. Four layers of white and pale green sheets enveloped me. A thin white curtain encircled my bed. As I always did, I touched my breasts to see if they'd grown overnight. Then everything came flooding back, Mother's betrayal foremost. A sharp pain pierced my throat as I caught my breath, about to cry. I felt absolutely bereft, as if a spirit had possessed me, then escaped with my soul. My head and neck ached from Conor's rough capture, and my inner thighs and tailbone were horse-sore. The faces of the cop, doctor, and the nurses who had pitied and stared at me the night before flooded my head. I pulled the soft sheets to my chin, shuddering to think that they had seen my body in its underdeveloped state. As attention-starved as I may have felt, this was not the notice I sought.

Somebody pulled aside the sheet hanging around my bed, then hurried to clumsily tie back the sheer gold curtains in front of the windows. She spun around, hands on her hips, and I read her tag and saw her name was Florence, and she was a nurse's aide. The creases around her mouth and eyes made her look as if she were chronically inhaling a cigarette. She was skinny as a twelve-year-old, and when she smiled, a gold cap flashed where one of her canines should be. A turquoise hairnet held back frosted hair, dark at the roots.

"Feeling better?" She had a deep, masculine voice and a Southern accent.

I shrugged, deciding to pretend to have lost the power of speech. Once, at theater camp, we'd had to carry on a conversation for ten minutes without speaking. I'd kept going for forty. I licked my dry lips and reached for a cup of water on the nightstand. I was utterly parched.

"I suppose you know the good news, darlin'," she said. "Your rape test come back negative."

I bugged out my eyes in a *Duh!* expression. Their very suspicion that Conor might have raped me enraged me. He wasn't like that. My understanding of rape had advanced somewhat since a friend and I had looked up its definition in the dictionary: the taking of a woman by force. I'd figured out since then that sex was involved. I might have been "taken by force," but I was still a virgin. But what perplexed me more was that I'd found something thrilling in the abduction. However much Conor had frightened me, my time in the woods with him was paradise compared to what had happened to me since. I'd actually felt moments of real happiness, riding on Conor's horse. I wondered if this was the sort of happiness Franny sought, but it seemed like she was looking for something else, something inside herself.

"You ain't surprised. Well, I wasn't neither." She walked over and released a tray from the side of my bed and lowered it in front of me. She smelled like cigarettes and lemony Jean Naté bath splash. Her long fingernails were painted tangerine. "I done told them you didn't have the look. Seen plenty of little girls who met the boogeyman in the woods. Those girls was spooked, all right."

I wanted to ask her about those girls. Like most children of the
era, I'd been well instructed not to take candy from strangers, to
beware of the boogeyman. Mother's prohibition against nighttime
woods-wandering had some of that flavor. But they were all wildly
vague warnings. Nobody ever showed up offering me Dum-Dum
suckers or Snickers bars. The very notion of an adult handing out
candy when it wasn't Halloween seemed far-fetched. They never
told you what this odd stranger wanted in exchange for the con-
fection. I always pictured the bad man in a black hat, wearing a
somber suit, driving a shiny sedan. There'd never been a Celtic-
king-on-horseback version.

Florence picked up my arm with her cold, leathery hand and
flipped up my wrist to take my pulse. I could see that she was
studying my palm. She coughed into her other hand and wiped it
on her pants leg. After a minute of glancing at my palm and at her
Mickey Mouse watch, Florence dropped my wrist and mumbled,
"Interesting." She went to the door and rolled in a food cart, then
pulled a tray from the middle shelf. "Had to do them tests,
though. Your mama's just like any mama. Wanted to be sure no
man done got inside her baby."

It was getting harder for me to maintain my silence. For one,
I wasn't a baby. For two, my mother was in no way like any other
mother. I glowered at Florence as she lowered the tray onto the
shelf in front of me.

"Old silent treatment, huh?" With a loud *tsk,* she rearranged
the items on my tray: a little house-shaped milk carton, a Styro-
foam cup of juice, and a bowl of cornflakes. "If you know what's
good for you, you won't be playing dumb for no Nurse Eleanor.
She loves provoking the silent ones. Then she can just poke 'em
with a needle and really keep 'em quiet. Dr. Keller's different.
He'll invent a diagnosis, especially if you won't talk to him. The
next thing you know"—she made a circle with her hands and
placed them on her head—"it's zappity-doo-dah!"

"Are they going to shock me?"

"Not yet, but could be. If you don't play it right."

I couldn't tell if she was telling the truth. She opened my carton of milk and poured it over the cornflakes as if I were two years old. The orange flakes disappeared in the milk, then floated back up, each cupping a drop of milk. I watched them slowly sink beneath the milk, taking my appetite with them.

"This is like the holding pen, see?" She made circles of her hands, then looked through them as if they were binoculars. She seemed to think the mime was necessary, that English wasn't enough to get the message through my head. "Observation. They're waiting to see if you try something funny."

"Like stab somebody with a plastic spoon?"

"Plan on sticking with that Celtic king story?"

"You're not even a nurse."

"Florence been here longer than all them nurses and doctors combined. They used to call all the girls hysterical. Now they're all schizo. I seen the way the wind blows. Keller's in around two hours a week. Eleanor's the one calling the shots. She's World War II. He's capital *M* Modern. Back in her day, they locked the crazy soldiers up and the nurses sat on the other side of the bars, tossing them food every few hours. He's all about making sure you're here for as long as your insurance pays."

I wasn't sure what my insurance would cover, so all I could say was, "I'm not crazy."

"I know you ain't crazy. Bet you a million bucks so does Keller, especially if your mama has high-end insurance. But you gotta play the game. Don't get all in a huff. Eleanor, she don't believe in talk therapy and all that. She just thinks y'all are just spoiled. Need a good kick in the ass is—"

"Florence!" A nurse stood at the door, tapping her watch face with a pen. She'd snuck up on us with her thick-soled nurse shoes. She was stout, with round full breasts and plump biceps. Tight salt-and-pepper curls were pinned beneath a white cadet's cap. She wore a silver pin on her lapel that read "U.S.," and her nametag said "Eleanor." Her authoritative vibe immediately repelled me, yet she had the pudginess of an old fat cop, not a fit soldier. "The other girls are waiting." She bustled across the room and readjusted the curtains so they hung with matching swoops. "Back in the Army, Penny, even the curtains had to be regulation!" She laughed as if this were a great joke, her false cheer readily transparent. I wondered immediately why she was trying to butter me up.

Florence ran to her cart and backed out the door, giving me a big wink, her eye disappearing into her wrinkled skin. Escaping Conor suddenly felt like a cakewalk compared to this place. Florence was right. I'd have to tell the adults what they wanted to hear. Since I'd left Conor in the woods, nothing had happened on my terms. I'd been rebelling in a stupid way. If I didn't wise up, I'd never see Conor again, and I could be stuck here a long time.

"Is Florence a former patient?" I asked.

Eleanor laughed, caught off guard. "You're feeling better."

"Much!" I reached for my cup of juice. A healthy appetite probably signified a healthy head around there. The juice was made from powder, pulpless and sugary Tang. I gulped it down. "Is my mother here?"

"She's speaking with Dr. Keller at the moment."

"What about?"

Eleanor wrapped a blood pressure band around my arm and pumped the rubber bulb. The band tightened, pulling my arm hair. "About what?"

Eleanor looked at the gauge. "Pressure's normal."

I dug my nails into my forearm to shut myself up. If I kept asking the same question, they'd call me hysterical. She'd heard me. I could wait. She unwrapped the blood pressure armband and dropped it in her pocket. When she leaned close to press the circle of her stethoscope to my chest, I smelled the coffee on her breath, felt her pillowy breasts on my arm. The pores on her nose were a million red pinpricks. White bobby pins held the salt-and-pepper curls beneath her cap. Her closeness made me shrink back into the pillow.

Eleanor looked at her watch and then held it to her ear. My silence finally registered, so she said, "They're looking over the paperwork. Ah, here she is at last!" Her tone made it sound as if Mother were late for an appointment.

Mother walked in the room and gave me a desperate look. I felt a wave of shame and pity for her, an amazing sensation considering I blamed her for my circumstances. From the circles under her eyes, I could tell she hadn't slept. Her long braid hung over her shoulder, and she sported a peasant skirt and a men's T-shirt that hung to her hips. Mother never bothered to press a tube of lipstick to her lips. Her tanned and freckled face looked exhausted, and she wore her leather peace sign, which even though the Vietnam War waged on, seemed outdated in 1974. She always wore it in oppositional environments: protest marches when Chicago cops were present and visits from her mother. I experienced that hyper-self-conscious constellation of emotions unique to thirteen-year-old daughters of oddball mothers. Shame. Sadness. Love. Anger. Hate.

"Would you leave me alone with my daughter, please?"

"Yes, ma'am," Eleanor snapped like a sarcastic high-ranking officer addressing a subordinate. She lifted her chin and glided out of the room like a great ship with white sails.

Mother put her hand on my forehead. I closed my eyes to avoid looking into hers.

"Did you sleep well?"

"I think they drugged me."

"Nonsense! Dr. Keller said they do that only in extreme cases. Thank God the tests were negative!"

"I told you they would be! Why wouldn't you believe me?"

"Penny, we don't have much time. Dr. Keller's on his way."

"Better check the hallway," I whispered. "That Eleanor's a snoop."

Mother went to the door and looked out, pulling it shut behind her. "Now you have to tell me more about this Celtic king."

"Ask Deirdre. It's her husband."

"I can't. If I say anything, then she'll know she's a Heroine."

"Oh, so *now* you admit that Deirdre's real!"

She ignored my challenge. "This is very bad. A Hero's come looking for a Heroine! It's the worst possible scenario."

"When can I go home? I'm supposed to meet him today."

"You can never meet him again."

"He needs my help to capture Deirdre!"

"You will absolutely not go near him. And you will not betray Deirdre!"

"You care more about her than you do about me."

"Nonsense."

"What are you going to do? Lock me in my room for the rest of my life?"

Mother swallowed and smoothed her hands down her skirt. She raised her chin and nodded her head. She kept nodding, as if the repetitive, up-and-down movement would affirm what she said next. "You'll be staying here a couple days."

"In the loony bin? You can't make me!"

"It's too risky for you to be back at home with that man running around."

"Send me somewhere. To Grandma and Grandpa's."

"They're in France."

"But I'm not crazy!" I shouted like a crazy person.

"Are they gonna find THC in your bloodstream, Penny?"

"I dunno."

"You told me you weren't smoking pot anymore. That it was just that once."

"A few hits with Albie aren't going to kill me."

"Well, that'll seal the deal!" She threw up her arms, reminding me of Grandmother Entwhistle. "You can blame yourself for being here, not me."

I could kick myself for getting high with Albie the day before, for going along out of boredom again.

"Talking things over with someone will do you some good. Everybody benefits from that. Dr. Keller said there are wonderful groups here."

"Right. You want me to tell Dr. Keller that Madame Bovary lived with us? Or should I tell him how you slapped me?"

"Don't—" Mother pressed the heels of her hands to her skull. "You need a haven, Penny. At least until I figure out how to deal with Deirdre."

"Can't commit *her,* huh?"

"I'm not committing you. I've checked into things." She glanced at the door and leaned closer. "If I sign you in, I can sign you out anytime. The doctor's insisting that if I take you home against medical advice, we'll lose our insurance."

Insurance didn't mean a whole lot to me. I started to cry, hot furious tears. "Lacrosse practice starts in two weeks! Why did you bring me here at all?" I felt a trickle of sweat drip down from my armpit. I couldn't believe what was happening. I was one of those girls who were put away. This did not fit my vision of myself, and I shook with the shock of it, my shoulders pinned up near my ears.

"Shhh." Mother stood up and watched me cry, afraid, I think, to disturb my sorrow, or maybe afraid to say the wrong thing. A few moments after I'd heaved a moaning sigh without manufacturing any tears, Mother put a hand on my cheek. "I found Deirdre's story. I went to the library as soon as it opened. It's an ancient Irish folktale. Pre-Christian."

I was glad to hear that Conor didn't come from a second-rate novel. His was just a very old story, maybe one of the first stories. "How'd Deirdre wind up?"

"The doctor's probably going to come in any minute."

"C'mon. What's with Conor? Good guy or bad?"

"Very bad."

I didn't want to believe this, but I could. The warm feelings I'd felt the night before flooded my body. I wished he'd ride up on his horse and carry me away from the hospital, maybe even transport me to ancient times. What would happen to him if I didn't return?

"Are the cops still looking for him?"

Mother shook her head. "They went to talk to your boyfriend. To Albie. That was the only possible lead."

"You know he's not my boyfriend." Albie and I had such a weird relationship. If we saw each other outside the woods, say in the library or in the town square, we'd ignore each other completely. "His mom'll have a conniption. Then she'll tell everybody about me. I'll be the big joke of the neighborhood!"

"I'll go talk to his mom this afternoon."

"Must be nice." I folded my arms across my chest. "You can go visit with neighbors while I'm stuck in here."

"As if talking to that woman's going to be easy!"

Albie's mom was a society type. More like my grandmother than my mother. But I realized that I had let Mother sidetrack me. "What happens to Deirdre?"

"She—"

The door creaked slowly open and Dr. Keller peeked in. "May I come in?"

"Doctor," Mother said, obviously relieved to have someone between us. I was becoming quite skilled at making adults feel uncomfortable. "What a long night it's been for you."

"I caught a few winks." Dr. Keller approached my bed. He looked terrifyingly *laid back,* with a crooked smile that could only be described as smarmy. He patted my calf. I spitefully glared at his hairy knuckles.

"Has your mother explained things to you?"

"How I'm stuck here?"

"We're just going to wait for the test results. Get you involved in group. You'll be feeling better in no time."

"School starts in three and a half weeks," I whined. Not that I was a stellar student, and I'd always felt like an outsider at the plush all-girls boarding school. But still, I didn't want to be held back a year.

"We're not going to worry about that now," Mother said.

"How can you do this to me?" I hissed.

Dr. Keller looked over his blurry glasses at me with his veiny blue eyes. Stray gray hairs were mingled in his dark eyebrows. "Penny, your mother thinks it's better if we give you a little break. Let you heal a bit from those injuries."

"I fell off a fence!"

Dr. Keller looked at the clipboard, avoiding my eyes. "Now it's a fence." His fingers trembled slightly as he looked at the sheet. "We just need to get to the bottom of what happened out there in the woods to cause those minor injuries."

"Conor's horse took off when a firecracker went off!"

"Yes, the king's horse."

He chuckled a little, which really lit a fire under me. He was trying to turn the most exciting night of my life into a joke or, worse, make me seem like a nutcase. My resolve to play it cool and tell them what they wanted to hear vanished into rage. "Yes, the king! Just ask her!" I screamed. Mother rushed over and tried to put her hand over my mouth. "Ask her about Deirdre, about all the Heroines!" I was sick of them both. He wasn't taking me seriously, and she was trying to shut me up again. I started to climb out of the bed, and my knee caught the tray and knocked it off the counter. The slam of the metal on the floor made Dr. Keller jump as if he'd been shot. I walked toward him. "Madame Bovary! Ophelia!" I truly felt psychotic.

"Another episode!" Keller said.

He wasn't much taller than I, so I ran and gripped his small shoulders. His eyes grew wide and his clipboard clattered to the floor. Mother rushed to pull me off him, and we both flew backward against the bed curtain. Dr. Keller ran to the door and pushed and yelled out into the hallway, "Mr. Gonzo! Room Sixteen, Mr. Gonzo."

In seconds, two big men in jeans and T-shirts swept into the room and pinned me to the bed before I could yell, *I'm not crazy!* They were like a couple of B-52s—high-speed instruments of precision targeting. They bound my wrists and ankles with leather straps, and one of them lifted up my gown and jabbed a needle into my ass.

"I'm terribly sorry," Mother said. "I don't know what got into her!"

Keller rubbed his shoulder and shook his head. "Another episode, I'm afraid, Ms. Entwhistle."

Eleanor marched in and picked the clipboard up from the floor. She pointed to the place on the form where Mother had to sign. I writhed against the restraints and yelled, "I hate you!"

Tears streamed down Mother's face as she squinted and committed her signature to the page, committed me. My childhood sailed away with the looping trails of her cursive.

PART II

+

The Unit

CHAPTER 12

Meeting the girls + *Kristina finds me
transparent* + *Life with pharmaceuticals*
+ *The pleasures of telepathy* +
Jump-in-the-Lake Jackie +

While I slept, they transported me to another wing, in another building altogether. I awoke in a steel bed behind a white curtain, my ankles and wrists freed from the restraints. I pushed back the drapes and found myself facing a wall of windows on an upper floor. Through the windows I saw a green, shimmering lawn and treetops. I thought of my night in the woods, the excitement of riding with Conor. The idea that I might never walk through the prairie, never wait for Horace by the pond, and never see Conor again seemed like a terrible loss. Something awful had happened to me, and yet the narcotics allowed only a vague recognition of it. I couldn't feel it.

I slowly sat up, my head spinning, and pulled back the other half of the curtain. The bed beside mine was empty. The floor was gray linoleum, the walls mint-green cinderblock, like the walls of the Academy's gymnasium. I blinked to make sure I wasn't seeing double. The sight of three doors with metal knobs reassured me.

The middle one turned, and Florence rushed in, reeking of Jean Naté and cigarettes.

"Atta girl, Penny. Up and at 'em. First, your meds. Then a little activity."

I dropped my feet to the cold floor, and she handed me a paper cup and a small round pill with a V etched out of the center. I popped it in my mouth and chased it with water. I stood up, not feeling anything, then let Florence lead me down a long hall. She held my elbow, chattering about some token system. We passed a locked and glassed-in bulletin board in the hallway, and she pointed out the brown construction-paper cones, labeled with a bunch of girls' names, with a tower of scoops stapled above.

"We'll getcha a cone, I guess," Florence said. "This is the new girl Peggy's big idea. I dunno if it works. I think she doesn't want the doctors to be the only ones giving out the privileges. Got a point. They're never around anyway. How it works is, if you earn enough scoops, we give you passes for day trips, phone calls, that kinda stuff."

"How do you earn them?"

"By being good. There's a list of criteria at the end of the hall." We turned the corner and entered a large bright room. "This is the Day Room," Florence said. "Time for you to meet the other girls."

The Day Room had orange vinyl chairs and turquoise couches. Sunlight poured through the blinds and shone on the bare floors. A TV blared. The other girls were dressed in everyday clothes, except for one girl, who wore two gowns at once: one tied at front, the other tied at back. The air-conditioning made my arm hair stand on end, and I was surprised to look down and see myself dressed in jean shorts and a striped tank top. Mother must have packed a bag for me. I was still too susceptible to fantasy to believe any of this was real. Not the stringy-haired girl pawing the window with an open hand. ("That's Maria," Florence said.) Not the double-gowned girl with the bloated face and messy ponytail, staring at a set-up chessboard and talking quietly to the empty metal chair across from her. ("That's Alice," Florence said.) It was some mad tea party of misfit girls. A couple others had what I later called the Mona Lisa Thorazine smile. To block out the grimness of the scene, I tried to focus on Conor, to replay every moment of our encounter so I wouldn't forget the feel of his arms, the galloping horse, the scent of the woods at night. I closed my eyes and held fast to the floor.

"Penny." Florence shook my arm. "This is your roommate. Kristina."

The girl lay on the couch with her feet on the arms, watching *Gilligan's Island*. She wore white cable-stitch knee socks folded below her scabbed knees, and a long second toe with chipped red polish poked through each sock. Her head rested on a pillow, and a long black braid hung over one shoulder and nearly touched the floor. I glimpsed a sliver of cleavage at the opening of her white blouse.

Florence grabbed the metal chair away from the chessboard girl and handed it to me. The chessboard girl went right on mumbling to her invisible opponent. I sat on the cold seat, my hands beneath my thighs, and watched the screen. The Skipper beat Gilligan with his folded hat. I struggled to find a resemblance between Conor and the Skipper, but the latter was too fat, too impatient, to match my king. I had reached the stage of infatuation where I compared every man to Conor. He could have pulverized Gilligan, the Skipper, and Dr. Keller in one fell swoop.

"What does your daddy do?" Kristina grabbed the braid and dragged it under her nose, sniffing it. With her deep, almost manly voice and her huge, bulging green eyes she reminded me immediately of a toad. A toad with intelligent eyes.

"He's dead," I said.

"Are you rich?" she asked.

"No."

"I thought all the girls here were rich." She stared at me, holding the braid under her nose; the tail hung beside her mouth like a lopsided Fu Manchu. She had a fine, arched nose and rosebud lips. If not for those froggy eyes, she'd be gorgeous. "My grandma bags groceries down at Henry's. So you know."

Henry's Market was an upscale grocery store in the Prairie Bluff town square, the sort of place where people bought caviar and put it on their account. Henry's accepted checks for $1.29. Most of the shoppers were hired help, housekeepers or nannies. Mother and I went there only when Grandmother Entwhistle came for a visit. Where else could you find ash-coated chèvre and figs in 1974?

"Why are you staring at my breasts?" she asked.

"I'm not," I said, staring at her breasts. My inhibitions were dwindling as the medication flowed through my bloodstream. I switched my gaze to the TV screen, watched Ginger Grant sashay across the sand and slam shut the door of her hut.

Kristina propped up on her elbow. She gave me the up-and-down, then smiled. "Just an observation, but you're flat."

"Hadn't noticed."

"Wish I was flat." She hit the sides of her breasts with the backs of her fingers. "I'm never going to have kids, so what's the use of having mammary glands? Most mammals develop mammary glands only when they're nursing. Only humans have them all the time."

"I know," I said. "We learned that in sixth grade."

"I got my period when I was ten."

She instinctively honed in on my insecurities. I reeked of them, and that aquiline nose of hers was extrasensory. But with the Valium Gulf Stream, I didn't mind one bit. Discussing my body when I was drifting out of it felt superb. Sublime. I could say anything and feel nothing. "I'm a bastard. An illegitimate child."

"Who isn't?" Kristina swung her feet to the floor and gestured for me to scoot in closer. "My mom's a classics professor. She said I was conceived during a one-night stand she had with some poet. What was your dad?"

"A football player."

"NFL?"

"Naw. Lincoln Park High School."

"My dad's in the wind. Split when I was two. Where's yours?"

"Dead."

"Oh. Sorry. You said that." Kristina looked down at her hands, and I looked at them too. There was something both spooky and sane about her. I couldn't put my finger on it, but it felt good to finally meet someone who didn't have a father either. "You know why I'm in here?"

I shook my head.

"I had sex with my drama teacher. I was playing Ophelia." She pulled the rubber band off the end of her braid and started to unravel her hair. I watched her fingers move, enthralled. "She's the one who kills herself when—"

"Hamlet kills her father." I knew Ophelia, better than Kristina might think. She had been at the Homestead after her father died, and, well, there wasn't a whole lot we could do to cheer her up. I'd found her paleness and red-rimmed eyes frightening.

"It's not like Mr. Dobson is *that* much older," she said. "People don't understand how love works."

"Wasn't Hamlet about fifteen years older than Ophelia anyway?"

"Exactly!" Her unraveled hair fell in a wavy cascade down her shoulders. She frowned and lifted her chin. "You're pretty smart for a middle-school kid."

I looked down at my hands, to hide my pleasure at her compliment.

She started to braid her hair as she snapped her gum. "They say I have anger issues. I broke all the windows in my house when they arrested Mr. Dobson."

"Did you get cut?"

"I used a broom handle. Doesn't that prove I'm sane?"

"I attacked Dr. Keller."

"Good for you. Did he give your mom the 'against medical advice' song-and-dance? That's his biggest trick for getting girls with good insurance in here. He tells them we'll have no insurance for the rest of our lives if we leave. It's a gold mine for the hospital."

I hadn't really understood it when my mom told me about AMA, and I'd been too mad to give it any credence. I had truly believed she'd committed me to keep me from helping Conor get Deirdre. But if Kristina believed the AMA routine, maybe it was true. "Really?"

"Yeah, they scare the parents into signing the kids in. Keller's shtick must work best with single moms, because this place is crawling with bastards. Eleanor says that's why I'm messed up. Because I'm a bastard. I'm just trying to get attention."

"Eleanor the Elephant is full of horseshit!" I said.

Kristina stopped and looked up at the ceiling with one eye closed. "Wait. That's a mixed whatchamacallit." She thumped the heel of her hand against her temple. "Damn meds! I learned it in English."

"Metaphor," I said, stunned that I had plucked that word from my medicated brain. Then we both started to laugh. I laughed and laughed and then acid churned up my throat. I slumped forward because I thought I was going to puke. The room spun—dusty windows, girl at her chessboard, TV screen filled with Mr. Howell's face—and then looped in my face. I swallowed back the burn of vomit.

"First time on meds?" Kristina patted my back. "Why the hell do they give us medicine that makes you nauseated when you laugh? They fucking *want* us to be depressed."

I squeezed my eyes shut, but when I opened them the room was straight again.

Kristina was sitting in a perfect lotus position, her palms turned up on her knees. The long waves of her hair seemed to vibrate like glossy snakes. With her unbraided hair, she'd transformed visually from frog into long-haired Renaissance Madonna. "Mr. Dobson's going to come rescue me," she said.

I turned my head cautiously to avoid the spins. The late afternoon sun filtered through the blinds and striped the floor. "When?" I whispered.

"I can feel him." She opened her eyes and stared at me with her dark eyes. She closed her eyes beatifically. "I send him messages telepathically."

"How?"

"You just concentrate. Lie on the other end of the couch. That's it. Now just think really hard about the person you want to reach. Send them messages. Say, like, *Think of me right now.* Or *Come here at midnight.*"

I laid my head against the armrest and closed my eyes. My legs touched Kristina's. I heard her take deep breaths, so I did the same, my hands on my stomach. *Come save me, Conor. Come save me. Get on that horse and save me. I'm right here.* I repeated it until I drifted off to sleep. Then Kristina was shaking my arm. "Soup's on."

I sat with Kristina in the dining hall, a narrow room with two long tables and oak chairs, French doors at either end. Eleanor and two other nurses sat at a small table, shoveling food into their mouths. Eleanor was the only one wearing a traditional nurse's uniform; the others wore street clothes. Two orderlies, one white, one black, stood at the kitchen doors, arms behind their backs, a stance that accentuated their biceps. They traded surreptitious comments. I knew they were making fun of us. Keys dangled from lanyards around their necks. The keys to paradise. Escape. I had the distinct impulse to try to pull one off their necks, but this was pure fantasy, as my bones felt wrapped in cotton rather than muscle.

Two women in vinyl aprons brought out bowls of green beans, a platter of pork chops, and canned apple sauce. They provided only forks and spoons. No knives. I broke my plastic fork trying to slice the pork chop. Kristina knew better. She picked up the cold meat by the bone and took a bite. She held her glass of milk in one hand, the chop in the other, and switched off methodically: bite of meat, swig of milk. She stopped talking only to swallow. It was Mr. Dobson this, Mr. Dobson that. Her mood seemed to have shifted. When we were alone, she was so composed, but once we got in the crowd, she was hyper, dominant. She'd wrapped her hair back into a tight bun, and she lectured us like a schoolmarm, or perhaps like a classics professor. When Mr. Dobson got out of jail, he'd be on his way to save her. As I ate the bland food, I felt less drowsy, but I drifted off during Kristina's monologue. I couldn't stop thinking about how mad I was at my mother, yet I wondered if Kristina was right: that Keller had tricked Mother into committing me. I didn't want to think about that—it made me feel so powerless—so I thought of Conor instead, how he'd chased me through the woods, how it felt when he held me on the horse. Memories of Conor might be all I had left of him, so I felt compelled to relive all the details, to brand them in mind.

"Dobson hasn't come yet, has he?" A tall skinny girl with a swollen face and a shaven head held out her fork and pointed at Kristina. She looked like a sick ostrich with a bristly scalp and bloodshot eyes. She sported the double-hospital-gown ensemble. "What's he waiting for?"

"Jealous, Jackie?" Kristina said, arching an eyebrow.

"Hey, new girl!"

"She has a name," Kristina said.

I looked down at my plate and then carefully up again, hoping she wasn't addressing me. The girl's face frightened me; the skin on her cheeks was dry and a handful of bloody pimples dotted her forehead. The trace of an old shiner still ringed her eye, green and yellow. Her shaved head made me think she'd had brain surgery.

"Yeah, you." Now she pointed her plastic fork at me. "Did you know Mr. Dobson's sixty?"

"He is not!" Kristina said.

"The old boy's gonna come cruising up in his Winnebago and drive her over the state line. Down south in Kentucky. Yeah.

Down there fifteen-year-olds can marry old men. Hell, you can marry your own brother in those states."

Kristina dropped her pork chop and raised her hand as if to slap Jackie across the face. "Refrain from describing your dear old dad."

"Don'tcha think Dobson would've made bail by now? He's been out for *weeks*," Jackie said. "What's taking him so long? Maybe he forgot about you!"

"Go jump back in the lake you almost croaked in, Jackie!"

Jackie's swollen face crumpled. "Nurse Eleanor! Kristina's talking about group information outside of group!"

Eleanor, too engrossed in her eating to get up, yelled from her table. "Don't start, you two. You want me calling Mr. Gonzo again?"

Kristina opened her mouth and then clamped it shut, sucking in her lips and sticking out her face toward Jackie. She fastened her lips into a sarcastic little button. She leaned in to me. "All the suicides and runaways have to wear their gowns like that."

"Jackie, be the bigger person," Eleanor said. "Move over to the other table. Kristina's helping Penny with her *transition*."

"Penny the horseback fantasy chick?"

I did a double-take. How did she know about me? But before the implications of that registered, Kristina clapped her hands and looked at me with wide eyes. "That sounds epic, little sister. You must tell me all! But later, back in our room. Where there aren't so many spies." She bugged her eyes at Eleanor. Jackie got up and moved to the nurses' table.

"Good job avoiding conflict." One of the other women handed Jackie a cloud-shaped cutout. "Here's an ice-cream scoop! I caught you being good."

"Don't I get a scoop for helping Penny?" Kristina asked.

"You can't ask for a scoop," the woman said. She filled Jackie's water cup from a plastic pitcher. "That's the whole point of the new system."

"That makes twenty-five scoops!" Jackie sang.

I'd checked out the scoops on my way to the dining room. Jackie and Kristina had the most scoops, whereas Maria (the one who'd been pawing the window), who hardly seemed to do anything wrong, had two. The biggest troublemakers obviously got the most attention, and thus the most scoops. It was a sign of my warped adjustment that I longed for a tower of scoops all my own. I also longed to have Kristina's command of the room, though not if it meant giving up her protection. She'd somehow chosen to take me under her wing, and I was grateful for the shelter, however capricious it might be.

CHAPTER 13

+ *More tales from the Homestead* +

Blanche DuBois, Kristina's idol + *Piggy the*

group therapist + *Kristina goes down* +

y madness (as defined by the hospital staff) was the most difficult thing for my thirteen-year-old mind to reconcile. I couldn't keep it straight. For me, if the Heroines were real, then I was sane (a); if the Heroines were fake, as the hospital staff maintained, then I was insane (b); but if I admitted that the Heroines and Conor were fake, then I was sane (to the hospital staff), but insane in my own eyes (i.e., I'd lived a whole life of complete delusion) (c). So I had to, as the armchair therapists say, *compartmentalize* my story. For (a), I could trust only myself and Mother (though my trust in her was rocky); for (b) I couldn't speak the truth of (a) to anyone in the hospital; so that (c) could take place and I'd be set free from the Unit. The tricky thing was that I sometimes doubted myself, doubted the Heroines, and wondered if Mother and I were insane. The medication added to this self-doubt, made me fuzzy and unable to remember when to apply (a), (b), or (c) to the right people. Plus I was angry and emotional and possessed at times by the urge to play insane by simply telling the truth to the wrong person.

Kristina wasn't one of those wrong people. She wanted to know everything about Conor. After dinner that night, I'd passed out early, but the next morning when I awoke, she was sitting cross-legged on her bed, staring at me. I didn't know how long she'd been up, but she was dressed in pedal pushers and a buttoned-up blouse, her hair in a braid so tight, her eyes were slanted. "Tell me about this king."

I blinked and climbed out of bed. I wanted to get dressed first. It was odd to have people besides my mother and me talking about the Heroines, but my outburst had made me and my story an object of curiosity—for Eleanor, Keller, the orderlies. And Jackie had made sure every other girl on the floor heard about it. Yet, in a strange way, I found a measure of comfort in the walls of the Unit. No other setting had accommodated the bizarre truth of my home life so well. Kristina would be the first friend I could con-fide in; my first girlfriend, period. She was (literally) a captive audience. I stepped behind the curtain and changed into shorts and a T-shirt. "You're not going to believe it," I said.

"I will, I will, I will!" she sang.

"It sounds really stupid."

"I don't care. At least it's interesting! It's gotta be better than all these super-boring, super-depressed girls."

Her words appealed to my vanity. I wanted to be singled out from the other girls. I wanted to believe that Kristina and I were the highest-functioning girls in the Unit. I whipped back the cur-tain and sat down on my bed. "All right. But don't laugh. These characters from books come to my house."

"Cool!" The story enthralled her; she believed every word of it. I was so grateful for the attention, and she asked so many ques-tions, that before long I'd given up everything. "You should have seen Ophelia!" I bragged.

"What was she wearing?"

"Just regular clothes."

"Bummer!" She hated the fact that the Heroines didn't wear

the clothes from their stories. "Have any other characters from plays come to your house?"

"This one Southern lady. Blanche Du—"

"DuBois! Blanche DuBois, I love her!" She jumped off her bed and zigzagged between the La-Z-Boys. "My dumb school wouldn't let Mr. Dobson do *Streetcar Named Desire*. They're so uptight!" She laid the back of her hand on her forehead and affected a Southern drawl. "'I have always depended on the kindness of strangers.' Mr. Dobson gave me the book. Oh, what was she like?"

"Drunk all the time."

"Where'd she get the booze?"

"From some guys who worked on the lawn."

"Let's do the scene where Blanche tries to talk Stella out of staying with Stanley."

"I don't know it by heart."

"I'll write down your lines." Kristina ran to her nightstand, her braid swinging down her back, and pulled out a notebook. I'd quickly noticed how her hairstyle and demeanor fluctuated with her moods. As she scribbled, I told her more stories about Blanche, who was always talking about being sweaty, needing a bath, wanting her talcum. Blanche had wandered the Homestead at night with a dripping candle. One afternoon I caught her making out on the power mower with the teenage lawn guy. She must have come to stay with us right before they put her away. At ten, I thought she was nuts. Usually the Heroines arrived in pathetic states of a different order: heartbroken, mourning a death, something. But Blanche's state was all her own. "I hadn't recognized her as a Heroine until this summer, when I'd read the play at theater camp," I said.

"There. I wrote only your lines," Kristina said. "I know mine by heart. You're Stella. You start." She unraveled her braid and undid two buttons on her blouse.

I looked down at the notebook and then faced her, thrusting my arm out like a knight about to duel. "You saw him at his worst last night!"

"On the contrary! I saw him at his best. What such a man has to offer is animal force and he gave a wonderful exhibition of that! But the only way to live with such a man is to go to bed with him. And that's your job, not mine! I have a plan for us both—to get us both out!" She looked at me expectantly, and I took the cue.

"You take it for granted that I'm in something I want to get out of."

"I take it for granted that you still have enough memory of Belle Reve to find this place"—she opened her arms and surveyed our cold hospital room—"impossible to live with!"

"You're taking entirely too much for granted!"

"I can't believe you're in earnest."

"No?" I said.

"I understand how it happened—a little." Kristina rested her hand on the bedrail and shook her head in disdain. "You saw him in uniform, an officer, not here but—" Kristina collapsed on the bed. "Ugh! I wish I knew the whole thing."

"That's so cool that you remember so much."

"Yeah, even on meds I have a good memory for plays." She turned on her side and pulled her hair over her face, running her fingers through the tangles. I could tell she was thinking about Mr. Dobson. "Why didn't your mother tell you who Blanche was?"

"She doesn't like me to know. She's afraid I'll interfere with their"—I rolled my eyes—"destinies."

"Could you?" Kristina sat up straight.

"How do I know? My mom's just paranoid and—" I cut myself off. As an only child, I wasn't used to discussing my mother with anyone. I felt guilty about betraying her, but the intense relief of finally speaking the unspeakable felt too good.

"What if when the Heroines went back to their stories, the plot changed? You could wreak havoc!" She jumped on the bed in a crouch, her knees sticking out like a frog's. "Do you think you could trade places with them?"

"I don't think so. I don't know how they get here. And then they just disappear. In the middle of the night, after breakfast, whenever."

"They vanish into thin air?"

"It's not like they go poof! It's just that you go looking for them, and they're gone."

"Have you followed them?"

"No." I hadn't thought of doing that. "The Heroines were mostly annoying to me. They stole my mother's attention. And Franny Glass was the only one even close to my age." I didn't want to admit how I'd lost Franny.

"You could so fuck things up!" Kristina punched the air, jubilant again. She swung her hair over her shoulder. "I would have totally warned Blanche that they were coming to take her to the nuthouse. Nobody deserves that! Anything beats being locked up. Even turning tricks."

"When I tried to warn Madame Bovary, my mom slapped me!"

"I'd've slapped her back."

"Slap your mom?"

"If she hit me first. Not that she's around enough to bother."

"My mom's just locking me up to keep me away from Conor."

"Man, she knows you're not lying about him, yet she signed you in." Kristina grabbed a pink plastic hairbrush off her nightstand. Tossing her hair over her shoulder, she brushed it all to one side. "Your mom's probably jealous 'cause this hunky king is into you. My mom's jealous of me. She'd kill for a guy like Mr. Dobson. Even if he only teaches high school and she's a full professor. She'd take him in a minute. Most men are afraid of her."

"My mom was afraid Conor raped me. They tested me."

"I had one of those too." She scowled. "They'll use any excuse to shove their hands up your twat." She trained her eyes on me. "I'm so jealous of you. Your life is so cool with the Heroines coming and going. It's probably never boring like mine."

"Don't be jealous," I said. Her confession disturbed me; something strong and almost hateful glinted in her eyes. "And you can't tell anybody about the Heroines. My mom swears that—"

"Knock, knock!" The woman who'd given Jackie the scoop at dinner the previous night poked her head in the room. Her voice had the high, squeaky singsong of a camp counselor. A batik poncho hung to her dimpled elbows. I hadn't noticed in the dining hall that she was so big.

"Group doesn't start for another half hour, Pee-iggy." Kristina called her Piggy, instead of Peggy, but in a garbled way that made it impossible to detect the slight vowel difference. Kristina pointed at the wall clock with the hairbrush. The clear bristles were thick with black strands.

"I realize that, Kristina." Peggy's smile involved clenched teeth. "I'd like to meet with Penny before group, to get acquainted."

She pointed at each of us with the hairbrush. "Penny, this is Pee-iggy. Pee-iggy, Penny. There. You're acquainted."

"Thank you for that nice introduction. But I'd like to speak with Penny a teensy bit more than that."

"Can I come?" Kristina asked sweetly.

"The sign-up sheet for one-on-one time is on my door. I'd love to meet with you individually when my schedule permits."

Kristina unfolded her legs and stuck her nose in the air. "Maybe. I'll see if my own schedule permits."

"How does a little Penny-Peggy time sound, Penny?"

I shrugged. She made it sound as if I had a choice, when I knew I didn't. I was having so much fun with Kristina, I resented the intrusion. "I still have to brush my teeth."

"We can stop in the bathroom on the way."

I got up and grabbed my toiletry kit from the dresser. As we walked out, Kristina yelled, "Don't tell her anything about Blanche and Ophelia!"

Their names struck me like bullets in my back. I actually checked over my shoulder to see if Mother was around. "Don't say anything—"

She giggled. "I won't! Gosh!"

I was suddenly afraid that I'd made a big mistake telling Kristina about the Heroines. It was the Big Family Secret, and while it relieved me to discuss it, my training was so inbred that I checked over my shoulder again to make sure Mother wasn't within earshot. I didn't know why I'd felt so free to tell Kristina everything. Hadn't I been feeling weird earlier about Jackie talking about Conor? But then I'd gone and blathered on about it again. It wasn't just the meds that were making me feel out of control. It was my own inexperience. I didn't recognize myself. I didn't know what I was doing.

After I'd washed up, I followed Peggy down the shiny hall to the group room, a windowless enclave brightened by inspirational posters of sunsets and kittens. One Norman Rockwell poster showed a little girl clutching her doll while a doctor held a stethoscope to its chest. The slogan read, "What wisdom can you find that is greater than kindness?" A framed diploma proved Peggy had received her bachelor's in psychology from Loyola two months earlier.

Peggy sat down at her metal desk, gesturing to the chair on the other side. Right behind her head was the coup de grâce: a close-up poster of pale pink ballet slippers, with the slogan, "If you can dream it, you can become it." I had the same one in my bedroom, and it irritated me to see it here, as mine was a prized birthday gift from my mother. Behind me, a horseshoe ring of folding chairs sat waiting for the others.

"Sooo," Peggy sang, opening a large manila file. "Dr. Keller says you're not talking much."

I shrugged and stared at the objects on her desk: a hollowed-out birch branch loaded with pens, a brown stapler, a monthly blotter covered in scribbles, an owl candle that had never been lit.

"Can you tell me, in your own words, why you think you're here on the Unit?"

"No."

Peggy picked up a pencil and pressed the pink eraser into her plump cheek. "Is there any reason why you don't want to tell me?"

I said nothing.

The eraser disappeared in her cheek. "Okay, let's move on, then." Her squeaky voice made her sound younger than Kristina. "You've met several of the girls, yes? Kristina, obviously, Alice—"

"Which one is she?"

"How shall I describe Alice?" Peggy looked up at the ceiling, tapping her temple with the pencil. "She likes chess . . ."

"With her imaginary friend," I said.

"Yes, imaginary friends . . ."

I'd bungled and backed myself into a self-revelatory place. Peggy let the silence grow. I avoided her gaze, focused on a poster of a rainbow straddling a sparkling stream: "Peace begins in the heart."

She squinted and gave me a sparked-with-tears look of pity, complete with frown and furious blinking. A sad clown face! People probably told her she had such a pretty face—straight teeth, blue eyes, pert nose; unfortunately, it was lost in fat. "Anything you want to say on the topic of imaginary friends?" she tried again.

"You ever have any?"

"This is about you, Penny. And why you're here. It's sooo important that you can articulate why. It's a first step toward healing, and toward getting you"—she grinned and stuck out her thumb like a hitchhiker—"the heck out of Dodge!"

Years of secret-keeping made speaking the truth a radical and liberating act. I both feared and relished it. In my inexperience, I wielded the truth as well I would have wielded an AK-47. "My mom's afraid an imaginary guy's going to get me."

"Yes, something about a Celtic king . . ."

"Conor MacNessa." Simply saying his name sent this new, alien flush of warmth through me. I loved the feeling. I told myself to keep my pipe shut, but I couldn't seem to do it. "Lord of the Red Branch Knights."

"Do *you* think he's trying to hurt you?"

"No." I lowered my voice and waited for Peggy to move in closer.

She did. She leaned forward in her leatherette executive chair, tucking a strand of long, dishwater blond hair behind her ear.

"He needs me," I said.

"Needs you." She scribbled on a yellow legal pad. "You believe that you and he had a special relationship? Kind of a father-daughter connection?

"More than that."

"Boyfriend-girlfriend?"

"If you can dream it, you can become it!" I sang.

"Funny!" She smiled and pointed with her thumb at the poster behind her. Then she shifted her weight and leaned into the desk, gearing up. "Now, I was just wondering, was your father Irish?"

"Wouldn't know. *He's* the imaginary character."

"What *do* you know about him?"

"He's dead. My mom was a teenager. He played football." I decided to throw an honest hardball. "My grandmother wanted my mother to give me up for adoption. She didn't think my mother could handle raising a child on her own."

"How does that make you feel?"

"I don't know."

The rest of our session passed in ping-pong banter about what constituted "reality." Then I clammed up and focused on my telepathic messages to Conor: *Think about me right now. Pick up the wave. Follow it here.*

Peggy then got some brown construction paper out of her desk drawer and a pair of round-tipped kindergarten scissors. She told me to cut out my ice-cream cone. Then she gave me a copy of a long list of behaviors that would earn me scoops: showing good listening skills, being responsible, helping somebody else, avoiding conflicts. At the end of the week, the scoops could be traded for privileges.

"Knock, knock." Alice stood at the door with one leg twisted around the other, staring at us. Peggy rose and directed her to take a seat in the half circle of folding chairs. I sat across from her, my thighs chilled by the cold metal chair. They cranked the air-conditioning to bacteria-annihilating levels in this place. As the other girls trickled in, Peggy introduced me to Maria (who'd been pawing the window) and a younger girl named Jennifer I'd never seen before. Her face looked more like a skull: dark circles under her eyes, sunken cheeks. Next came Jackie, pulling faces that alternated between owlish (wide-eyed and shocked) and shrewd (slant-eyed and sneering). It almost seemed that she was looking at herself in the mirror, practicing her intimidation techniques. Kristina skipped in, her hair undone again, and her blouse unbuttoned to just above her bra. The tongues of her Keds flapped around her feet, the shoes laceless, and she'd changed into a daisy miniskirt. I immediately sensed another mood shift—the wild and destructive energy was unleashed. The comment she'd made in front of Peggy about Ophelia and Blanche had set me on edge.

Peggy rolled her executive chair around the desk and filled in the empty spot in the horseshoe. She waved a stack of ice-cream scoops at us. "I first want to say that everybody gets a scoop just for being here today. If you behave well, and share your feelings, you may earn another. Today we're going to talk about responsibility." She looked around, waiting, out of habit I guessed, for a sarcastic comment.

Kristina grinned and sat on her hands, shaking her head as if to suggest that she could say something very smart, but she was trying really hard to be *good*. She tucked in her lips and shook her hair over her cheeks.

"Responsibility means," Peggy continued, "that we accept the consequences of our actions. What I'd like to do today is have everybody in group name one thing they did that led them to being here today."

Nobody said anything. Peggy's act was bombing, and I was not inclined to make it easier for her. What I needed to think about was *not* how I got there, but how the hell I would get out. Sheepish and peevish, I resisted playing Peggy's game. She was too uncool to win us over; anybody who fell for her act was, I sensed, immediately demoted in the nuthouse hierarchy written by the patients. In fact, everybody seemed to behave worse in group—more crazy, more cocky, more show-offy.

Finally, to break the silence, Kristina yelled out. "I fucked my teacher!"

"I jumped in Wonder Lake!" Jackie yelled.

"That's wonderful, you two," Peggy said.

I gave her a quizzical look, so she added, "It shows a lot of growth that you're both willing to acknowledge what behaviors led you to your current situations." She turned to another girl. "Jennifer?"

"I can't sleep," said Jennifer.

"Well, that's a *symptom* of what's going on with you, not an actual reason for why you're here. But you're new. So I'll give you a pass for today."

Jackie leaned back dangerously in her chair, balancing on the tips of her slippered toes. She'd gotten a hold of some orange lipstick, which clashed with her shiner. "She set her mattress on fire!"

"How do you know?" Kristina said.

"It's true! I heard them talking about it." Jackie continued to teeter on the back legs of her chair. It disturbed me that she had insider information on everybody, including me. I pictured her tiptoeing down hallways, hiding under beds, crouching on the toilet with the stall door locked so she could listen to the staff converse. Jennifer turned her face and gave Jackie one of the dirtiest looks I'd ever seen: teeth clenched, eyes narrowed, and lips trembling. Something between a growl and a purr came out of her mouth. Then she turned back, lifted her chin, and stared straight ahead at the rainbow peace poster. A quiver of fear shook my shoulders.

"Jackie," Peggy said. "You know better! You're not supposed to speak for other people in group. Sit up straight, please. You could fall and crack your skull. Let's move on. Penny, are you ready to tell us why you're here?"

"My mom's crazy."

"No, no, no!" Alice jumped up. She waved her arms over her head as if she were flagging down someone three blocks away. "She has to talk about what *she* did."

"The blame game will get you nowhere!" Jackie said. She wagged a finger and closed one of her beat-up eyes. The shiner had turned yellow-brown, and when she smiled, I saw discolored teeth.

I affected a zombie monotone. "I didn't do anything. I don't know why I'm here."

"Well, that's what you need to think about," Peggy said. "Let's hear from some of you girls who've been at this a bit longer. It takes time to get used to talking about our feelings."

"I know why she's here," Kristina said. "And it's really, really not her fault!" Her tone was sincere, but there was something sinister underneath it. "All these Heroines come to her house. From plays and novels. Really!"

"Enough, Kristina," Peggy said.

"It's true. And she thinks they're real."

"Shut up, Kristina," I snapped.

"She's soooooo important, all these famous ladies want to stay at her fancy house."

"I said *enough,* Kristina," Peggy said.

I clenched my fingers, imagined wrapping them around Kristina's throat. It was bad enough that I had to tolerate the Heroines' antics, my mother's attention to them but not to me. But to have somebody say that I'd made them up to get attention really burned me. I'd expected as much from the adults. But Kristina was acting like I was a spoiled brat. "Just shut up!" I yelled. What a mistake to have told her anything! I hardly even knew her, and now she was making me look like a nut. I'd given her all the ammunition she needed.

"Both of you! You're on warning. Let's all take a time-out. Silence! We'll all close our eyes and breathe deeply."

Peggy, Jennifer, Alice, and Maria all closed their eyes, but I stared Kristina down. She bugged out her eyes at me, but then turned them on Jackie, whose delighted eyes moved back and forth over our faces like a pendulum on a cuckoo clock. The others breathed in and out, and the sound of their whistling noses became excruciating. Kristina, still seated in the metal folding chair, kicked her leg high and started to sing, "I'm in love with a man, that I'm talking about! I'm in love with a man, that I can't live without."

"Leg down, please. You're exposing yourself," Peggy said.

Kristina gripped the seat of her chair and kicked even higher, her pale blue underwear flashing beneath her miniskirt. "But I must have picked a bad time for being—"

"A slut!" Jackie sang. "A bad time for being a slut!"

Kristina's laceless Ked fell to the floor while her foot, in its holey sock, hung in the air for a moment. She swung the toes into Jackie's face, an inch from her mouth. Everybody froze. Then even Jackie was rigid, looking at Kristina's chipped red toenails poking through the sock. Kristina's arms trembled as she balanced on her chair, but her leg was firm, tan, the hamstring curved as a bow.

"Kristina! You're on warning." As Peggy struggled to her feet, her chair flew back behind her.

Kristina cast a winning smile around the group, her gorgeous leg still high, then she opened her big and second toes and squeezed Jackie's nose hard.

Jackie screamed and pushed Kristina's foot off her face, and the chair slipped out from under Kristina. She landed on her hands, her ass on the floor. She pushed herself up and back into her chair. The group went wild. Alice stomped her feet, crying, "Not fair, not fair." Even stone-faced Jennifer cracked a smile, leaning back in her chair as if to distance herself from joining the melee. Maria covered her face with her arm. The dexterity and audacity of Kristina's move stunned me, and I burst out laughing. Jackie jumped from her seat. She balled her fists and stuck out her ass and squatted, her bottom lip swallowing her top lip. She looked like an angry monkey. Then I heard the trickle and tinkle of her pee splashing on the linoleum.

The next thing I heard were the wheels of Peggy's chair, as Maria careened around the room in it. As Peggy rushed to the door, a bunch of ice-cream scoops flew off her lap and fluttered to the ground. Jennifer leapt up and started sweeping them into the crook of her arm.

Peggy ran and pushed the intercom button and yelled, "Mr. Gonzo! Mr. Gonzo, Group Room!"

The pee pooled at Jackie's feet, bright yellow and pungent from vitamins and meds. Kristina sat back in her chair, cool as a movie star, one leg draped over another, smoking an imaginary cigarette. She swept her hair over one shoulder and static snapped and crackled between her fingers.

Two orderlies ran into the room, and each grabbed one of Jackie's arms. Jackie kicked her legs and howled. Then she jumped in the air, her heels tucked into her ass, and the men carried her over the puddle of pee. Jackie stayed frozen in her tuck, as they passed sideways through the door.

"Everyone back to their rooms!" Peggy yelled. "Group is over. And you're on probation, Kristina."

"Boohoo! Like I care about that."

"You better care. It's your fifth this week. That means isolation." She swung her head out the door. "Mr. Gonzo!"

Kristina pointed at the puddle of pee. "This one's shaped like a kidney bean!"

Two more goons stormed through the doors, their keys bouncing off their developed chests. Peggy pointed at Kristina. "Get her! Isolation!"

They grabbed Kristina's arms and yanked her out of the chair. She wasn't going down easily. She jabbed one in his side, kicked the other in the shins. They tightened their grip on her arms, then one stepped behind her and pushed his knees into the back of hers to make them buckle. She held fast. Alice started to keen like a banshee. The men lifted Kristina up and slammed her, face forward, to the ground. Her forehead bounced off the tile floor, and blood spurted out of her nose. Her skirt rose dangerously close to her ass. They pinned her legs with their feet, and pressed her arms behind her back. I saw one of the orderlies twist it.

"You're breaking my arm!" she cried.

"When are you going to learn, Kristina?" Peggy asked. "You've got to change your behaviors."

One of the orderlies laughed. "She likes it rough."

When Kristina switched into her Blanche DuBois voice, "What such a man has to offer is animal force," they pressed her shoulders into the floor. "What a display we have tonight!" Then she let loose a cackle. "They told me to take a streetcar named Desire!"

"Stand her up!" Peggy shouted.

They lifted Kristina from the ground; she held herself rigid as a stretcher. Blood dripped onto her shirt. Alice's keening had reached a pitch detectable only by hounds. She started to stomp her feet, marching in place like a psycho majorette.

I'd never seen anything like this, and it terrified me how brutally they treated Kristina. But something even more horrifying registered: Kristina was used to this. Her lip was curled in the corner and she nodded and winked at me. The sight of her flowing blood started a hum in my head, and I lowered my forehead between my knees to keep from fainting.

"That rattletrap streetcar that bangs through the Quarter!" she cried. "You can't lock me up!"

Then she made a move they'd taught us in drama camp. The rag doll. She went suddenly limp and slumped to the floor. "Penny! 'I have always depended on the kindness of strangers.' And it fucked me every time!" The two men pulled her by the elbows and dragged her like a mop across the tile. Her hair fell across her face, into the blood.

When I stood up, the room spun. The sight of blood always made my knees buckle. I closed my eyes and held out my hands. *Come save me, Conor. Please hurry. I'll do anything!* The soles of Kristina's feet disappeared across the threshold.

"Sit down, you!" Peggy huffed and puffed, winded by the trips across the room to ring the bell. She leaned into her desk, a hand on her heaving chest. "Back to your rooms. Everybody."

But I stood there, eyes closed, holding out my hands to steady the spinning room, and silently mouthing the words, *Conor, come quickly. Come now!* I fancied myself a statue, still as marble. An overhead vent blew an air-conditioned gale that nearly parted my hair. *I'll help you get Deirdre. I'll do whatever you want.* A cold hand grabbed my elbow and shook me.

"Quit acting crazy," Florence whispered.

I wouldn't open my eyes. I let her lead me like a blind girl down the hall into my room. I didn't want to see anything, didn't know anymore if I wasn't crazy. I counted my footsteps back to the room, and with each step some sense returned to me. I knew one thing for sure: I had to stop talking about the Heroines if I was ever going to get out of the Unit.

An hour later, I lay on my bed, sulky and sullen, with the shades drawn. The bare room with its corduroy recliners depressed me, felt nothing like home. However much I took the Homestead and Mother for granted, I'd never felt threatened there. I couldn't figure out how Kristina had led me to talk so freely about the Heroines. She'd seemed so trusting, so intrigued, and yet she used the information to get back at me. It was almost as if she envied me, an unusual response to a lonely teen like me. Still, I couldn't blame Kristina entirely. I'd broken one of Mother's strict codes, and now

I understood the consequences. Mother's chief aim with the Heroines had always been containment: provide a safe haven and meddle as little as possible. I was finally realizing what a volatile compound their existence created; I'd expected Kristina to think I was nuts, but not to be envious. If I was going to survive the Unit, I had to be tougher and smarter. I rolled to my side and closed my eyes. The face of a Heroine came immediately to mind. Though her visit to the Homestead last winter had been brief, I saw enough to know that there was something to admire about Katie Scarlett O'Hara.

CHAPTER 14

✦ *What would Scarlett do?* ✦

Seven months earlier, one late December afternoon, I sat at the front desk thumbing through the registry. We rarely had guests at the Homestead during the winter break. I had talked my mom into paying me two dollars an hour to sit at the front desk (I was saving for new bedroom decorations), and I always enjoyed listening to the top songs of the year on WLS while reviewing the guest registry. Visits from Heroines in 1973 had been a little slim. March had brought Daisy Buchanan (a real pain); in August Ophelia had arrived.

The mantel clock ticked, and I was so bored I almost wished another Heroine would waltz through the door. As if I had some gift for conjuring (which I didn't), the door banged open and a woman staggered into the foyer. Her black hair was wild, her face as white as the snowy birch trees outside. She had mauve circles beneath her eyes, but one glimpse at their jade color and her tiny waist told me instantly who she was, though she wasn't quite as beautiful as Vivien Leigh. She reached a shaky hand to the desk for support, then collapsed on the cold tile with a sickening thud.

"Gretta! Help!" I ran around the desk and sat on the floor. As I lifted her head, I felt a lump swelling at the base of her skull. Her eyeballs fluttered beneath her lids as if she were having a nightmare. "Mom!"

Gretta ran in, yellow rubber gloves dripping soap suds. "What's all the commotion? Oh, my!"

"I think it's Scarlett O'Hara!"

Tossing the gloves to the floor, Gretta swept her arms beneath Scarlett's thin body and lifted her off the cold tile. Scarlett wore a rabbit fur coat with a leather belt. Calves bulging, Gretta took the stairs two at a time, transporting Scarlett as if she were carrying a feather bed.

"I'll get some ice for her head!" I cried.

"Put on the kettle! She's froze to the bone!"

As I sped through the dining room, I collided with Mother on my way to the kitchen. "Scarlett O'Hara's upstairs!"

Mother's eyes widened and she clapped her hands to her mouth to hide her smile.

"She passed out!"

"Must still be the middle of the war," Mother said. She rushed through the dining room and I heard her run up the stairs.

By the time I'd prepared the tea and ice pack and brought them up to the Top of the Stairs Room, Scarlett was awake. She sat in the four-poster bed with her head propped on pillows. Although the room had a private bath and a large sunporch, the sleeping area was small. We three crowded around the bed, spellbound by her powerful eyes, and grateful for the diversion, as the snowy days had left us with cabin fever.

"I'll fix some soup," Gretta said.

"Let me find her a warm nightgown," Mother said.

"I'll get more pillows," I said.

Lifting her hand to shield her eyes from the overhead light, Scarlett glared at us. "Corn whiskey. I told Pork I needed some now!" Her weakened voice still held a touch of saucy Southern belle.

"I don't think—" Mother said.

"She been in a war," Gretta said. "Whiskey it is."

"You're most kind," Scarlett said, falling back into the pillows again.

Gretta leaned in and whispered to Mother, "She is tougher than Catherine Earnshaw, this one."

Mother nodded, immediately dropping her eyes. One mention of Catherine Earnshaw, from *Wuthering Heights,* and Mother backed off like a scolded dog. Whenever Mother and Gretta referred to Heroines I didn't remember, I always felt left out, and though I'd often tried, I could never get Mother to tell me about that particular Heroine's visit. I sensed that Gretta knew not to speak of it either. There were many things she wouldn't speak about, especially the war. I was somewhat surprised that Gretta knew Scarlett's story, but I realized later that *Gone With the Wind* had been a big hit in Germany. Generally she kept a respectful distance from the Heroines, but wartime refugees evoked her deepest sympathy. Scarlett might be thin and ill, but Gretta knew that she had a colossal personality, more than Mother could handle alone.

The first hour of a Heroine's arrival was always the most delicate. One never knew how she would adjust. Ophelia had paced the halls; Franny had curled up on the window seat, staring out at the prairie. We hadn't yet determined at what point in the narrative Scarlett had arrived (and it was always important to Mother that she knew, so she wouldn't give away anything), but she seemed in dire need of sleep. I couldn't stop staring. Her frail beauty disturbed me: she was so small, yet so womanly. Her skin seemed translucent and her eyes twitched beneath their lids. I quietly backed away from the bed and looked out the sunporch window. Snow had drifted into the southern corners of the porch, foot-high waves like the caps of dwarfs. The wind whistled through the last of the Dutch elms, and I was happy that Scarlett was safe in bed. As I often did, I said a quick prayer that Franny was safe and warm somewhere, preferably back in her story. Mother tiptoed to the window and lowered the shade, then released the heavy maroon curtains from their sashes. The radiator clanked, and Scarlett moaned in her sleep.

"Ashley!"

Mother and I locked eyes, and she shook her head gravely as if she knew that I wanted to rush to the bed to talk Scarlett out of loving him. Mother gave me too much credit. This was a few months before Emma Bovary arrived, before my rebellious hormones kicked into high gear. I'd seen *Gone With the Wind* enough times to know that nobody could talk Scarlett out of anything.

Gretta came in, holding a bottle of Jameson by the throat. She plunked a glass on the nightstand and poured out a hearty portion. Shaking Scarlett's shoulder, she said, "Wake up now."

Scarlett opened her eyes and shook her head. "The cow needs to be milked. And little Beau is starving—"

"You drink!" Gretta pushed the glass toward her.

Scarlett held the glass with both hands and took a sip; her eyes opened wide and she shuddered. Color flooded her cheeks, and she peered into the glass, blinking. Raising it again, she knocked back the rest and then started to climb out of bed.

"No, you stay!" Gretta pushed her back down.

"Leave me! I must check the garden for sweet potatoes."

"I'll bring you soup! Stay put."

Things sometimes took this course with the Heroines in the beginning. Gretta had the firm hand to make them rest and eat, whereas Mother would have caved in and let them run the show. Mother understood the dynamic, and she put her arm around me and led me toward the door.

"Stupid woman!" Scarlett hissed.

We closed the door and stared at each other on the landing. Then I snapped my fingers. "Attic!"

"Yes!" Mother said. We charged down the hall to the attic door to retrieve *Gone With the Wind*. Mother opened the padlock with a key tied to her wrist. We always kept the attic secured, to prevent any wandering Heroine from discovering her fate. Mother opened the door and we climbed the steep wooden steps into the chilly space. Mother ran her hands along a crossbeam and found the keys to her bookshelves. Frost laced the dormer windows. I tugged a shoestring to illuminate the bare overhead lightbulb. Mother plugged in a space heater and the red coils glowed. Along the northern slanted walls were dusty trunks, cobwebby baskets, box fans, a clothes dummy, a birdcage, and the dollhouse replica of our house that I'd abandoned years before. But the flat western wall held Mother's treasure: six ceiling-high bookshelves, with rough pine doors, latched with metal locks. Each door was labeled by continent: European (French, Italian, Russian, Spanish); Asian (Japanese, Chinese, Indian); and English Literature (Irish, Scottish, Welsh, and American) had its own case. This was Mother's treasure, her insurance policy, her prized stock. She didn't care if a book was a cheap paperback or a leather-bound first edition (and she had both types). The collection simply needed to be vast and well organized (alphabetized by author name), to allow for speedy retrieval. Mother wanted to be sure that we didn't slip and reveal something to Scarlett—that the missing Ashley would show up eventually, that her mother was dead—that she didn't already know.

"I've a good idea that she's just escaped Atlanta," Mother said. She turned the dial of the combination lock and popped it open. The hinges creaked as the doors swung and banged against the wall. I propped a bucket against one to keep it from swinging back again. Mother reached up to the *M* shelf and plucked a hard-backed copy of *GWTW* from the shelf. She thumbed through the first few hundred pages.

"She said something about asking Pork to get her whiskey," I said.

"And needing to feed Beau. Melanie's milk didn't come in." Mother licked her finger and flicked through the pages. She had a near-photographic memory. "I can almost see the page. Here it is."

We stood there together in the cold attic, hovering under the lightbulb, reading. Scarlett had arrived, like most Heroines, at her worst moment. She had narrowly escaped the fires of Atlanta, after she had waited for Melanie to give birth in the midst of a siege. Abandoned by Rhett, she drove the carriage through the Georgia woods, which felt haunted by the ghosts of slain Confederates. When she finally reached Tara, she discovered that her beloved mother was dead. Typhoid fever gripped her sisters and her father had lost his mind. The stored cotton had been burned, the fields were ruined. Seriously, few Heroines had it so bad. Yet it must have been her mother's death that precipitated Scarlett's need for a respite at the Homestead. Scarlett worshipped her mother, Ellen, a model of perfect Southern female deportment, possessing not only beauty but gentleness, self-sacrifice, and restraint. The only one of these attributes Scarlett possessed was beauty. She always struggled to meet Ellen's high standard of Southern female conduct. But passivity and altruism would not help anybody survive a war.

Mother pointed at the page. "Here she is, asking for whiskey."

"She's kind of mean to the slaves," I said.

"Impatient," Mother said.

"Same difference."

"Try not to judge." Mother closed the book. "Scarlett's from another era."

"But racism is wrong."

"Of course!" Mother said. "And I'm glad that you understand that. But there's no sense trying to point out that fact to Scarlett. In fact, I want you to steer clear of her altogether. She's a firebrand. She's liable to bite your head off."

"But you spent all that time trying to make Franny a feminist. Why can't I try to make Scarlett less of a racist?"

"That was different. Franny's almost a contemporary and—"

"You care more about feminism than you do about racism," I snapped.

"I just know what battles to pick. It's based on the character herself. Not on my agenda."

I shrugged and snatched the book from her hands. Mother didn't like how I'd begun challenging her approach to the Heroines, pointing out her inconsistencies. "If I'm not allowed near her, then at least let me stay up here and read the rest."

"It's too cold and——"

Just then we heard a crash downstairs and a door slamming against a wall. I dropped the book on the floor and we raced down the stairs. Mother scrambled to close the padlock, while I hurried down the hall.

"Oh, my God . . ." I said.

Gretta had Scarlett by the waist, and Scarlett was flailing and thrashing, beating Gretta's legs and arms. The maroon bedroom drapes were piled around their feet, looking oddly like the discarded robes of a Greek goddess—though the figure they presented was more like a Gorgon emerging from the stomach of a barbarian. Gretta took a step backward to brace herself against the doorjamb, but her foot caught in the drapes and she bounced against the wall and then tumbled forward. Gretta's arms flew open, and Scarlett scrambled out, her arms sprawled in front of her and her face planted on the worn Persian runner. Pinned at the waist beneath Gretta, Scarlett let out a shriek that made me happy there were no other boarders in the Homestead.

"Damn woman!" Scarlett tried to reach behind her and gather the drapes, but they were so twisted around Gretta's ankles that she only succeeded in tightening them, which made Gretta cry out.

Gathering the drapes meant Scarlett was scavenging for fabric, just as she had in the novel, turning the drapes into a dress and bonnet. Mother ran in and extended her hand to Gretta, who lifted her chest off Scarlett and propped herself on her knees. Scarlett wiggled out and fixed Gretta with an angry glare. "How dare you?"

Mother got Gretta to her feet and offered a hand to Scarlett. "Now, Miss Scarlett, you must lie down and rest. You've had a terrible time of it."

"This is no time to lie down! I have a million things to do!" As she rose, the color drained from her face. She tilted to the left, and Mother braced her shoulder against Scarlett's arm.

"You really must rest," Mother said, in her softest voice. She paused for a moment while Scarlett steadied herself, then slowly turned toward the bedroom door. "The whiskey's making you woozy."

Scowling, Gretta collected the drapes, folding them over her arms in neat layers of tumbling maroon velvet. She picked off lint and muttered under her breath.

"I—I suppose," Scarlett said. She allowed herself to be coaxed back in the room and into bed. This is where Mother always fared better than Gretta. Sometimes a heavy hand was needed with the Heroines; sometimes a gentle one. With Scarlett good and dizzy, Mother could ply her with kind words and sympathy in a manner that Gretta could rarely muster. Gretta got busy with her more pedestrian skills: shaking out the drapes, finding a stepladder, and fixing the hooks on the curtain rod. I quietly sat down in the wing-back chair to watch. I knew they'd shoo me away if I made any noise, and Mother's gentle persuasion—her soft voice, her careful stroking of Scarlett's tiny hands—comforted me as much as Scarlett.

Once the drapes were hung again, and Scarlett's breath fell into the rhythms of deep sleep, we crept out the door. Mother locked it from the outside, turning the old skeleton key with a gentle click. We went down to the kitchen and quietly ate a simple supper. Our ears stayed cocked for commotion from above, but the hallways remained quiet.

"Battle fatigue's probably set in," Mother said.

"She'll sleep a week, if we're lucky. If the nightmares don't wake her," Gretta said.

We went to bed early that night, afraid that any noise from the television might wake Scarlett. In the morning, Mother's footsteps woke me, and I jumped out of bed. She and Gretta stood at Scarlett's door, Mother's ear pressed to the wooden panel. Gretta knocked first—lightly, then harder and harder, until the door, which was supposed to be locked, swung open. Mother knelt and picked up the skeleton key from the floor.

"How in the world— Oh, there was another key in the night-stand!"

We pushed through the door to discover a ravaged room. It looked as if a cyclone had hit. The drapes had been torn down and dangled from their rods. Potatoes and yams were scattered across the carpet. A pile of apples made the old mattress sag. It looked like a silverware explosion on the floor beside the sunporch. Sunlight streamed through the bare windows, reflecting off Grandmother's tea tray. On the nightstand rested three sharp cooking knives with wooden handles, including Gretta's well-worn meat cleaver.

"She tried to rob us!" Gretta cried.

"She thought she could take this all back with her," Mother said, her voice full of pity.

I pointed at the cleaver. "She was going to kill us!"

"Nonsense," Mother said. "She was desperate."

"She killed that Yankee soldier," I said.

"These are tools for survival," Gretta said. "She could sell the silver, eat the vegetables."

"She must have snuck out in the middle of the night."

"Sneaky like cat!" Gretta said.

"I knew she wouldn't stay long," Mother said.

"Not even a day," I said.

It took the three of us two hours to put everything back in place. The odd assortment of items made a deep impression on me: root vegetables and silver, sharp knives and candlesticks. She had pared down the Homestead's possessions to the essentials. For a girl like me, who'd never given a thought to survival, it struck my imagination, made me wonder how I would fare in desperate circumstances. Survival had never been a concern, not until I'd found myself locked up in the Unit.

CHAPTER 15

✦ *The limits of telepathy* ✦ *I hatch lame*
schemes to contact Conor ✦ *Florence*
catches me red-handed ✦

The evening after Kristina's group debacle, I found out what isolation meant. Maria had emerged from her catatonia long enough to inform me that a nurse had to check on Kristina every ten minutes.

"The nurses hate isolation!" she said. "It means they have to get off their fat butts and quit watching TV."

I loitered in the hall outside the isolation room on the way back from dinner. It was right next to the nurses' station; I had to investigate, to find out what the punishment was for acting out as Kristina did. As I waited for the nurse to do her check on Kristina—she took much longer than the requisite ten minutes—I read a hand-drawn poster that listed the behaviors that earned you scoops: showing respect, apologizing, ignoring provocation, being helpful, avoiding conflict, etc., etc. I thought about how Scarlett would handle this situation. She'd wrestle up a passel of those scoops and scheme her way out of the Unit.

Finally I heard the nurse's chair legs squeak and the heavy pad of her feet moving toward the door. I crept around the corner, and when the door cracked open I got a glimpse of Kristina's bare feet. She lay on a bare mattress—no pillow, no blanket, no linens— strapped at the feet and ankles. The almost empty room, with its cinderblock walls and steel door, made their voices echo. When the nurse entered, Kristina cried, "I'm gonna sue! This is the last time you fuckers do this to me! You have to let me out! I got only two weeks left on my insurance anyway!"

"Keller knows how to get it extended. And you just gave him the perfect excuse!"

Shocked, I ran to my room and collapsed on the bed. How many times had Kristina been through that drill? Her empty bed, tightly bound in white sheets and a cotton blanket, looked luxurious com- pared to the isolation bed. I turned away from it, stared at the lumpy asbestos tiles overhead. No matter how much I regretted trusting Kristina too quickly, I wouldn't wish isolation on anyone. Mother was right about not talking about the Heroines. People could use it against you. I'd never get off the Unit if I confided in anyone again. With Kristina's empty bed beside me, I felt incred- ibly lonely. Even memories of Conor couldn't comfort me.

Though covered in cotton, my pillow was sheathed in plastic, and beneath the sheets was a plastic liner. The whole bed was ready for fluids: tears, piss, blood. I wanted my mommy. I wanted to be in the Homestead, where violence didn't lurk in the halls, didn't arrive at the push of an intercom button. Violence was at home in the Unit. I was not. I soaked the pillow with my tears, right down to the plastic, cried till I grew weary of it, then decided I had to do something. I inhaled and focused hard, pressing my temples. *Conor, think of me now. Follow these thoughts! Save me!* I fell asleep for hours (Florence had given me what I now know was Valium at dinner), and I awoke with heavy limbs and a racing head, think- ing, once again, of my new inspirational figure: Scarlett. Sending telepathic messages wasn't enough.

It dawned on me suddenly what I needed to do to get off the Unit: earn enough scoops to get a phone pass to call somebody.

There was no getting near a phone without a pass, as patients had to use the phone at the nurses' station. But who could I call? The only person I could think of was Albie, and he was probably pissed that my mom had sent the cops to speak with him. But he had long suspected something was up with the Heroines, never buying my murky explanations of the bizarre coincidence of literary names and boarders. He'd once happened to read the registry and saw Daisy Buchanan's name. I felt guilty for ignoring him in public the way I had, but still, he was my only hope.

I must have dozed off, because I woke to somebody tapping on my shoulder. Florence slipped a cigarette out of the pack in her shirt pocket, wriggling it between her fingers without lighting it. "Wake up, sugar cake. You need to get in the hall. It's time for Dr. Keller's midnight drive-through rounds."

I didn't know what she meant, but I followed her out to the hall and into the Day Room. A crowd of girls in pajamas clustered around Dr. Keller, who was sporting a burnt orange leisure suit. The fifteen girls, some of whom I'd never seen before, clamored for his attention. Everybody seemed wide awake and not the least bit put out at having to traipse into the Day Room in the middle of the night. One of the night nurses, an unsmiling, middle-aged Pole named Josephine, handed Keller a clipboard with papers and pointed to where he should sign. The girls pressed in closer.

"Okay, girls, one at a time!" Dr. Keller laughed and smiled.

Jackie jumped up. I didn't understand why she hadn't gotten isolation when Kristina had. "I've been really good, Doc. Can I please have a phone pass?"

"Well, looks like your eyes are healing nicely. Are you feeling better?"

"Lots!"

"Glad to hear it." He handed over a half sheet of paper, then patted Jackie on the head. "Here you go, sweetie."

"No fair!" Maria cried. "She has to earn her scoops!"

"Scoops, schnoops!" Dr. Keller said.

"Yeah, scoops, schnoops!" Jackie said.

Florence shook her head and muttered under her breath, "Peggy's gonna be teeeee-ed off."

I had no concept of normal psychiatric care, but this struck even me as a totally cockamamie checkup.

Josephine pulled on her cigarette, then said in a bored singsong, "Okay, girls. Line up, now." She waved down the hallway with her fuming cigarette. "Make a straight line."

Everyone rushed into line and waited to approach Keller like kids on their way to meet Santa Claus. Some of them bounced on their toes, while others crossed their fingers. I wound up at the very end of the line, watching as he doled out privileges to kids who hadn't earned them, told others he was upping their meds per Eleanor's instructions. The privileges were simple: pass to the hospital cafeteria, phone calls, visits, weekend passes (nobody got one of those, although Jennifer whined for one). When my turn came, he took a noticeable step backward, no doubt remembering our last encounter when I'd attacked him. My face burned with embarrassment.

"Calmed down, have we, Penny?" he asked.

"She's compliant," Florence piped up.

"Still . . ." He flipped through the pages. "No recommendations yet for passes. Too early. How are you sleeping?"

"Not great."

"Appetite?"

"Not for this icky food."

"That could be the meds. I'll mix that up a little and check back in a day or two to see how you're adjusting." He flipped through the pages again. I could smell his cologne and the trace of coffee on his breath. He started to scribble "Here's the new dosage, nurse." He flipped another page. "Lookie here. Sorry to say, little lady, but your tox screen came back positive for marijuana. *Tsk! Tsk!*" He waved a finger at me, then looked down at his watch. "Better run back to the ER. It's the witching hour!" He handed the clipboard back to the nurse. "You know how those interns hate to deal with psych patients." Patting my arm, he smiled and showed his tobacco-stained teeth. "Be a good girl, now!"

I made an effort not to shrink from his touch. "I'll be good, Doctor. And I'm sorry about the other day."

"That's fine, honey. I understand you were upset." He patted my head again.

On the way back to my room, I said to Florence, "Don't I get a scoop for apologizing?"

"For what it's worth, yes. But don't tell them I gave it to you when you asked. You can't ask for the damn things. But, Lord knows, you can ask for the moon with that charlatan."

Staff had to write their names on the scoops, so I knew I couldn't milk Florence for too many. "Thanks, Florence. That'll be my first one. How many do I need to get a phone call?"

"Ten, I think. Gotta get your cone up there first. Wait a minute. You plan on getting the king on the horn?"

"Like he has a phone."

"Get to bed."

I lay in the dark, plotting my strategy of compliance. I'd noticed that the most scoops were handed out at dinner, and my mother was coming to visit the next day, so maybe there was a scoop-earning angle there. She was coming to visit because Peggy had called and told her I wanted to talk about my father.

CHAPTER 16

More nonsense from Mother about

my father ✦ My meds are upped ✦

Contact with Albie ✦

"Lie to me, then!" I shouted at Mother. We sat on a stone bench on the manicured lawn around the psych wing of the hospital. Daylilies circled the elms, the orange blossoms withered and replaced by dead stalks. Fastened to the back of the bench was a plaque that read "A gift of Dr. and Mrs. William Stanton. In memory of Susan Marie." Some girl who probably hadn't made it. I was starting to wonder if I would. Peggy had insinuated that my lack of knowledge about my father was the source of my problems, and I was beginning to worry that she might be right. I hadn't hassled my mother too much about my father, not since I was a small child, so my sudden interest startled her. There was a bag at her feet, and through the opening I saw a cookie tin and the September issue of *Seventeen*. I crossed my arms like a real brat, scorning her objects of truce, though I ached for the cookies, the fashion updates, and most of all, I ached for her sympathy.

"It was one of those things. One of those silly nights."

"Great. So now you're calling my conception silly."

"No! You'll understand when you're older."

"I'm almost fourteen! Thirteen and a quarter."

"Fine, Penny. If it means you'll stop being so angry with me. He was very tall, like you're going to be. And athletic."

"I already knew he was tall. How long were you together? Didn't you care about him at all?" I asked this boldly, though I feared the truth. My mother had never called my conception a one-night stand, but I'd begun to suspect that it might have been one.

Mother stared at her hands, then ran one thumbnail under the other, dislodging a smear of dirt. She had probably spent the morning in the garden, where she always retreated when frustrated, yanking out dandelions and crabgrass as if each stalk were a personal insult. On better days she would wax philosophic about their right to exist. She wiped the dirt on her skirt and looked up into the tree. "I thought I was in love with Cliff, your father. He was very handsome—dark and moody. It all happened so quickly, and I was so young, so infatuated."

"But you always say sex is wrong if you're not in love."

"Now you know why I always say that. It gets too complicated." She reached into the bag and pried the lid off the cookie tin. Lumpy, sweet chocolate chips with M & Ms. My favorite. She held the tin out for me. "Penny, I made mistakes. But, look, I was lucky. I got you out of the deal!"

I took a cookie, unable to resist the offer of chocolate. "Were you two a couple?"

Mother laughed. "Not really. To be honest, I don't think he cared very much about me. Still, it took me a long time to get over him. Love's strange like that. It's not logical. I knew I shouldn't pine for somebody who hadn't been very nice to me. He just left one day, and I never spoke to him again."

I understood very little about love at this point. All I'd known were crushes, romances conducted principally in my daydreams. I was uncomfortable even hearing my mother use the word *love*. When I looked at her I saw overgrown eyebrows, the mole on her left hand. "I love you" wasn't part of our everyday repertoire. I assumed that if you said *I love you* to a boy, that meant you were bonded for life. If she had said *I love you* to Cliff, and he had broken up with her, then she was forever cursed. The idea of this guy hurting my mother upset me. I didn't like the sound, feel, or taste of it. I didn't understand how heartbreak felt, nor could I imagine being as vulnerable as my mother obviously had been. Desperate. The mother I knew was full of quiet strength. Maybe that was how she'd learned to be so sympathetic with the Heroines. Yet the thought of her as a defenseless creature was more than I could stand, and it somehow kindled my anger.

"When are you going to get me out of here?"

"I'm working on it. I didn't think it would be this hard."

"What's going on with Deirdre?"

"Still here."

"Any sign of Conor?"

Mother raised a cookie to her lips, opened her mouth, but didn't bite it. She looked across the lawn and I followed her gaze. Eleanor was heading toward us, her breasts bouncing as she bustled along, a hand on her cap. The other hand held a tray with meds. I knew she'd be pissed that she'd actually had to get out of her chair and find me.

"Great. Here comes the Elephant." I rolled my eyes. "Tell me quick. Have you seen Conor?"

"That's disrespectful, Penny." Mother straightened up her spine. "There have been signs of him. I went out to the woods to see if I could talk with him. I saw footprints and panicked."

"Remember. He can't cross to our side of the prairie. There's a spell on it."

Mother folded her arms and squinted at me, the way she did when she thought I was lying.

"Really! There's a druid's spell. Deirdre's got some kind of magical spirit looking out for her." I told Mother how the horse had reared up when it approached the prairie. "And I know Conor wouldn't hurt you."

"I know a little more about Deirdre's story than you do."

"Conor has honor!" I said, pissed that Mother was making judgments about somebody only *I* had seen. He was *my* Hero. Then I heard the cups rattling on Eleanor's tray. "Wait." I saw my chance to earn another scoop. I ran up to meet Eleanor and took the tray from her hands. "Sorry you had to run out here."

"Why, thank you!" Eleanor called. "You'll get a scoop for that. Time for your medicine, Penelope. Thirteen hundred hours." She handed me the medication.

"Wait a minute." Mother stood up, extending her hand to ward off the pills. "Dr. Keller said Penny wouldn't be medicated unless absolutely necessary."

"Oh, these are very mild, Mrs. Entwhistle, very mild. Take your meds, like a good girl," Eleanor said.

"Drugs are nothing, Mom! You don't know how it is here! They gave Kristina a bloody nose!" Even though I was trying to be a goody-goody, I was quick to use Kristina's predicament to stir up trouble.

"That can be explained, Mrs. Entwhistle," Eleanor said.

"Ms. Entwhistle. Mrs. Entwhistle is my mother."

"Ms. Yes. This particular girl, she's one of our toughest cases. Combative with the staff and other patients."

I swallowed the pills, then stuck out my tongue to prove to Eleanor that I'd taken them. I was so angry I didn't even protest when Eleanor spun the Kristina-attacked-staff story. Adults. They were all in cahoots, and they just didn't *listen*. I counted to fifty and pasted a phony smile on my face.

"Do I get a scoop for helping?"

Eleanor looked at Mother. "Yes, dear. When we're back inside."

It took only another day to earn ten scoops. I participated in one of Peggy's groups—that was an automatic scoop—plus I "confessed" to having made up the Conor story to get some attention and to distract my mom from the fact that I was getting high. Peggy was beaming. Most of the other staff didn't even pay attention to the new system, but there were two nurses and one orderly who kept pocketfuls of scoops and doled them out pretty freely. After I'd earned the ten, I pestered Peggy into letting me use the phone right away. She even defended my desire to stretch the cord around the corner of the nurses' station to get some kind of "privacy." The only problem was that Eleanor had just dosed me with my new meds: two more pills. I knew I had to act quickly before the drugs kicked in. I should have napped away the first pitch-and-roll of it, but it was three on a Saturday afternoon, the perfect time to call Albie. I figured Albie would be, as usual, lying around reading comic books in the air-conditioned comfort of his suite. He was the only kid I knew with a private phone line. Albie's great-grandfather had invented the plastic tube on the end of a shoelace. His house was one of the oldest and biggest in Prairie Bluff. He'd transformed the loneliness of his childhood into a splendid adolescent isolation. He had a La-Z-Boy in his room, a reel-to-reel tape recorder, a TV console, a miniature fridge, a giant microwave oven, and a stupendous collection of Stan Lee comics, including vintage *Fantastic Four, Spider-Man,* and *X-Men.* I didn't really dig comic books myself, but I'd shown Albie a few old issues of *Hulk* that had belonged to one of Mother's cousins, and he'd dropped to his knees in the attic and bowed before them. Every Saturday he went to the Village Newsstand and bought fresh issues of his favorite comics, then lay around reading them till dinnertime.

As I stood in the hallway, some staff headed toward the dining hall to start setting the tables. They never paid much attention to us. Eleanor had made one of the orderlies take everybody for a walk around the grounds, but I'd gotten out of it. I pulled the phone up on the countertop and dialed Albie's number. I felt the first wave of dizziness as I worked the cord around the corner. The hallways smelled like Pine-Sol and cigarettes, and with the overhead lights turned off, the floor was cool and gleaming. Albie picked up on the second ring. "Hullo."

"Albie, it's Penny."

"Traitor."

"I don't have much time."

"I'm grounded for the summer, thanks to you. Your mom told mine about the weed."

"Your mom will cave. Besides, isn't she going to France or something?"

"Yeah, they leave for Biarritz. I can probably work around my grandmother. She's—"

"I gotta hurry, Albie. I need a favor."

"After siccing the cops on me, you want a favor?"

"It wasn't my fault. I have only a minute. There's this guy in the woods. He kind of looks like a king. You have to tell him to get me. I'm in the hospital. Locked up in the loony bin."

"Your mom said you were in Europe."

I hugged the phone to my ear. "Just go to the woods behind the prairie. Tell Conor I'm on the second floor. I'll have a sign on my window."

"You expect some king to rescue you?"

"I'll put a sign on my window. A big star." I felt the floor shift. "It's like those other boarders. Bovary, Karenina. He's from a book. He's come to get Deirdre back." The meds were kicking in, just as I heard footsteps coming down the hall.

"I knew something was up! Penny?"

"I know it sounds crazy. I'll give you the *Hulk*s!" I hung up the phone and grabbed the cord to keep from keeling over.

CHAPTER 17

✣ Medication overload ✣
Deus ex homo imaginarium ✣

Dr. Keller's midnight visit was the only time I'd seen him since I'd checked in. Just because I'd said the food was bad that night, he'd upped my meds. Once my new drug regimen began, I sleepwalked for days, was spoon-fed soup and cereal, sucked juice and milk through straws. Incapacitating doses of narcotics comprised the treatment *du jour*. I suppose they felt they could strip down my defenses, pare me down to my thinnest self. But the therapeutic value of a thirteen-year-old transformed into a thumb-sucking three-year-old escapes me. All this for saying the food was bad? I was present just enough to notice that Kristina had gotten out of isolation, but it didn't really affect me. I couldn't feel it. Nothing could penetrate the walking-through-water sensation. The blur. The TV in the rec room had a rainbow aura, and I watched Nixon's flabby and sagging face with a mixture of awe and pity. My doped-out sisters—Jennifer, Maria, even Jackie—seemed cloaked in angelic light. I was glad I'd managed the call to Albie before I got so doped up.

One night, I heard footsteps heading toward my door. I'd slept through dinner again. From the light at the window, I figured it was about nine. Florence opened the door and came over to shake my shoulder. I smelled her cigarettes and Jean Naté bath splash. She held the three pills in her palm, then tucked two under her thumb. I remembered that she had done something similar the night before, holding back one of the pills. As she passed one pill into my hand, her curved fingernails brushed my palm. "Sit up, now, sugar. Drink up." Florence handed me the paper cup of water.

I swallowed the pill, then Florence tucked the others in her apron pocket, winking. I lay back down. Then I remembered. I had to hang a star on my window! I grabbed some paper and a Magic Marker from the nightstand and fixed a lopsided gold star to the window with a Band-Aid. Even with the smaller dose, I fell into a disturbed sleep.

Later that night, I woke up a little more lucid, with a heightened sense of my body. When I asked my toes to flex, they did. When I blinked, my eyes cleared, and I saw the white curtain around my bed rippling in the air-conditioning breeze. I'd been having a vivid dream about chasing my mother across a football field. It had something to do with running from my father. My father. A moody guy with dark hair. Maybe a one-night stand. No matter how I tried to envision him, to make him some icon of paternity, my mind continued to wander to Conor, the strong, handsome Villain on horseback. I vaguely remembered making the phone call to Albie, and for the first time in days, I wondered if he had found Conor, and what that meeting had been like. I sent him telepathic messages. *Conor, come now. Rescue me!* I propped myself up on my elbows and looked over at Kristina's empty bed. I'd been keeping my distance from her, partly because I wanted to be complacent, partly because I'd lost all my energy. And Kristina had been sneaking over to the boys' wing at night.

I had half dozed off again, when a rattling noise worked its way into my dream and dragged me out of it. As I pulled back the bed curtain, I heard the rattle again. Something hit the window. A handful of stones. Maybe Kristina's boyfriend, Mr. Dobson, the drama teacher. I jumped out of bed and rushed to the window, cupping my hands to the glass. At first I couldn't see anything, and then my night vision sharpened. I saw the outline of a horse's mane.

"Are you there?" a man called. A man with a deep voice and a snorting horse. *Conor!* I broke into a sweat. At last! I was ecstatic, jumping up and down in my bare feet, and my heart started to thrum. In the last two days only my mounting collection of ice-cream scoops and Conor fantasies had kept me going. The adrenaline rush I felt outpaced the effect of the meds and I almost felt like myself again. Albie had done it. I struggled to raise the window, but it still lifted only four inches, too little for me even to swing a leg through. I whisper-yelled out the window, "I'm up here!"

Conor grasped the trunk of a large tree outside the window and disappeared in the leaves. I heard rustling and snapping twigs. The branches shook and then his face emerged in front of me, followed by his shoulders. He had his cape bustled in his arm, and there was a look of irritation on his face.

"Why did you not meet me?"

"They locked me up!"

"Where is Deirdre?"

Leaves were tangled in his hair, and I smelled the wood smoke in his clothes and his sweet sweat. He'd been living in the woods for weeks, and it showed in his rough and wild breathing, his overgrown beard. Still, my relief felt close to salvation, as if he were rescuing me from the jaws of death. "She's back home."

He looked the building up and down. "There doesn't seem to be any spell around this place." He squinted at me. "Is this your castle?"

"My prison! Please help me get out of here!"

"They imprison children in this kingdom?"

"And Mother says *you're* bad."

"Bad for wanting to save my wife!"

"Save me first!"

He sliced through the screen with his sword, then ripped off the frame, the screws popping against the glass. With a swift punch, he pushed out the whole inner window, crank and all. I grabbed it before it hit the floor, and I tore off the paper star. An alarm started to blare, a rolling, clanging bell.

"They've sounded the battle call!" He jumped soundlessly into the room and strode over to Kristina's bed. I couldn't believe he was this close again, and I wanted to crawl into his arms, to feel the press of his broad chest. At the same time, I feared the sheer volume of him, his sturdy legs, his billowing cape, his bulk. The jewel at his throat glinted green.

I went around to the side of my bed, looking for my shoes. All I could find were paper slippers. I slid my feet into them. There was no time to change out of my sailor-print pajamas.

Conor drew his sword and pointed it at the door. "The battle calls!"

"You can't fight them!"

"The Lord of the Red Branch Knights fears no man!" he roared.

"But they're not armed. Really!"

It was too late. Two orderlies rushed in, clenching their fists. They were the same two guys who'd restrained me the first night I was there. The black guy held a needle, and the white one drew back in shock, staring at Conor's sword. They stopped and looked at each other like a couple of Keystone Kops. Florence squeezed in between them, standing there in a daisy T-shirt, a cigarette in the corner of her mouth. "Holy hell, he's real!" she cried.

Conor swung the sword and held it in front of his chest, the tip a half inch from his forehead. "The Master of the Twinkling Hoard does not battle unarmed men!"

"Let's go!" I screamed. "They'll arrest you, Conor. We can set up a—a—a duel later." I had no idea if duels existed in his world.

Conor pointed the sword at the white orderly, who raised his hands in surrender, his eyes wide. "I'll send a messenger to arrange a meeting at a battle ford."

"Hurry!" I shouted.

He slid the sword into its sheath, strode across the room, and scooped me up. Resting in his strong arms, I felt pale and small in my thin pajamas and paper slippers, more like a baby than a rescued damsel. He leapt to the window ledge.

I looked up into his handsome face, then over my shoulder at the cowering orderlies. Florence shook her head and fired up a cigarette. "How did you find me?" I asked.

He said something about a crow and a riddle, but before I could ask what he meant, he jumped from the ledge, and I closed my eyes. We dropped straight down, through the warm night air, the leaves slapping our faces. Sirens were approaching and the alarm continued to ring. The horse seemed to sweep up to meet us, and I buried my head in the itchy cloth of Conor's tunic, breathed in his smell. When we landed on the horse, it was like a jolt through my spine. The horse reared up, nearly throwing us off, then took off across the dark lawn. I hadn't felt night air on my skin in weeks. Conor held me by the waist, and I grasped his arms and let my body fall into the rhythm of the galloping horse. I believed again! Dreams could come true. Deus ex machina. Deus ex homo imaginarium. I looked up at the dark night sky, at stars and treetops, holding fast to the arms of an imaginary man.

CHAPTER 18

+ *Camping in the woods, Celtic-style* +

Talk of severed heads + *The odd sexual mores*

of Celtic kings + *Musings on magic* +

Prairie Bluff was a well-wooded suburb—a green spot on the aerial map—so we followed forest preserve trails most of the way back to the woods behind the Homestead. Once in a while we burst from the woods into a paved cul-de-sac behind a nouveau mansion, or galloped across a train track. We avoided the open stretches beside the railroad tracks, which would have provided more direct paths, because Conor mistook the looming power line towers for giant effigies, humming with druidical spells. He asked if I'd heard talk of the giant Finn McCool. My blank response, "Who?," yelled over my shoulder, did not dissuade him from suspecting that the great giant's henchmen lurked in the vicinity. So we stuck to the forest trails.

Once we reached the woods behind the Homestead, I recognized everything immediately. Even in the dark, I knew those woods so well my mother would have been shocked. I spotted the path to Horace's pond, the arching oaks, the railroad tracks on the other side of the trees. The horse galloped straight to the edge of a stream, but Conor held it back so I could dismount. The fresh night air helped to clear my wooziness from the ride and the latent effects of the medication. I walked up the path and looked around. Something in the brambles caught my eye. I walked closer and divined the outline of a hive-shaped shelter. Conor had camouflaged it masterfully, weaving reeds and cottonwood branches with leaves. It was like a thatched roof, though I glimpsed a white plastic sheet beneath it all, probably scavenged from some construction site.

"Imagine the Lord of the Red Branch Knights in such a hovel!" he roared. He led the horse up from the pond and tied it to a pine tree.

"It looks kinda cozy," I offered.

"At the Twinkling Hoard, you'll find all the javelins and shields and swords. I tell you, the place twinkles with gold and silver, shields and goblets and javelins. At the Ruddy Branch, I keep the severed heads and spoils of battle—"

"Severed heads?" Thank goodness I'd kept him from attacking the orderlies.

"With the sparkling torques still around their necks!" He rubbed his hands together. "We've got to get Deirdre!"

"Tonight?" I was wiped out, still murky from the medications. And I was in no rush to share Conor with Deirdre. Or risk running into Mother. "I'm really too tired to do anything tonight."

"You must devise a way to trap her at dawn!"

"Why do *I* have to?"

"You assured me you could lure her to the woods with the promise of cresses!" His eyebrows drew together in anger.

"That's out the window! I can't go home now. They'll toss me back into the Unit. The prison."

"You're clearly in favor with the sidé. Perhaps a night's rest will bring a dream of entrapment." He lifted the plastic opening of the shelter with the tip of his sword. "Now sleep!"

I crouched and crawled in over the rocks that held the plastic to the ground. At the center was a young oak trunk, and the roof was held up by curved branches, dug into the dirt. A confusing web of ropes crisscrossed the ceiling. Conor had fashioned a bed out of brown paper lawn bags stuffed with leaves. The tent smelled musty and damp, and it killed me to be only acres away from my own bed. I ached for my feather pillow, my pink satin duvet—the sheer peace of my posters and windows and rugs on the worn oak floors. I'd drive Deirdre out in a minute to have all that again. But I didn't know who might be waiting for me at the Homestead—cops, doctors, orderlies—and I couldn't trust that Mother wouldn't hand me back over to Dr. Keller and Eleanor. What if they brought bloodhounds to comb the woods for me?

Conor crawled in the shelter after me, then stood up, his hair brushing the ceiling. I hadn't noticed before how short he was—probably about five-foot-five.

"Have you started to bleed?"

I looked down at the thin scars on my arms.

"Not there," he said. "Below. Have you had your first gush of blood?"

I felt color rise in my face. He was asking about my period! "No."

"Then I shall not bed you. It's written that every woman must sleep with the king before she sleeps with any other man. And any Ulsterman who gives me a bed for the night must give me his wife to sleep with as well. But you're still a girl. It would not be kingly to bed you. Are you promised to any man?"

"I'm only thirteen!" I neglected to tack on the "and a quarter" bit. He could have raped me! Just like Mother had said.

"Sure the girls are marrying young as that!"

"Not around here!"

"For what are they waiting?"

"To finish high school?"

"Now you're speaking nonsense. Take the bed, then. I'll make do on the ground."

I crawled onto the "bed" and curled up. I felt ridiculous, lying there in my sailor-girl pajamas. I had to get some real clothes and bug spray. A mosquito buzzed around my head, and I would have killed for a hairbrush. Despite all the physical discomforts of the woods and my relief over having escaped the Unit, what really rocked me was that Conor had considered having sex with me. I listened to him breathe heavily through his nose. Naïve as I was, I still believed sex was for married people (especially after what had happened to Mother), and he was already married to Deirdre! I'd be a mistress. It was weird to think that because I didn't have my period yet, I could lose my virginity and not have to worry about getting pregnant. What a freaky window of opportunity, yet Conor would never do it. The Celts might have collected severed heads and believed in Druids, but sex with children was taboo. Even I saw something wrong in a man having sex with a girl who hadn't started to menstruate, and I didn't want to have sex with Conor anyway. My sexual curiosity hardly went beyond kissing. I feared sex, and the shock of Conor's proposition melted into comfort. Having him bluntly spell out the sex issue had actually helped me. I felt safer than I had in weeks. And my crush on him could continue without the reality of his manhood intruding.

"Your lordship?" I said.

He grunted and awoke with a snort. "What is it?"

"What did you mean when you said a crow told you where I was?"

"Exactly that. Your thoughts took the shape of the Morrigan—"

"What's a Morrigan?"

"A shape-shifter. She tried to trick me into giving up on Deirdre, but I solved her riddle and then a boy appeared to lead me to the prison."

"Was the boy's name Albie?"

"I do not know. A boy with a pox on his face."

"Sounds like Albie." I lay back on the leaf bed and stared at the white plastic sheet overhead. I didn't get what he meant about the crow appearing. Maybe Conor was deluded, prone to see druidical interference where none existed. Part of me wanted to believe in shape-shifting birds. Part of me, reared on *Lord of the Rings* and *Narnia,* believed that magic had actually existed in bygone days. I thought the world had changed at some point from being a magical place to being a rational place. I couldn't have articulated when I thought this monumental change had occurred. I guess I held the childish sentiment that things used to be better. I couldn't believe that magic existed in the present. That's truly odd, since I believed in the appearances of the Heroines. But I'd never attributed their arrival to magic: they appeared out of some literary imperative. Shape-shifters and witches were such obvious fabrications that I wouldn't have expected them to visit the Homestead. That was another class of character altogether. So I chalked up the whole crow issue to Conor's pre-Christian ideas for explaining the way things worked, and figured that Albie had saved the day. Still, as I drifted off to sleep in that damp hovel, I struggled to reconcile it all. Could the man really converse with crows?

CHAPTER 19

÷ I'm stricken ÷ The deer slayer ÷
The semi-solace of peppermint ÷ Valium
cravings ÷ Serious male desire ÷

A howling train thundered through the shelter. Or so it seemed. The plastic sheet shook with the downdraft, and outside, the horse whinnied and brayed and clomped its hooves. I opened my eyes to the first migraine of my life, my mouth so dry, my lips cracked at the corners when I closed it. I felt incoherently angry with the train, annoyed by the horse. I pinched the web between my thumb and index finger to redirect the pain from my skull. It didn't work. I should have been happy not to wake to the reveille of curtain rungs screaming across the rods, courtesy of Eleanor, but I wasn't. I was ready to dive in the murky pond to quench my thirst. I squinted at the other side of the shelter. Conor's cape hung from the young oak at the center of the hovel, but he was gone.

I crawled out of the shelter and looked up at the boxcars. The moist dawn air was a relief compared to the musty hovel. A Soo Line car rumbled past, a washed-out red peace sign spray-painted on its panels. A gold flatbed held huge spools of wire. Albie and I always loved to count the cars, but the clank of the wheels felt like

a stake through my head. Between the boxcars, I caught a glimpse
of the pink horizon, though the sky between the trees was still
midnight-blue. I got to my feet and headed toward the stream,
stepping carefully in my bare feet over twigs and moss-covered
stones.

As I walked, my vision blurred, and I stumbled off the path, net-
tles and arum brushing my knees. I squeezed shut my eyes. When
I opened them I was staring at a tall Queen Anne's lace plant. The
reddish brown floret at the center was like a spot of blood on a veil.
Water trickled in the creek. Where was Conor? I jangled my hands
and tried to shake off the feeling, then ran down to the water. I
kneeled at the edge, then cupped the cold water in my hands, gulp-
ing it down in a panic. The relief was instant. I plunged the crown
of my head in the water, hoping it would ease my headache and
dispel the visions. I wanted to shake off my skin, or scratch at somebody else's. I must be going through withdrawal! A murder of crows
landed in the tree above me, as if on cue, cawing and croaking and
polluting the air with their ugly arguments. I looked up into the
oaks at their shiny black wings and curved beaks. First some creature had taken the crow's shape to communicate with Conor. Now
it felt as if my migraine had conjured a hundred of them.

An overwhelming longing for home gripped me. If Conor was
gone, I could give up this whole misadventure. It wouldn't take
much to convince Mother not to send me back to the Unit. I heard
the snap of a branch and looked up. What I saw coming toward
me made me drop to my knees.

Conor strode down the path, his hair wild, a smear of blood on
his cheek. Over his left shoulder dangled two dun-colored legs,
tipped with black hooves. On his right shoulder rested the head
of a doe, her eyes wide open and twitching. One of her forelegs was
bent forward like a hockey stick. Blood trailed behind Conor as he
walked. His head pressed the doe's furry side, her ribs rising and
falling with labored breaths. He stopped suddenly and grabbed
the doe's legs, lifting her off his back with one strong heave. She

writhed in the dirt, tossing her head from side to side. Conor drew his sword.

I turned away quickly, crawled up the embankment, wet leaves plastering my knees, and grabbed the polished stones that buttressed the creek bank. When I reached the trail, my head spun as I stood up. I wanted to run, but I felt too weak. My headache had reached a grueling peak. I had never seen Conor like this. One word rang through my mind: *brutal, brutal, brutal.* It drummed in my skull. As I staggered past Conor's horse, it dropped manure that splattered on the ground. I felt bile rise in my throat, tried to force it back with my hand on my mouth. Too late. I projectile-vomited the remains of the previous night's Salisbury steak and potatoes. I heaved until I was empty.

My legs trembled so much I couldn't go any farther. I backed into the shelter. I'd have to pretend to sleep and make my getaway later. *Brutal, brutal, brutal.* I heard him coming closer. I crawled across the dirt floor and lay down, draping an arm over my eyes. I remembered how Mother's headaches used to incapacitate her for half a day. I started to worry. Maybe my time at the Unit had actually made me crazy. Maybe now I was a hallucinatory psychotic. Maybe Conor was an illusion. Maybe the deer was a nightmare. Maybe the musty hovel was a figment of my imagination, and this was all a bad dream! Maybe not having a father had finally unhinged me. Something was missing, something was off.

I ached for my mother's migraine medicine. I'd fetched it a hundred times, popping off the child-protection lid and shaking out two pills. I could see the clear green container in her medicine cabinet. My fingers mimicked the action, thumb depressing the plastic tab; my other hand clawed the air. I could scale the walls of the Homestead, slice the screen, and raid the cabinet, pry off the lid with my teeth. I could do it! I crawled across the floor and poked my pulsating head out the doorway.

My eye met the dull eye of the deer that was hanging upside down from two forked poles. The deer had been sliced through the side. I saw meat and blood and sinews. Conor crouched in the dirt, smashing rocks against each other, trying to get a spark. He didn't notice me watching. I felt the vomit rise again in my throat, but I forced it back this time, swallowed the rancid burn in my mouth. I backed into the shelter and sprawled on the dirt.

I was truly ill. There was no doubt about that. The shelter spun as I dug my fingernails into the dust. When the spinning waned, I dragged myself to the bed and lay on it face down.

I must have slept for at least an hour. The smell of fresh peppermint woke me. Conor was squatting in the tent, grinding peppermint leaves with two stones. His calves bulged with muscles, and he bit his lip as he worked. The headache had ebbed somewhat, but I was afraid to move or breathe a word in case it came roaring back. So I lay still, eyes open, watching while he ground the mint leaves and placed the pulp in a McDonald's cup. He must have felt me watching him then, because he looked over and his face broke into a ferocious smile.

"I see you've been sick. We'll get you sorted out with this." Conor brought the cup over to me and held it under my nose. "I'll add some water, but a good sniff will settle the stomach. There you go."

I carefully propped myself up on my elbows, inhaling the peppermint. It smelled wonderful—cool and light—but when I sniffed too hard, the headache intensified again. Just closing my eyes felt like a strain, and when I did, I saw a piercing light and short spasms electrified my brain, more startling than painful, but as they passed, the headache mushroomed.

"I'll get you some meat after it's roasted. You need to eat again."

The thought of eating the once-frightened, now-disemboweled doe repelled me, but I held my tongue and tried to banish the thought of slaughtered doe from my mind. I lay back on the paper mattress in slow motion and wondered about Conor. I couldn't square it: the brutal hunter and the kindly king. Then the headache rendered thinking moot.

I practiced breathing deeply as Mother did, stretched out on her four-poster bed, the shades and drapes drawn so not a glimmer of light snuck into the room. She had told me she focused on something peaceful and beautiful, so I thought of my pink satin duvet, inhaled and exhaled, pretended it was rising and falling on my chest. Condensation dripped from the plastic ceiling onto my leg. Though the shelter was warming up, my teeth started to chatter. I couldn't tell whether I could control them. It felt like I could and couldn't. The tooth-on-tooth pressure offset the headache. For a while. Then my thoughts started to race, and all I could think of was, *Valium, Valium, Valium.* I spelled it backward and forward: *Muilav, Valium, Muilav, Valium,* chanting like a cheerleader. My headache leveled into lofty numbness. I stood up, teeth clattering, and danced from foot to foot. Conor came in, holding a slab of meat on a garbage can lid, and shook his head at me.

"Working your spell, are you?"

"Valium, Muilav, Valium, Muilav," I sang. I rushed over and grabbed his shoulders. "I must have it now!"

"Girl, you must eat! It will return you to your senses. An empty gut works ill on the mind."

I took a chunk of greasy, smoky meat and lifted it to my lips. I tore off a chunk and chewed. It was tough but tasty, and I chewed and chewed, relishing how my grinding teeth offset the headache. Conor studied me; he seemed to be counting my chews. Then he held up the McDonald's cup filled with water and peppermint.

"Thanks." I was shocked by how good the meat tasted, even though I couldn't bear to think of how it came to be in my hand. I accepted the cup and the water cooled my throat, while the peppermint eased my stomach. Once I'd eaten the chunk of meat, I lay back down, exhausted.

"There'll be no going after Deirdre till you've rid yourself of this sickness. I'd say someone in the prison laid a mighty curse on you."

"For sure."

The curse of meds. I'd never been this sick without having my mother around. Conor was the only one I had. He was the first man besides my grandfather to care for me. I had a confusing mix of romantic and daughterly feelings toward him. The daughterly feelings were both wonderful and painful, as they came with a sharp ache for the father I'd lost, that moody man who'd died in a fiery car wreck. Before Conor, I hadn't really registered how much I missed having a father. Timing had something to do with it. All this chaos made me wonder about the man I'd lost, made me wonder if I would have wound up in the Unit if I had a father.

I, typically and unoriginally, took out my anger on my mother. Before that, she and I were happy in our tidy twosome. I'd always been told that I had been an easy baby, an easy child. I think Mother longed for those idyllic days for the rest of her life. Now she had turned away from me. She was most responsible for my being in this state. I didn't know who to trust anymore. Conor could single-handedly catch and slay a deer; imagine what he'd do if I crossed him. If by some fluke my period started, I'd have to sleep with him. How could I hide it? Yet he was taking care of me, so it seemed incongruous to fear him. I looked down at my chest; it had been weeks since I'd measured it, but I felt my nipples and was shocked to discover that they were bigger. I couldn't believe it. I'd been too doped up at the Unit to notice. I wished I had a measuring tape. I looked across the shelter and discovered Conor staring at me. He lay on his side, one hairy knee bent toward me. The blood on his cheek had turned brown.

"I've never gone this long without a woman." He rolled over on his back and reached for a thick walking stick that lay beside him. His knuckles turned white as he gripped the wood and drew it across his calf. He cracked it in two on his shinbone. He took the two smaller pieces and cracked each of those in half. "You need to get Deirdre to me."

I felt a new urgency to do that.

CHAPTER 20

÷ Albie appears ÷ Finally, a decent scheme ÷
Weaning with weed ÷ I come clean to
the right person (for once) ÷

When my headache subsided somewhat, I rolled off the mattress and tried to sort my thoughts. My to-do list was short but herculean: get to the Homestead, trick Deirdre into coming to the woods, all while avoiding Mother. I also wondered what was happening in the Unit. Mother must have been called by now. The cops would come looking for me. It was only a matter of time. I remembered TV news reports of cops and hounds and locals combing the woods for a missing girl. The humiliation of having my face broadcast over the local news terrified me.

I was pretty sure it was Sunday, but I didn't have a watch, so I had to determine the hour by the sky. By the level of heat and the angle of the sun through the roof, I figured it was early afternoon. Conor was outside stuffing another lawn bag with decayed leaves from the forest floor when I heard a familiar voice.

"Did you get her?"

"She's resting in the shelter."

Albie! I crawled out of the hovel, and when I stood the trees spun. Albie lent me an arm and I squeezed it tight. "You're here!"

I said. I'd never been so happy to see him. Next to Conor he seemed like a garden rake, with his bony legs and wild hair. Despite his pimply face, the stoop of his shoulders, and the whiff of body odor, I was delighted to see him. A friend.

"Hey, Penny. Nice outfit."

I looked down at my pajamas and crossed my chest with my arms, ashamed of the corny anchor print.

"I got away as soon as I could," he said. "The Prairie Bluff fuzz was all over me."

"Cops came to your house?"

"With your mom. They know you escaped. After forty-eight hours, they'll start searching the woods."

"We better move," I said.

"Sure a humble place it is, but—" Conor said.

"We'll be safer farther back in the woods. They're bound to come looking for me. The guys at the hospital might have—"

Conor jumped to his feet, turning on me angrily. "The High King runs from no one!"

"I'm not saying you should run . . ." I felt a hint of my old self returning with Albie's presence. I could manage Conor a little better. His brazen courage had gotten me out of the Unit. I'd read enough Tolkien to understand the code: he was driven by pride and honor. "I just think *I'll* feel better going out on raids if the base camp is secure."

"I don't know, Penny," Albie said. "They're getting close. Maybe you should go back farther. Back where we used to build the forts. I told them I hadn't heard anything from you. I admitted that you'd called me that one time, 'cause they could probably check the phone records."

"Shit, Albie. I'm so sorry you're getting in all this trouble."

"Good thing my parents left for Biarritz. My mom would be going nuts. Grandma's just vacuuming. Vacuuming upstairs the whole time the cops were there. But I've got her snowed. She won't squeal."

"How'd you get out?"

"She went to church. No dragging me there. She can't stand parading me in front of the High Episcopalians anymore with my long hair. And there's some luncheon thing going on afterward."

Albie looked over each shoulder, as the super sleuths in his comic books probably did. "I got an idea about how to ward off the cops. I was eavesdropping on them. They kept asking your mom if they'd found a note saying you'd run away. See, if you're a runaway, then they don't really look. If they think you've been abducted, then it's a totally different scenario. Bloodhounds and stuff."

"So I should write a note—"

"And I'll sneak it to Gretta. Around the back. That way they'll back off some."

"What do they think happened?"

"All the cops said was that a nurse went in your room this morning and you were gone."

"The orderlies aren't talking?" I asked.

Albie shook his head. "Why would they?"

"Long story. But I guess they don't want to say some guy in a cape hoisted me out the window."

Albie pulled a pack of cigarettes out of his pocket. "Not if they don't want to wind up as patients."

Conor lifted the bag of leaves off the ground and walked toward us. "What about Deirdre? Can you bring her here?"

"I don't know about all that," Albie said.

"We'll focus on Deirdre tomorrow. I promise, Conor. One more day." I turned to Albie. "But I don't have a pen!"

Albie took a sheet of folded loose-leaf from his back pocket and a Bic pen.

I searched the ground for a smooth writing surface, finally settling on a shorn-off tree trunk. Though I had no idea what would happen if they found me, I felt fairly certain that Mother wouldn't sign me back into the Unit. What I didn't know was whether

Keller could do it without her consent. I squatted on the ground and scribbled a messy note:

Dear Mom,
I've run away. I will call you when I reach a new town.
I'm OK.
I can't go on in that hellhole of the Unit. It's not fair!!!!!!
                                        Your daughter,
                                        Penny

"What's up with your hand?" Albie asked.

My hand was shaking and my penmanship a nasty scrawl. "I think I'm withdrawing from the medication they gave me."

"What'd they have you on?"

"I don't even know. Maybe Thorazine or Valium or something." I handed him the note.

"My cousin was on that. Strong shit." He slid the note into one pocket, then extracted a tightly rolled joint from his Marlboro hard pack. "This'll take the edge off."

"Really?"

"It'll relax you." He gestured toward the trail with his chin. "Let's clear out for a while. Not sure what would happen if the Lord King of the Ruddy Hoard got a toke off this."

"He told you who he was?"

Albie smirked. "Kinda. He went off about a bunch of titles. Lord this, king that. But you need to lay the real sitch on me. Let's hike up to the other side of the railroad tracks."

"I don't have any shoes," I said.

Albie turned his back, squatted, and held his arms out like a wiry monkey. "Jump on my back."

"No!"

"C'mon. You're like a sister. And you weigh about two pounds."

"You weigh about three."

"Exactly. I'm bigger."

It seemed to be my destiny to ride the backs of horses and boys. But Albie was right. I didn't want to smoke pot around Conor and I was too woozy to go anywhere on my own two feet. After everything he'd done, Albie deserved an explanation. I jumped on his skinny back, wrapping my legs around his waist. I didn't know what to do with my hands, so I let them rest on his bony shoulders. As he straightened up, he staggered, gripping the back of my legs to find his balance.

"What'd they feed you in that place?"

"Puke food." As we headed down the trail, I called over my shoulder to Conor, "We'll be right back!"

"'Tis a strange transport!"

Albie hoofed up the trail and crossed a broken bridge that led to the ditch along the tracks. I squinted as we emerged from the woods and into the sunny prairie. I hadn't been out this far since Franny had disappeared, two summers before, and I felt a queasy feeling of guilt. It was almost the same time of year. Purple-spiked thistles waved in the air; sunflowers drooped on their fuzzy stalks. Albie galloped through the weeds, huffing and puffing up to the tracks, where he paused to catch his breath. Despite the heat I shivered at the sight of the woods on the other side, which had swallowed up Franny.

"Let's stop here," I said. "You're tired."

Albie didn't object. His smoking habit hadn't exactly done fine things for his lungs. He crossed his legs and sat down on a crosstie. I faced him, cross-legged on the other side, my legs on the splintery crossties, my feet on the warm rocks. There was something wonderful about sitting in the middle of the tracks, the sun blazing down and glinting off the rails. It wasn't really dangerous—you could see trains coming a mile away—but still it felt risky. My sailor pajamas, unfortunately, diminished the rebel stance, reminding me that I was a nuthouse escapee.

Albie pulled out the joint and lit it, peering down the tracks. "Maybe we should just jump the next freight train."

"Yeah, I can just picture it. Me tooling around the States in pajamas and bare feet."

He flicked open his Zippo lighter and said in a fake British accent, "Shoes are a mere contrivance!" After a long hit, he handed me the joint. "My cousin weaned off his meds with grass."

I took a deep drag, and the end of the joint sizzled. My lungs filled up and burned my insides. Blinking and frowning, I coughed out all the smoke and passed the joint back to him.

"Easy, there," he said with a laugh. "Haven't I taught you anything? I wish your mom could see what a tame stoner you are." He squeezed the joint between his fingers. "Like this." With his pinky lifted, Albie had a gangly, Jagger-esque elegance when he smoked a joint. After he inhaled, he talked through clenched teeth, careful not to let the smoke escape. "Hold it in for a little bit, like five seconds, then let it out real slowly." He exhaled a steady stream, then reached across the crossties and handed the joint back to me. "This'll take the edge off. Grass is way more natural than the shit pharmaceutical companies cook up."

Usually when I smoked with Albie, I didn't try that hard to catch a buzz. This time I inhaled carefully, counted to five as I held in the smoke, then exhaled as if I were blowing out a single birthday candle. My nerve endings jangled, then went calm. My senses expanded from the pot; the wild grasses throbbed a deeper gold, and I stared at the swirling pinwheels on Albie's tie-dye. Even the birdcalls were amplified. The humidity no longer felt like a wool blanket, but more an element I had to glide through with composure.

"The birds are so loud," I said.

"You're stoned." Albie laughed.

I felt suddenly elevated inside. Being high made me feel like a leavened version of myself: lighter and loftier. I had to confess everything. My mind started to race and I blurted out, "Albie, you have to know. You probably won't believe me. But these Heroines come to our house. It's crazy. It's—"

"Yeah, what's the story?"

So I told him everything, and it felt different than telling Kristina, who'd lapped up the story like juicy gossip. Albie stayed calm, almost neutral, merely nodding his head like a stoned wise man. The most he ever said was, "Yeah, I always knew something was up with your mom."

I told him about Scarlett and Madame Bovary, about Daisy Buchanan and Blanche, but I couldn't bring myself to confess what had happened with Franny. The pot made me paranoid enough to fear even uttering her name within earshot of the woods on the other side of the tracks.

"How old were you when you figured out what was up?" Albie asked.

"Five. My mom sat me down. Told me about Rapunzel visiting when she was a kid."

"It couldn't have mattered before you could read, right?"

"But it did matter. Or it started to matter. When Hester Prynne came, with Pearl." I rarely thought about that visit. But it all started to come back to me.

"She brought the kid?"

"They were never apart."

"Grim, man," Albie said. "*Scarlet Letter*'s a sad tale."

"I didn't really get what happened till last year, when I trudged through the book and started to remember what they'd said. It had always been there—you know, fragments of memories, but they never really added up."

"I have memories like that. Like I can't remember if I dreamt them or if they really happened."

"I think this really happened."

CHAPTER 21

Hester and Pearl hit the Homestead ✦
Puritanical child's play ✦ Mother
finds a kindred spirit ✦

They came in with a bang, feet stamping, girlish shrieks, the door slamming against the stop. I ran down from my bedroom to see what the commotion was all about. A little girl was screaming, pointing at her mother's breast. She was around my height, and her mother stooped to hush her with her finger. When Mother heard her say the name Pearl, she knew immediately that another Heroine had arrived.

"I am terribly sorry, mistress," Hester said, then turned to the girl. "Naughty Pearl, thou art a disgrace to me."

Pearl continued to jerk her body, shriek, and point at Hester's chest. Her eyes were wild, her hair flying about. She flung herself on the settee and kicked her feet behind her. I found her fascinating and disturbing. I wasn't prone to tantrums myself, and the sight of her flailing legs and fists filled me with both dread and awe. Pearl was a beautiful girl, with dark thick hair and pale skin. She held a fistful of half-dead sunflowers, which she must have picked from the prairie. The browned petals showered the velvet cushion each time she threw a punch.

"I know what ails her," Hester said. "Pray thee, mistress, have you a scrap of red fabric?"

"I'll get the sewing kit."

Mother remembered that Pearl couldn't bear to see her mother without the scarlet letter upon her breast. I, of course, didn't know what was going on, so I followed Mother out to the kitchen. Gretta stood at the sink, scrubbing potatoes in a large aluminum colander.

"What all the noise about?"

"I need your sewing basket. And a scrap of red fabric."

"Another one here?"

"Hester Prynne."

Gretta shrugged and wiped her hands on her apron. She rushed to the cupboard and extracted her sewing basket. On the shelf above were fabric scraps, folded in neat rectangles and organized by color. She slid a square of crimson silk out and handed it to Mother.

"Why is that girl screaming?" I asked.

"Her mother lost something that she usually wears. And it bothers her to see her mother without it."

"What is it?"

"A letter. Her initial."

I didn't understand why this would disturb Pearl so, but I didn't argue. I had no playmates beyond recess in the schoolyard, and even there I often spent a solitary half hour drawing faces on the blacktop with stones. At seven, I didn't insist on my version of the world. People behaved in ways that I didn't understand, and I was learning that observation made a more fruitful study than talk. But it was more shyness than slyness. I didn't know how to demand knowledge and understanding, and back then I would never have pitched a fit like Pearl's to get my way. Instead I clung to my mother's bell-bottoms, shadowing her like a loyal pup.

"Are they from a book, too?" I asked.

"Yes."

When we returned to the foyer, Pearl had calmed down some. Although she sat quietly beside her mother on the settee, what

had soothed her was the act of picking petals off the withered sunflowers and pressing them into an A shape on her mother's chest.
Hester endured it with a weary frown. "Thou dost torture me so."

Mother showed Hester the basket and cloth, and then we all
followed Mother down the hall to Sidney's Room at the north-
west corner of the house. It had a private bath, and the previous
boarder had cleared out two days before. Mother pushed open the
door to reveal a dark room with beamed ceilings, yellowed wallpaper, and dormered windows. The bed had a horsehair mattress
and a frayed tan-and-maroon quilt. The windows overlooked the
prairie, which was in the last golden throes of autumn, halfway
toward its November decay to gray. It was strangely warm for
mid-October, and Mother opened the French doors to the porch
to let the air circulate. Wicker chairs were stacked on a sunporch
that led to the Blue Room next door, which was currently empty.

Hester sat down in the wingback chair and searched the sewing
basket for scissors. Mother covered her mouth and watched. This
was the first time a Heroine had been disturbed by her change in
clothing. Would their clothes disturb them beyond the issue of
the red letter? Pearl wore a pair of corduroy overalls; Hester a
jumper and blouse. They'd arrived without coats, as the temperature was nearly seventy degrees.

"Pearl, how old are you?" Mother asked. I'm sure she was cal-
culating the plot point.

"Seven years," Pearl said.

"Same as Penny! Penny, why don't you show Pearl your room?
Maybe she'd like to play with the dollhouse."

"Okay," I said. It was unusual for children to come to the
Homestead, and as wild as Pearl seemed, I relished the chance to
have someone to play with on my own territory.

"Toys are for the idolatrous!" Pearl cried. "And I shall not leave
Mother!"

"Shush, child," Hester said. "This is not one of the children
from the village. She shall not harm thee!"

Pearl ran up to me with her fists on her hips. "Should thou tri-est to pelt me with stones"—she stomped her foot close to my sneaker—"I shall harm *thee*!"

"Mom!" I cried, running behind Mother's legs. Pearl's cheeks flushed and her dark eyes flashed wild. I couldn't believe she'd threatened me like this, right in front of our mothers.

"Was there ever such a child?" Hester said.

"Penny is very friendly, Pearl," Mother said, stroking my hair, unfazed by the child's vigorous threat. I hid behind Mother's legs; she was a kind, protective tree in the woods, and Pearl a mercurial sprite. "She's never mean to anyone. Right, Penny? You'll promise."

Pearl pouted and crossed her arms, and there was something in her trembling lip that touched me. The beautiful bully was afraid, and I so longed for a playmate. "I promise I won't be mean."

"Thou hast a house just for dolls?"

"Yes. It has three floors and real furniture!"

"Dost thou hear?" Hester said. She had folded the fabric in three, and without a stencil began to cut a cursive A. "Penny still wishes to play with thee despite thy strange and elfish outbursts."

"Did thy father make this house for thee?" Pearl asked me.

"Her grandfather," Mother cut in.

"C'mon. I'll show you."

"Thou speakest strange!" Pearl said.

"So do *thou*!" I said.

"Thee!"

"Thou!" I said. "It sounds like you're praying."

"If only Providence would hear thee," Hester said.

In my room, Pearl quickly got to work. The dollhouse held her attention for only a minute or two. The small rooms couldn't contain her wilderness-bred imagination. Her dismissal of the spool-of-thread table and the tiny plastic dolls discouraged me. But they were hard to move about, and Pearl was interested in drama.

Instead, she arranged my stuffed animals in a circle on the floor. She picked up a panda bear and placed him at the top of the circle.

"Hither the governor!" Beside him she set a fuzzy gray shark, a turtle, and a dog with floppy plastic ears. "These art the elders!" She pushed me toward the center of the circle. "Thou art the minister. Stand on the pillory and have thy sentence read."

I complied, jumping over the stuffed animals and planting my feet in the soft rug. I didn't really understand what was unfolding, didn't know what a pillory was, but I figured it was akin to a guillotine, and anyway her fierce commands inspired obedience.

Pearl picked up the panda bear and spoke from behind its head in a deep voice. "Minister, why dost thou go about with thy hand on thy heart? What hidest thou thither beneath thy shirt?"

"Nothing!" I said.

"Liar! Some evil sin is in thee!"

I didn't know what to say. Mother and I went to church only at Christmas with Grandma and Grandpa Entwhistle. The concept of sin intrigued me, though, despite Mother's efforts to shelter me from it. I had reached the age of reason, knew that lying and disobeying were considered sinful behaviors in school and at home, so I ventured, "I lied."

"Speakest of thy lies and thy hidden ways! Is it not true that thou hast met with yonder woman in the woods to plan escape?"

"I did!"

"Why dost thou plan to leave the people who hast made thee their leader?"

"I can't take it anymore!" I spoke in the dramatic voice of a TV housewife.

"Thou shall pay for thy sins!" Pearl picked up a long stuffed snake with a vinyl forked tongue and started to flail me with it. I dropped to my knees, cowering beneath the soft lashes of the furry toy. I got a peculiar pleasure from her punishment, was stirred by the sound of her English accent as she repeated, "Repent, repent, repent."

After several minutes, Pearl collapsed on the floor, and we stared at each other across the felt fins, button noses, and clawless paws of the pastel and primary-colored animals. Her eyes bored into mine, her chest heaving from exertion.

"We shouldst go and listen to the mothers. Tell me, dost thou know a way to listen to them without their knowing?"

"We could hide outside on the sunporch. If the doors are still open, we can hear everything from there. C'mon."

We ran down the hall and then silently crept into the Blue Room, which shared the porch with Sidney's. The desk and bed were painted marine blue, and a bluebonnet paper lined the walls below the wainscoting. I put a finger to my lips, then tiptoed across the creaky floor. The trick was getting the door open without their hearing. Pearl was stealthy and catlike in her movements, soundless and slant-eyed. I turned the knob and slowly opened the door to the porch. Our mothers spoke in quiet tones, and we pressed against the side of the house and slid closer to the French doors.

"In three days' time, we shall be at sea. My Pearl will have a father."

"That'll be wonderful," Mother said, pretending, as usual, not to know Arthur Dimmesdale's tragic fate. "Raising a child alone can be difficult."

"Where might be the father of Penny?"

"He's gone," Mother said. "Like you, I was never married. And like you, I never told anyone who Penny's real father was."

I froze. So rarely did Mother even speak of my father that I hardly thought of him myself. He wasn't a person to me as much as an absence, a void that made me different from the kids at school. I knew that most people had a father hanging around, going to work, but I didn't really understand the biological imperative of father, that a woman couldn't have a baby without a man.

"Thou hast felt the scourge of the people's disdain," Hester said.

"I have," Mother said.

I squirmed, wished I understood what Hester meant. But I heard the bond growing between them; I understood that Hester was sympathizing with Mother. They had something in common: their girls and their singleness. Yet, it would be years until I could read *The Scarlet Letter* and truly understand what Mother had risked to keep me. What it would have cost her, centuries before, and how certain puritanical ideas still pervaded the Protestant culture of Prairie Bluff. And how the men could escape any responsibility.

I heard the chair being pushed back, then Mother said, "Are you done stitching it?"

"I am, thank thee."

"Let me help you get back into the jumper."

"I shouldst check on Pearl. Glad she'll be, to see me wearing again my badge of shame."

Pearl and I backed out of the porch then, and scampered across the floor and back to my room.

The next day, Pearl and I made our way from the garden to the prairie and into the woods. Our mothers were in such deep conversation on the patio, they didn't notice when we slipped beyond the hedge. It was another Indian summer day, the leaves golden, the sun warm on our heads. We ran like unbridled weeds, though I always trailed her. Even though it was my territory, Pearl led the way. She was one of the fastest girls I'd ever met, and she had no fear of charging into the marshy cattails along the prairie path and muddying her sneakers. Running her hands along the wildflower stalks as if she were strumming a harp, she loosened thistle seeds and dried grass pods. When we entered the woods, under the shadow of the trees, her eyes flickered like the sun between the leaves. The trail of oaks made a golden canopy over our heads. The woods were her true home, and she danced and gathered a bundle of dried-out grasses.

"Stand thee against the tree!" She pointed with the grasses to one great oak.

I stepped against the tree and wrapped my arms behind it, as if bound.

"Witch!" she shouted. "Dost thou know why thou art here before the people?"

"I have sinned." I lowered my chin to my chest in shame. The strange wave of pleasure ran through me again. I squeezed my eyes shut waiting for her next words.

"Thou hast met the devil in the woods at night. Thou must pay for thy sins!"

She lashed me with the stalks, striking my chest and arms, making thin white scratches on my skin. I pretended that it hurt more than it did, thrashing against the trunk and moaning. "I am not a witch! I swear to God!"

"Witch, witch, witch!" she sang, until she was thoroughly winded.

I relaxed my arms, let them drop to my side, while Pearl caught her breath. "Do you know any other games?" I was growing tired of being the naughty one, however perverse a pleasure it gave me. "Let's play princesses!"

Pearl fixed me with a stern look. "But where is thy king, thy father?"

"Back at the castle."

"I mean thy true father. The father who made you."

"He's in heaven," I said, and the images of a father playing a harp and frolicking with angels filled my head.

"Not thy heavenly Father. The earthly one."

"I *said*. In heaven. He's dead." I didn't like to say the word, so I softened it. "He passed away right after I was born."

"Art thou certain?"

I didn't understand why she would say such a thing.

"Sometimes the father is closer than you think. Mine is in the village. He shall join Mother and me in a new land."

I looked around the woods, a creepy feeling coming over me; I didn't understand or like what she was saying. The shadows deepened around us. Night was falling more quickly in those October days, and I didn't want to get caught in the dark. "C'mon!" I said. "We better get back home. Our moms will be worried."

She merely smirked, then turned away, making me chase her down the path, through the rocky trails and over the extension bridge. Once, she ducked behind a tree and then jumped out screeching like a cat. When I screamed, she merely giggled and headed back toward the prairie, as if she knew, by instinct, that staying in the woods beyond sunset was an unwise thing to do. I was so relieved to see her turn toward home that when we emerged from the woods, I decided to forgive her for everything.

Hester and Pearl stayed for almost a week. Every day, Pearl and I reenacted our drama of the pillory. She was always the governor or the punishing cleric, and I the minister or the disgraced woman, who had to pay for sinful ways with lashings or by holding my arms in the air till the blood drained out. The games always felt terribly serious, intense, but only mildly painful. I succumbed completely to Pearl's will. And for months after they disappeared, I longed for the thrill of her shaming. I never told my mother about the nature of our play.

CHAPTER 22

÷ Albie heads to the Homestead ÷
I worry and wait ÷ Conor and I retreat
farther into the woods ÷ I long for Gretta ÷

I t's hard for me to explain the confessional mode that struck me while sitting in the sun on the hot railroad tracks with Albie, my mind foggy with weed. Perhaps the Unit had made me appreciate the freedom of talking to a peer who actually knew me, not to Peggy or some nurse who was trying to unearth some golden nugget that would set me "free." I felt perfectly at ease confessing to Albie the strange games with Pearl. They had always confused me, made me feel an odd shame. Albie understood it completely.

"We talked about that in class," Albie said. "How Pearl always created mean imaginary characters. Plus, my theory is that all kids are basically cruel."

"But why did I go along with it?"

Albie shrugged his shoulders, and curved his scoliosis-prone back. Strands of dark hair brushed his collar, and I noticed some sparse hairs above his lips. "She didn't actually hurt you, right?"

"No. She just bossed me around."

"You're an only child." He held up one finger, then made a

peace sign. "If you had a big bullying brother like I do, you'd have learned to defend yourself."

Albie's brother was one of those prep-school dream boys, who'd gone off to a boarding school in the East. He lorded his perfect grades, skin, and looks over Albie like a preening snot. "Maybe," I said. "I didn't have a lot of friends my own age back then. Pearl was the only kid Heroine who ever showed up."

"Cool. Old Anne-Marie's like a witch or something, drawing these characters to her. What a head trip."

The word *witch* made me cringe, mostly because it had crossed my mind a million times, and because Pearl had chanted it so gruffly in the woods. "No surprise I wound up in the Unit."

"Man, your mom sure looked like she could use a break from *her* story line."

"What do you mean?" I felt the headache creeping back, the inklings of paranoia that (I'd later learn) came with a diminishing buzz. I didn't want to think about my mom's feelings; if I let that in, I'd be swallowed up.

"The cops were grilling her pretty hard."

I looked down at my palms. The creases somehow made me sad, feel older. My hands felt heavy and yet somehow detached from me. Everything they'd done in the past few weeks, all the ways I'd changed. I couldn't fathom it. I couldn't fathom what my mother had been through either. I didn't want to. "I bet she's getting one of her migraines."

"If we're lucky, she will. Isn't she down for the count with those? It would work great if she were asleep. I think I can handle it if I run into Gretta. She won't send in the cops, I bet. Does she know the deal about the Heroines?"

"She's hip." I looked up from my lap. The sun was starting to drop behind the trees. "You better hurry, Albie. Get that note under the back door."

"Jump on." Albie squatted and I jumped back on his back. "I'll come back later tonight to check on you guys. But like I said before, you should move farther in. Out where we used to build the forts. I'll find you."

After Albie left for the Homestead, my paranoia got stronger. He left me a joint to fend off the withdrawal, and I took a few tokes to take the edge off. But as the sky darkened and the crickets started to chirp, fear took up full residence in my bones. I paced the ground, stirring up the dirt and blackening the soles of my feet. Conor and I had to move.

"My mother knows I met you in these woods. Better to throw them off the trail by going to a different part."

"The High King hides from no man!"

"It's not like we're hiding. Just finding a better spot for the final battle."

Conor finally agreed, so we broke camp, wrapping the plastic sheet around the branches and roping the mattresses to the horse's rump. I had to talk him out of carrying the deer on the horse's back (I couldn't stomach it) by telling him we'd move faster without it. He could retrieve it later if he wanted. Horse trails wound all around Prairie Bluff, so we could have easily passed for a father and daughter out for a late Sunday ride. Of course, Prairie Bluff residents had fabulous saddles and riding gear, whereas we were bareback, me in PJs, he in a tunic, and carting trash. Conor's sword would be a little tough to explain as well, but I figured I'd sell him as a fencer, if anyone got close enough to ask.

Within minutes we cleared my normal stomping grounds and wound along rarely traveled trails.

"I nearly set up camp out here," Conor said, "but I was afraid that you and Deirdre would never find me. 'Tis true that it's a far better spot for hiding."

Albie and I used to have daylong expeditions on these trails, pretending to be chased by giants or constructing feeble forts. This past summer, we were too lazy for hikes; we just sat on logs and listened to WLS on his blue plastic transistor radio. He smoked grass while I did interpretive dances to "Don't Let the Sun Go Down on Me." It seemed like kid stuff to me now, yet as Conor directed the horse along those dark and narrow trails, I longed for those simple days.

Conor and I rode to the edge of the woods, where the train tracks curved along the river. As we approached the water, we scared up three ducks, which flapped into their heavy-bottomed flight, and annoyed Canadian geese honked at us. Other than the birds, the woods felt deserted, though with the horse at full gallop, it was hard to see anything but a blur of leaves. Conor started to slow down, then brought the horse to an abrupt halt, which made my head spin. He jumped straight off, but I closed my eyes and tried to find my balance before I allowed him to lift me off the horse and down to the ground.

I needed to lie down, and I watched through glazed eyes as Conor reassembled the shelter. As soon as he'd finished, I crawled inside and lay down on one of the mattresses. I imagined how close Albie might be to the Homestead just then. He was so lucky! I only hoped he could reach Gretta without my mother noticing. I wondered if Gretta knew I'd been at the Unit, and what she might think of me. I stared up at the plastic-sheet ceiling, the black outlines of fallen oak leaves. I'd never really thought about it, but Gretta was sort of like a father figure to me. She managed the Heroines well whenever one of them flew into inexplicable outrages or tears, and I knew better than to cross her myself. She was so Old World, played the heavy when needed, and yet when I thought about it, she was actually warm and flexible. There was so much about Gretta that I didn't know then, and yet I longed for her steadiness nearly as much as I longed for Mother's Valium. That was the thing about her. Gretta never had a migraine, she never even caught cold. She was the iron force in the household, and yet at thirteen, I knew so little about her life. Yet within days I would learn unimaginable things about Gretta, my mother, and the real truth about my father.

PART III

The Girlhood of
Anne-Marie Entwhistle

CHAPTER 23

✦ Gretta's back story ✦ A rain-drenched
Heroine appears to Gretta alone ✦
A nineteenth-century plot device foiled
by German ingenuity ✦

Gretta had been the cook at the Homestead long before Mother converted it to a bed-and-breakfast. She'd been a fixture throughout the Entwhistle family's summer visits, and her Old World reticence and relentless perfectionism utterly suited Grandmother. Born in a small impoverished Bavarian village in 1929, she knew the meaning of the word *want*. She never wasted a grain of salt. She gathered windfall apples for latticed pies and warm compote. Gretta assaulted food when she cooked. She beat eggs into a froth, chopped meat with a sharp and whistling cleaver; she made quilts from discarded clothes. She cut out dishtowels from old linen tablecloths, pressed them with a steaming iron, and folded them into perfect rectangles that draped the towel bars. Gretta was never idle. She actually darned socks! In late summer I helped her pick blueberries, and we'd make jam the old-fashioned way. After we'd boiled the berries in a huge copper pot she wrapped them in linens, strung the bundle from a stick wedged between the fireplace grates, and let the juice drip for hours into an earthenware crock. It delighted her that I took an interest in cooking, when Mother had scorned all housewifery.

Gretta had come from Germany in 1947 with an American soldier when she was only eighteen. Within one year of her arrival, she was married and divorced, though I never dug up more than scant details about the circumstances. Grandmother took little interest in Gretta's story. She'd snapped her up when Gretta had answered an ad for a cook and housekeeper in 1948, and she'd served the family well for years. But the most important thing about Gretta was neither her culinary expertise nor her spartan housekeeping tactics. No, what really made her vital to my mother was that she had been present for the most problematic Heroine. And the first intruding Hero.

The story, which I pieced together over the years from different conversations with Mother and Gretta, begins the summer of 1960, just after Mother turned eighteen. Gretta stayed in the Homestead year-round, though the Entwhistles spent only summers and two weeks at Christmas away from their Lincoln Park home. In late June, on a night of thunderstorms, Gretta was up late ironing tablecloths, preparing for the family's arrival the next day. Lightning cracked, followed immediately by thunder, and it sounded as if a tree had been struck. When the electricity flashed off for an instant, she remembered the Allied air raids, unplugged the iron, and instinctively ran to the pantry. As stalwart as Gretta was, thunderstorms made her tremble like a shell-shocked vet. She slammed shut the door, and inhaled deeply, counting the length of time between the lightning and thunder. Grandfather Entwhistle had told her that every five seconds equaled a mile, which meant the lightning had struck one mile away. Between the growing intervals of crashing lighting and thunder, she discerned another rapping sound. Somebody was pounding at the door. When three raps were audible between the lightning and thunder, she left the pantry and ran to the back door.

A young woman stood under the porch light, soaked to the skin. Her long skirt clung to her legs, and raindrops dripped from her darkened hair down her nose. Gretta opened the door and shooed the girl into the mudroom. Though she was under strict orders from Grandmother Entwhistle never to have guests, she didn't hesitate to let the girl in. Having watched refugees and soldiers emerge from the Bavarian woods, Gretta could never turn away a person in need. Not when the Entwhistles had plenty to spare.

She searched the cabinets for the beach towels she'd washed for the Entwhistles. Taking care of somebody else immediately steadied her hands. Before she wrapped the towel around the girl's shoulders, she demanded that she take off her wet clothes. (Gretta had no false modesty about the human body.) The girl peeled away her dress and blouse and started to shiver the moment the towel hit her shoulders. Gretta plunked her down in the old wicker chair and wiped her feet dry, scolding her for being out on such an unseasonably cold night. The young woman was disoriented, didn't know how she'd found her way there. Her accent was closer to the English Gretta had learned in school in Germany. Deciphering where the girl was from was less important than remedying her chill, and Gretta hurried her up to the second floor and ran a bath for her in the bathroom connected to Mother's room.

While the girl soaked, Gretta searched Mother's dresser for a warm nightgown. The girl and Mother were nearly the same size—thin and long-limbed—though the English girl, even in her shivering delirium, had a high forehead and proud lift to her chin that didn't match Mother's bearing in the least. Gretta had never understood Anne-Marie Entwhistle. She saw clearly that Mother hid her intelligence, but always had her nose in a book, and it seemed to Gretta that Anne-Marie did her simple chores with an almost studied carelessness. Gretta was always remaking Mother's bed before Grandmother's inspection, refolding the crooked towels in her linen closet, or touching up the botched cakes Mother inevitably began to frost before they'd cooled. Mother cared only about exploring the woods or pedaling downhill a half mile to the Lake Michigan beach. Gretta understood Grandmother's perfectionism completely, yet even she hated to see Anne-Marie berated. Mainly because it had no effect and was a waste of precious time. It was faster to fix things herself than to go to the trouble of having Anne-Marie reapply herself.

Gretta found a flowered flannel nightgown balled in the corner of a drawer and shook it out, trying to decide if she should iron it. A quiet flash of lightning answered that question; Gretta wouldn't go near an electrical outlet during a storm. Also, she didn't want to leave the English girl alone; she didn't seem to be in her right mind. Gretta gave the nightgown a good shake and sniffed the armpits. It smelled like Tide. Mother wore only her father's oversized T-shirts to bed, never the Victorian gowns that she received without fail from "Santa Claus" each Christmas.

Gretta knocked on the bathroom door, then barged in. "Here is nightgown, miss!"

The girl was submerged beneath the water, her eyes open, her cheeks puffed out like a corpse. Bath oil gave the water a blurry sheen, made the girl look more pale, her nipples bright red. Her hair fanned out above her and clung to the porcelain of the tub. She looked eerie and half dead, and Gretta clapped her hands to snap the girl out of it and ordered her out of the tub.

Mother had twin beds in her room, each with a mahogany headboard and four carved posters. Every bed in the house—all fifteen of them—had received fresh sheets that morning, in anticipation of the Entwhistles' arrival. As soon as Gretta had tucked the girl into the guest bed and plied her with warm milk and sandwiches, she became more animated rather than calmer. She raved about the disappearance of someone named Heathcliff, and vowed to punish someone called Linton. She sat upright and tore at her wet hair. She spoke of searching the moors, passion and hate. Confused and disinterested in all the blather, Gretta lay a plump hand on the girl's forehead and pushed her head back against the pillow. She forced a thermometer into her mouth and held it there, ignoring the girl's wild eyes. One hundred and two degrees. Nothing a couple of Bayer aspirins wouldn't cure. Cutting in amid all the hysterical talk, she managed to get the girl to say her name: Catherine.

"Swallow these, Katerina." Gretta held out the aspirin and passed her a glass of water. "Big gulp."

The girl tipped the glass and swallowed the pills, coughing dramatically afterward.

And with this act of practical kindness, a subtle interference with a Heroine's destiny occurred. In early nineteenth-century novels, fevers worked wonders for authors. They caused madness and protracted death. They dragged on for months; they brought on visits from country doctors, with dramatic scenes with leeches, meals of water whey and gruel, powders and sponge baths. They gave many a lovelorn spouse or dutiful child, servant, or maid sleepless nights. But with a twelve-hour course of plain old Bayer aspirin (Gretta woke her several times to dispense it), Catherine Earnshaw's fever was cured.

CHAPTER 24

✢ *Fever cured, Catherine remains distraught*
✢ *Gretta won't suffer Catherine's*
torn-between-two-lovers act ✢ *Gretta's accused*
of witchcraft ✢ *The Hero pounds the door* ✢
Enter the young Heroine, my mother ✢

Catherine slept late the next day and descended the stairs in her nightgown around one-thirty, oblivious to how she was inconveniencing Gretta. Catherine had regained her color, but her tangled hair was a mess. When she entered the kitchen, Gretta was vigorously arranging the big refrigerator. Grandmother Entwhistle liked it perfectly ordered and gleaming: a clear pitcher of milk and a pitcher of lemonade on the top shelf, red fruits and vegetables in one bin, green in the other; cheeses and lunch meat layered carefully in their drawer; eggs snug in their holding pens on the door; aluminum ice trays full and ready to be snapped for Grandfather's scotch. Squeezing lemons was Gretta's final chore—that and the more troublesome task of sending Catherine off (though she didn't know where) and tidying Mother's room before the family arrived at three.

She'd baked bread that morning, and she cut a thick slice for Catherine and layered it with last summer's blueberry preserves. Catherine sipped breakfast tea but ignored the bread. Seeing lack of appetite as a sign of illness, Gretta brushed aside Catherine's matted hair and felt her forehead. It was cool and dry.

"I'm dying," Catherine said. "I'll be deep in my grave before—"

"Nonsense," Gretta said. "You are fit as a horse." She pushed the plate of bread closer to her. "Eat."

"I shan't eat another crumb until Heathcliff returns."

"When will that be?" Gretta checked the clock on the fireplace mantel. The brass pendulum swung back and forth. "He will come here? My employer does not like—"

"He ran off to the moors last night. Who knows if I'll ever see him again?"

"Is there another place you could meet him?"

"He left without bidding adieu! I'm torn in two! Why can I not have them both? Why must I choose?"

"You have two men in love with you?" Gretta sliced through a lemon with a serrated knife, then plunked the glass juicer on the table. Shaking her head, she wrung the last drop of juice from one rind, then grabbed another. "Two men, two times the trouble."

"What should I do?"

When Heroines asked those questions, Mother was always evasive, encouraging them to speak, rather than offering her own opinion. She would have pretended not to know Catherine and Heathcliff's fate (nor that of their troubled offspring), and like a mediocre therapist, she'd say, "What do *you* think you should do?" Gretta, who knew nothing about Catherine or *Wuthering Heights* or pop psychology, asked a more basic question.

"Which one you love more?"

"My love for Linton is like the foliage in the woods. Time will change it. My love for Heathcliff resembles the eternal rocks beneath!"

"*Sheisse!* I don't believe in this in-love-with-two-men-at-the-same-time *sheise*. You know who's the one! Only guilt keeps you from admitting it!" Gretta shook her fist, a juiceless lemon rind in her hand. She zipped the knife through ten more lemons. Catherine had obviously struck a nerve. Gretta poured the lemon juice into the pitcher. At the sink, she turned on the tap and flicked her finger under the stream to gauge the temperature. "You don't make up your mind, one of them make it for you!"

"How can they make the choice?" Catherine lifted her chin and a haughty look seized her face. "It is mine to make!"

"This Heathcliff. He ran off already. Some men don't want to play the second violin to another man. Women too!" She cracked a tray of ice and poured it into the pitcher. "They rather be alone than share."

Catherine jumped out of her seat and pulled the ends of her hair. She tugged on Gretta's arm, trying to derail her lemonade-making. "You think he'll never return? I will die surely! I can see them all gathered around the parlor after I'm gone. Edgar and Isabella—weeping. Even Hindley might shed a tear. And Heathcliff, wouldn't he be sorry to see my eyes forever closed, tucked into my coffin—"

"You getting carried away, miss! You listen." She shook off Catherine's hand and started grinding another lemon against the juicer. "You light in the head from hunger. Nobody's dying in this house! Not when Frau Entwhistle arrive in one hour!" Gretta led Catherine back into a chair and pointed so fiercely at the bread that her finger picked up a spot of blueberry. "Now eat!"

"I can't!"

Gretta licked the jam from her finger. "Eat or it's out on the street!"

Catherine picked up the bread and held it before her mouth without biting into it. Her eyes narrowed as she glared madly at Gretta and climbed up to crouch on the chair. "I see what you are! Only a witch would predict such a thing as Heathcliff's desertion." Her eyes grew misty. "I see you, hag! You are gathering elfin bolts to kill our heifers! You'll poison the well with a glance!"

As if casting a spell, Gretta stretched out her arm and wagged her index finger at Catherine's nose. "Eat!"

Just then someone rapped hard on the back door. The fierce knock made Gretta jump, and Catherine's hands began to tremble.

"Does he know you're here?" Gretta asked.

"Where?"

The pounding grew furious. Gretta dropped the lemons, put her arms under Catherine's armpits, and dragged her off the chair. She pushed Catherine into her own bedroom, which was just off the mudroom, a forbidden zone for all children. She turned the old skeleton key and locked Catherine in. If only she had set her free! But instinct made her protect the half-crazed girl. The man's violent knock reminded her of when the SS pounded on her own door, sweeping the village for Jews.

The mantel clock chimed twice and Gretta ran to the door and pushed aside the eyelet curtains she'd ironed and pressed earlier that week. Through the glass she saw the face of a young man. He had gaunt cheeks and dark skin and wavy black hair. She immediately thought that he'd have been rounded up as a Gypsy during the war. He peered at her with dark eyes and struck the glass with a hard thin branch.

"Open up, woman!" Even through the glass his words were clear. "Catherine!"

Just then Gretta heard the front door burst open and someone running back toward the kitchen, calling, "Gretta, I'm here!"

Catherine pounded the bedroom door and wept and wailed. Gretta double-bolted the kitchen door and yelled, "Go away! I call police!"

Heathcliff folded his arms and glared at her. He raised his stick again but held back.

"Here they come! *Polizei!*"

And in she swept, my mother at eighteen. Clear-skinned and freckled, her auburn hair in a fresh flip-do, a thin belt around her geometrically patterned pink dress. She wore low white pumps and a matching white headband. Her face glistened with sweat as she kicked off her shoes and ran to see who had been pounding the back door. When she joined Gretta at the window, she saw Heathcliff's handsome face. Her mouth fell open and she covered it with a gloved hand, as a powerful and unfamiliar desire snaked up her spine and streamed through her veins like warm water. Like many a Heroine, she fell in love at first sight.

CHAPTER 25

+ *Mother consoles Catherine* +
Gretta gets her gun + *Mother's plot to change
the plot* + *The new Catherine Earnshaw* +

Gretta pushed Mother away from the window and pressed her back into the wall. "Where your mother?"

"Who's that guy?" Mother asked, her flip-do bouncing as she jumped and waved her hands.

"When she come your mother? Why you alone?"

"She let me come up by myself on the train. They were taking forever to get ready, so they said if I helped you, I could come up alone. Who's that guy?"

"When she get here?"

"Is he related to you?" She got on her tiptoes and reached over Gretta's shoulder to draw the curtain back.

"No!" Gretta pushed Mother's hand away. "When she come? Five minute? Two hour?"

"Around three, like they planned."

Heathcliff rapped on the door again, this time less furiously. "Why don't we find out what he wants?"

"I need your help!" Gretta said.

"Making beds?"

"No. House ready. Go in my room. Calm down that girl. Another one of those Heroines, I think. She your age and she out of control. Crazy! And I can't turn her out! Not with him out there."

Mother finally noticed the muffled weeping on the other side of the door. "You let somebody in your room?"

"Just go in and talk to her!"

"Is that her boyfriend?" Mother asked, her heart sinking. "She must be beautiful. What's her name?"

"Katerina. She crazy. Two boyfriends. Him and somebody else! Go."

Gretta turned the key in the door lock and Mother stepped inside Gretta's room. The scene inside stunned Mother. For one, she'd only glimpsed the room when Gretta slipped in and out of it. Entrance was strictly forbidden, and Gretta kept it locked at all times, the key fastened inside her apron pocket with a yellow duck-shaped diaper pin. Mother had imagined a million versions of Gretta's room throughout her life. That the headboard and nightstands were made from gingerbread. That the room spanned the length of the house, with a spiral staircase to the basement. That she had trunks full of gold doubloons. The real room stunned Mother because it was half the size of her own; it was spare and neat with a simple oak dresser, an old rocking chair, a lamp with a curved gooseneck. The dust ruffle matched the eyelet kitchen curtains, but the bedspread and drapes were a masculine brown with yellow and blue pansies. But the most shocking feature was what lay across the single bed: a weeping blond girl in bare feet who wore Anne-Marie's own Christmas 1959 flannel nightgown.

Another girl might have been outraged to see somebody wearing her pajamas, but clothes meant little to Anne-Marie Entwhistle, since her mother chose every article of clothing for her. Even the dress she was wearing was her mother's choice. She had insisted that my mother dress like a lady for the train ride, and Anne-Marie was ready to do anything to avoid the long hot ride in the station wagon with her tense parents. No, she was a simple girl when it came to accoutrements; what interested her were stories, people, drama. The girl's spectacular weeping impressed Anne-Marie. She quietly moved to sit on the edge of the bed.

In a gentle voice, she asked, "What's wrong?"

"I'm dying!" Catherine propped herself on her elbows. "That hag won't let me see Heathcliff! She's trapped me in here. I'll go mad!"

"It's Heathcliff!" Mother said, snapping her fingers. "From *Wuthering Heights*!"

Catherine sat up. "You know the Heights?"

Mother nodded.

Catherine gave her a puzzled look, then tried to tear off the sleeves of her nightgown. "I'll go mad! I will! That hag is just like Nelly! She'll betray me the same. She has no pity for my situation. Choosing between day and night. Edgar and Heathcliff!"

Mother observed Catherine's long blond hair, porcelain skin, ethereal beauty. And the guy outside looked tortured and dark and gorgeous, even beyond what she'd imagined when she'd read *Wuthering Heights*. "I'm Anne-Marie Entwhistle." Mother pressed her gloved hand to her lips again and sat down in the rocking chair.

Catherine ran to pound on the door. The key turned in the lock, and Gretta burst into the room. Her face was wild and she opened the bottom drawer and pulled out a dark object from underneath her clothes.

"What's that?" Anne-Marie rushed to the door.

"Only one way to get rid of this man!" She held up a black gun with a mahogany handle.

"You can't shoot Heathcliff!" Mother yelled.

"The hag is mad!" Catherine cried.

"I just scare him away with a few shots. He no understand! Frau Entwhistle be here in half hour!" She ran out of the room and as she tried to lock the girls in, they charged the door and found their way out. Gretta gave up and ran to hold the pistol up to the window. She still didn't dare open the door.

"You two back up!" she yelled.

Catherine and Mother stepped backward. Heathcliff yelled through the door, "I will wait on the moors all night!" Then they heard him turn away and clomp across the patio.

Once he'd gone as far as the back garden, behind the apple trees, Gretta opened the door and stepped onto the porch. She checked over her broad shoulders. Mother held Catherine back, but the girl trembled with rage, her fingers curved like claws. Gretta ran to the end of the brick patio, stood beside the barbecue, held the gun with both hands, and fired two shots into the trees.

Anne-Marie pulled Catherine into the house and they charged up to her room to watch Heathcliff from the window. But by the time they climbed the two flights of stairs and wrestled open the bolted sunporch door, they caught only the last flash of his cape disappearing into the prairie. Catherine assumed her prostrate pose on the bed, the back of her hand pressed to her forehead. Anne-Marie sat on the edge of the bed, waiting and wondering about the appearance of this Heroine. But most of all, she was stunned by the presence of this Hero, Heathcliff, who had somehow followed Catherine here. He could rightly be called an anti-Hero. Never before had a man followed his Heroine here.

"Do you ever have odd dreams, Anne-Marie?" Catherine said, her voice muffled and monotone.

"Sure," Mother said.

"Once I dreamt I was in heaven, and it's horrible to say, but I was unhappy there. Can you believe? Unhappy in heaven? What kind of person am I? And one of the angels became furious with my lack of gratitude, and he cast me out, and when I landed on Wuthering Heights, I awoke with a sob of elation! Pure delight and salvation. What can this mean?"

"It's like you want to be with Heathcliff, but some part of you feels it's sinful. And yet, you would rather be a sinner than an unhappy saint."

"Precisely!" Catherine sat up, her eyes bright with tears. "Why is it so?"

"You two are so alike."

"I am Heathcliff," Catherine said.

Mother nodded slowly. "That makes perfect sense."

"Oh, a kindred spirit at last! How I wish my mother had lived to give me a sister like you."

"I've always wanted a sister too!" The two girls hugged. For a bookworm like Mother, a Brontë novel sister was better than a biological one. Catherine must have arrived at the Homestead at the moment when she was trying to decide which man to marry. Mother had to convince Catherine not to wed Edgar! She'd never been tempted before to meddle in a Heroine's fate, and it meant she had to ignore her own attraction to Heathcliff for the sake of a happier story. Anne-Marie often helped her prettier friends win the handsome guy. This always-the-bridesmaid, never-the-bride role marked Mother's life. If she could alter the fates of these characters, she'd be working miracles! She petted Catherine's hand. "Everything will work out! Let me think!"

Mother looked at the clock on the nightstand. Her mother's imminent approach overrode any other plans. She had to get Catherine cleaned up and presentable, out of the sweltering nightgown, for starters. She would tell her mother that Catherine was a friend from the boarding school up the road (Prairie Bluff Academy, which I would later attend). Her mother was sure to welcome the pretty young Englishwoman and consider her a good influence on Anne-Marie. (Grandmother, like many upper-crust Americans, was an unrepentant Anglophile.) As Mother ran to her closet to find a suitable outfit for Catherine, Gretta stormed into the room.

"She must go! I can't have that Gypsy man pounding on door!"

"He's not a Gypsy!" Catherine leapt off the bed and charged toward Gretta with her hands outstretched and ready to strangle her.

Gretta didn't back off at all, but dug her fists into her hips.

Mother jumped between them, facing Gretta. "Please. Let me handle this. You know we can't just kick her out. It doesn't work that way. Is everything else in the house ready? Mother will be here in ten minutes."

"Yes, miss." In the end, Gretta was the servant, and Anne-Marie had reached an age when she could give an order as directly as her mother. Gretta highly doubted that the spoiled American girl, who'd wanted for nothing her whole life, would have the wit to handle the Katerina problem. She was mistaken. Mother might not have known how to roll out pie dough, fire a pistol, or survive a grueling winter on nothing but rutabagas, but she knew how to get Catherine around the most towering obstacle of her own life: her mother, Edith Entwhistle.

She rifled through her closet of pressed summer dresses and found a pale yellow sundress she'd worn last year. It had capped sleeves and a vinyl belt, and she grabbed a shoebox that held yellow flats with white bows and handed them to Catherine. "Try this on."

Catherine glared at Gretta. "Only because *you* asked me to, Anne-Marie."

Mother turned to Gretta. "We'll tell my mother that Catherine's a friend I met on the train, and I invited her to stay a few days."

"As you wish." Gretta pulled a bottle of Bayer from her apron pocket and handed it to Mother. "Keep these. She had a fever." Then she marched downstairs, grabbed her cleaver, and took out her frustration on five pounds of New York strip steak.

"Now, Catherine, when my mother comes—"

"You're so fortunate to have a mother still!" Catherine pulled off the nightgown, and lifted her hands in the air so Anne-Marie could pull the sundress over her head. It hung loose on Catherine's lean frame, but it was one of those cheerful, virginal dresses Edith adored.

"And I know she's going to love you—but. Please don't pace like that. Sit. Let me brush out your hair."

"We have to find Heathcliff!"

"Don't stand at the window. Come here." Mother finally coaxed Catherine to sit on the edge of the bed and pulled a hairbrush through her tangled curls. "See, Heathcliff's a little bit of a problem. My mother's very strict about dating and boys."

"But he is my foster brother! Couldn't we tell her that? Oh, why does the world always turn against him?"

"I know, it's not fair. But it would be such a big huge favor to me if we just sort of"—Mother gently pulled the brush through a tough tangle of Catherine's hair—"*pretended* like Heathcliff wasn't around. Then at night, when everyone's in bed, we can sneak out and go look for him."

"Yes, we'll take excursions in the moonlight! With torches and hounds!"

"Right. So for now, let's just say you're visiting. There's a boarding school up the road. We'll say you're staying on for a few weeks this summer. And I'll ask if you can spend a few nights here." Mother figured it would take a few days to convince Catherine to choose Heathcliff to marry instead of Edgar.

"You brush my hair so gently!"

With every stroke of the brush, Mother said calming words to Catherine. "You're going to be fine. We'll find Heathcliff tonight." Catherine closed her eyes, and Mother felt empowered. In the novel, Nelly had always seen Catherine's temper as an affectation, an exaggeration. But Mother believed that with kind words and compassion she could, perhaps, avoid disaster. Even if Anne-Marie's knowledge of passionate love was derived only from books, she did know how it felt to be misunderstood and to have her feelings mocked. Every summer she'd been stuck with her irritable mother. She was starved for the companionship of girls her age, and she'd do anything to keep Catherine close. As she pulled the brush through Catherine's hair and watched the sun light up the curly ends, she heard the crunch of tires and the rumble of the family car pulling into the circular drive below.

CHAPTER 26

÷ *The Entwhistles arrive* ÷ *A rollicking*
thunderstorm ÷ *Catherine swoons* ÷
Mother heads out to the prairie alone ÷

Mother ran to the window and saw the family wagon, with its dolphin-blue finish and shining chrome fins. Her father honked twice—which meant, *We're here!* The first glimpse she had of her mother was a shot of red light, the sparkle of a ruby on her right hand, which she tapped against the frame of the open window, waiting. Her father, who was lean, red-haired, and dressed in a seersucker suit, ran around the front of the car and opened the passenger-side door. Grandmother stepped out of the car and pulled a cigarette from a silver case and tapped it three times against the cover. In 1960, Edith Entwhistle was forty-five years old, but she was still a perfect size six. She arrived at the Homestead dressed for chance encounters with the ladies of Prairie Bluff. She wore a magenta linen dress and pearls, and her lipstick matched her dress perfectly. Her long brown hair was swept away from her head and tied at back in a chignon. Anne-Marie always thought her mother's penciled-on eyebrows were exactly like the wings of a seagull. Grandfather pulled a lighter from his pocket and lit her cigarette, then he reached back in and shook a Winston out of his pack. Edith shielded her eyes with her hand and looked up toward Anne-Marie's window.

Anne-Marie pulled Catherine's arm and they ducked beneath the window. Then Anne-Marie peeked out again. As her mother pointed at the window, her ruby caught the sun again. "The trim around the window is starting to peel, Henry."

And thus, the inspection began. The screen door slammed and Gretta emerged on the front step. "Herr und Frau Entwhistle. Your trip, it was good?"

"No problems," Grandfather said. "Though it got a little muggy! I could do with a stiff one."

"Come inside, I get you a scotch."

Edith blew cigarette smoke out the side of her mouth, then waved it away. She smoked as if disgusted by her own habit. "Did Anne-Marie arrive safely?"

"Yes. She met friend on train. English girl. They are upstairs together."

"That's terrific!" Henry said. "How nice for A-M to have a girl her own age around."

Mother gave a silent cheer; her father would lay the groundwork for Catherine's stay. Trust him to see things from Anne-Marie's perspective.

"How in the world does Anne-Marie know an English girl who happens to be riding the commuter train?" Edith took a final drag, then pushed her cigarette butt into the antique milk pail filled with sand on the front porch. Grandmother never smoked indoors or inside cars.

"From school up the road."

"The Academy? Why in the devil would an English girl be stuck at that old convent during the summer? Don't people usually go to the Isle of Man or Brighton?"

Gretta shrugged. "I don't know, ma'am. You have to ask her."

Anne-Marie pulled Catherine from the window and sat her on the bed. Her mother's skepticism set her nerves on edge. She held

Catherine's hands and stared into her eyes as if casting a spell. "You have to tell my mother your family's going to the Isle of Man in August. And you've been asked to stay at school to . . . I know! Because your parents are traveling in Egypt! No, that's too weird. But it can't be Europe, because otherwise, why couldn't you join them?" Mother dropped Catherine's hands and paced the Persian runner between the beds. She snapped her fingers. "Tell them your mother's ill and having special treatment. No, then they'll have all these questions about medicine—"

"You're confusing me, Anne-Marie!" Catherine's face buckled. "How can I keep any of this right in my mind when Heathcliff is out there alone somewhere? Chased away by that wench with the pistol."

"I'm sorry!" Mother sat back down on the bed and breathed deeply to calm herself. "Let me make this simple. Tell them school isn't over in England till the end of June. You're joining your family on the Isle of Man when your brother's classes are finished at Cambridge."

"Yes, Heathcliff's at Cambridge."

From the bottom of the stairs, Edith called Anne-Marie's name.

"*Maybe* don't call him Heathcliff. How about Heath or Cliff?"

"Cliff—that sounds like a rocky outcrop. But Heath is too soft for a man like—"

"Cliff, then. Like Clifford."

"Anne-Marie! Come down here, please!"

"Cliff doesn't really suit him."

"It doesn't matter!" Anne-Marie said, exasperated. "They won't ever see him. If he comes raging at the door again, Gretta'll shoot him."

"We must find him tonight!"

"We will. I promise. Later, after they're all in bed. Now come and meet my parents."

* * *

From what Gretta told me much later, the dinner went fine. Edith interrogated Catherine about her family, but Catherine managed to make it sound plausible; when she stammered, Anne-Marie filled in the blanks with both truth and invention. Catherine's father was a businessman who owned a large estate; her mother died when she was young. When Edith heard that Catherine's brother Cliff was at Cambridge, and that the family planned to spend the end of summer on the Isle of Man, Edith nodded triumphantly at her husband. Everything fit her notion of gentrified English people, right down to the widowed and wealthy landowner. The wine left Grandmother in good form, and she praised Gretta's cooking, while damning her Lincoln Park housekeeper, who routinely overcooked the steaks into "tough, inedible hides."

Grandfather drained his wineglass and motioned to Gretta for brandy. He'd been drinking more lately, which made him sentimental and flush-faced. "Sounds lovely, Catherine. And we're honored to have you here with us." When he hiccupped, Grandmother rolled her eyes at him.

"Henry, really!"

Over the previous month, Anne-Marie had been so caught up in the whirlwind of graduation parties in Chicago that she hadn't noticed the change in her father. Although she'd heard her parents arguing lately about money, she hadn't really paid attention, sailing along on the flotilla of her accomplishments: valedictorian, admission to Vassar, top honors in biology. She suddenly feared that the isolation at the Homestead would accentuate the tension between her parents. Edith wasn't the type of mother to confide in her daughter about her marital difficulties: they weren't the least bit chummy. But her parents had been fighting that morning about a property on the west side of the city, and Anne-Marie had been glad to escape them by taking the train. She'd hoped that Catherine's presence would temper her mother's blatant disdain, but Edith never felt compelled to censor herself in her own home.

Edith clapped her hands to hasten the end of dinner and thus the end of Grandfather's drinking. "Gretta, come clear, please. Anne-Marie, give her a hand. And watch the goblets!"

That night, after everyone had finally headed to bed, Anne-Marie and Catherine set up cots on Anne-Marie's sunporch. The humidity had suddenly climbed, and the bedroom air was stifling. Anne-Marie also used their sleeping on the cots as an excuse to raid the linen closet for extra sheets. She worked in the dark, knotting three sheets together so she and Catherine could lower themselves from the porch onto the roof below. From there, it was an easy shimmy down the wisteria trellis to the garden. Her parents' suite was on the other end of the house, but Anne-Marie could see the square of light from their window lighting up the dark lawn below.

As the girls waited for the light to disappear, they lay on their cots listening to the wind in the big elm tree outside. The sky between the branches turned midnight-blue. It was June 15, nearly the first day of summer, so the lengthening days meant an even longer wait for dark. Something boomed in the distance. Anne-Marie hoped it was a firework, though Catherine feared it was a cannon. The noise soon distinguished itself as thunder. Lightning flashed in the distant trees, the trunks and branches in black relief.

"It'll pass," Mother said. "Sometimes it's just an electrical storm. It doesn't even rain."

"To think of Heathcliff in such a storm!"

The thunder and lightning grew closer and the wind picked up. The elm leaves rustled, then stopped, then rustled again. The nighthawks ceased their calls, though the bullfrogs continued to chirp and croak. Usually Anne-Marie delighted in thunderstorms, but not on this night. A few raindrops plinked against the metal window frames of the sunporch, and then the downpour began. Sheets of rain angled through the screens. The girls jumped up and pushed their cots against the wall of the house.

"Jump in your sleeping bag!" Mother ordered. She gathered up the sheet rope and climbed onto her own cot.

"Poor Heathcliff!"

"He'll figure something out," Mother said.

Catherine pushed down her sleeping bag and tried to wiggle her feet free. "I must go now!"

"You can't! Their light's still on!" Mother jumped out of bed and rushed toward Catherine. "You're shivering. Come on. You'll catch your death in the rain. Come back in the house."

Catherine argued for immediate departure, but Mother felt Catherine's burning and sweaty forehead, and coaxed her to lie down inside. She pulled back the bedspread and patted the sheet, as if cajoling a pup to jump up. Catherine succumbed quickly to Anne-Marie's care. Having lost her mother at a young age, Catherine longed for mothering; Anne-Marie knew precisely the kind of mothering she wished she'd received. She gave Catherine aspirin and cool water, she stroked her hair with the hairbrush, uttered soothing remarks. Mother knew how easily Catherine could drive herself mad, and that neither her maid nor Edgar could ever talk her out of it. Isolation from society on the gloomy moors hadn't helped Catherine's volatile disposition. So Mother stroked Catherine's hair and plied her with soporific words, until the distraught young Heroine fell asleep.

By that time, the rain had stopped, and the lawn outside Anne-Marie's parents' window was dark. This was her chance. She looked at the sleeping Catherine and realized she'd have to go find Heathcliff by herself. She put on clam diggers and laced up her tennis shoes. In truth, leaving Catherine behind was a relief. Though Mother worried about Catherine's fever, she secretly wished to encounter the handsome Hero by herself. The image of his dark and ruddy face, seen through the kitchen window, flashed in her mind. She'd made little effort to convince Catherine not to wed Edgar so far (and there had been ample opportunity while they lay on the cots, waiting for her parents' light to switch off). Of course, she was too naïve to admit she had ulterior motives, but at eighteen, having finished high school without incident, my mother yearned for an adventure. She was so close to being free from her mother, yet it was still months away. She couldn't wait! She wanted something to transform her, to drown out her dawning fears about her family's financial situation. She knew she was missing something, but she didn't know what it was. She could only recognize girls who had it, and Catherine Earnshaw definitely did: men vying for her affection, striking beauty. Experience. Now adventure had landed on Mother's doorstep.

She tied back her hair with a scarf, then tiptoed to the sunporch and raised a screen. Looping the sheets around the beam between two windows, she secured it with the best Girl Scout knot. As she lowered the sheet out the window, she pretended there was no self-interest in her going alone to find Heathcliff. She felt proud of her pure motives. She'd get a happy ending for the principal characters in *Wuthering Heights*. She stepped over the window ledge and rappelled down to the first knot. She shimmied down the soft sheets and landed quiet as a cat on the living room roof. The air had cooled significantly. She tiptoed across the tar, careful not to slip in the puddles, then climbed down the wisteria trellis, her face in the wet and fragrant blossoms. When she landed on the slippery grass, she fell to one knee, then stood up. Everything smelled clean and earthy. Being back in the country exhilarated her, as did the prospect of seeing the handsome man whom she'd glimpsed behind the kitchen curtain.

CHAPTER 27

Mother seeks the Hero ✦ *She loses her innocence to gain Heathcliff's trust* ✦

Mother ran straight down the path, the prairie alive with its usual nighttime creatures: the fireflies throbbing between the cattails, the rattling cicadas, the crickets. The thunderclouds had cleared, and the Big Dipper popped out of the blackness, along with the rest of the many constellations that Mother could name on sight. One of her favorite childhood wishes—one she passed on to me—was that the Dipper would scoop her onto its ladle and swing her through the Milky Way. On that night she made no such wish. In fact, her deepest wishes were coming true. She was having a daring adventure. She focused not on the stars, but on the woods that blocked the horizon and sheltered Emily Brontë's troubled Hero.

Taking a bridle path through the trees, Mother called Heathcliff's name, wiping silky spider webs from her legs and face. At first she kept her voice low, but soon realized that it didn't matter. Who would hear her out there? The wind shook the trees and splashed so much rain on her head, she thought it had begun to storm again. Soon her shoes were soaked, her shins and calves splattered with mud. She sat on a fallen tree trunk to catch her breath. Acorns and pinecones fell through the trees around her.

Twigs snapped and small animals scampered through the fallen leaves. The extent of her solitude suddenly struck her. She was alone and not alone. For all she knew, Heathcliff might be out there watching her.

She pulled the wet scarf off her head and wrung out the rain. The dampness enlivened every smell in the woods, giving the air an earthy scent. "It's no use," she said, almost feeling skittish enough to tear back to the Homestead. If Catherine awoke, she might go downstairs and wake up everyone in the house. But having climbed out the window and gotten this far into the woods, it would be pathetic to give up now. If Heathcliff showed up tomorrow and pounded the door while her parents were home, anything could happen. If he wound up in jail, or shot by Gretta, what would happen to the novel? How could *Wuthering Heights* exist with a slain Heathcliff? She had to warn him.

"I know you're out there!" she yelled. The strength of her voice surprised her.

"What do you want, girl?"

His voice startled her even more than her own. She jumped to her feet and looked around. "Where are you?"

A freight train blasted its horn just then, the wheels rattling against the steel rails as it sped down the distant track. The horn sounded again, its warning moan. She couldn't tell if Heathcliff had answered. It sounded as if his voice had come from the right of her, so she stood up and headed down the path. "Where are you?" Then a bit of genius struck. "I'm here about Catherine Earnshaw."

She heard footsteps crunching through the leaves, and suddenly a black silhouette stepped onto the path. In his cape he cut a dramatic figure, and his deep voice seemed to make the leaves tremble. "Where is she?"

As he stood on the path, his hand on his cane, his strong masculine presence overwhelmed Mother. In the book, Nelly the housekeeper had said that Heathcliff had the tough air of a soldier of fortune. There was nothing soft about him, and he stirred longings she'd never felt before. She was drawn to him, felt a reckless attraction, physical and aggressive. The urge to press against him, to feel his weight against her, to be lifted in his arms.

Making him forget about Catherine would be like asking the wind to forget how to blow, Mother thought, but he had to prefer a girl whose attraction to him was complete, undivided. It occurred to her that maybe she wouldn't need his love—only a few nights of experience, something to gird her against the family's troubles, the anonymity of college life that awaited her.

"I asked, where is she?"

"Back at my house."

"Is that wench with the firearm still on the premises?"

"And my father too!" Anne-Marie was bluffing, of course. Grandpa never fired a gun; Edith Entwhistle was the sharpshooter in the family.

Heathcliff pointed in the direction of the Homestead. "Is that your estate?"

"My family's summer home."

"Any male heirs?"

"No," Mother said, missing the implication, forgetting how he had married Isabella to get her property. Mother stared up at him with wide eyes, her flip-do flat and dripping rain on her shoulders.

"Interesting." His gaze stirred her, his glance drifting down to her chin, her shoulders, and farther down.

Mother felt exposed, naked. Her mind started to swim. Before she knew what she was doing, she said, "Catherine wants to marry Edgar."

"That half a man!"

His every movement—the sweep of his arm, the lift of his brows—seemed choreographed to arouse her. Mother's plan to work for Heathcliff and Catherine's union was out the window. Who was she to try to effect a happy ending for them? she thought.

And now she was more interested in her own story: innocent girl meets dashing man in woods. Her skyrocketing attraction to Heathcliff overpowered all her benevolent aspirations.

"What's your name, girl?"

Mother told him.

"Are you promised to anyone?"

"I don't even have a boyfriend. I'm not looking to get engaged."

"What are you looking for?" he asked.

Heathcliff's seductive tone flew right over Mother's head, though she thought his accent made everything he said sound sexy. She was inexperienced, hadn't done more than neck a few times with her Edith-approved-and-appointed prom dates. She was like many girls in 1960, off to college soon: to lose her virginity would mark her as tainted, a bad girl. The actual mechanics of sexual intercourse were unclear for Anne-Marie, but the tingle she felt around Heathcliff exceeded anything she'd experienced before. "I don't know what I'm looking for," she answered.

He stepped forward and took hold of her arm, staring down at her as if deciding whether to fling her to the ground or kiss her. She looked up at him, frozen. He took her other arm and drew her to him, so her head was beneath his chin. Her face nearly touched his chest, but not quite. When he spoke, his chin pressed into the crown of her head. She held herself perfectly still, afraid any false move would anger him or make him step back.

"I have to see Catherine. If only to tell her farewell. She will not scorn me again! She has thrown me off for the last time."

Mother wanted to stay in this position forever, to smell his damp clothes, to feel his strong arms around her. Even if the man who held her spoke about another woman, it was the closest she'd ever come to a passionate embrace. She understood that her only chance of staying close to Heathcliff was through Catherine. So she fooled herself, as many have done before and since, into thinking that if she became his friend, Heathcliff would eventually see that she was more loyal, stable, and good-natured than Catherine, and thus more worthy of his love. "I'll help you reach her. I just made her stay inside tonight. She was getting feverish."

"She's ill?" He pushed Mother away, yet tightened his grip on her arms.

"She started talking crazy," Mother said, disappointed her words had precipitated the end of their quiet moment.

"Another bout of mania!"

"No, she just wants you to leave her alone now. She wants a peaceful life with Edgar."

"She said that?" Heathcliff dropped his hands and took a step away from Mother. "How can she choose that half a man?" He sat on the stump of a tree trunk, and buried his face in his hands.

"I'm sorry." Mother stepped toward him, then pulled back, genuinely ashamed of her sabotage, unused to this conniving side of herself. She longed to place a comforting hand on his shoulder, but knowing he could be volatile, she held back. So she waited with her hands clasped behind her back while her lie about Catherine sank in, hoping it would work to her advantage. While Heathcliff wept into his hands, she stood in the dark woods, swatting mosquitoes and watching. Good breeding stepped in and told her to leave him for the moment, no matter how much she longed to comfort him. He wouldn't want a witness to this weakness, and her own guilty conscience made her timid. It was still hard for her to admit she'd deliberately caused this pain.

She walked a few paces down the bridle path, far enough so that she no longer heard his sobs. It was the right move. At Wuthering Heights and Thrushcross Grange, people were always poking into each other's business. Family members shouted and nagged at one another, servants gossiped, dogs yelped. By keeping a respectful distance, Mother gained Heathcliff's trust. She broke a branch from a pine tree and counted as she pulled off the needles. By the time she'd reached thirty-three, she'd thought she'd blown everything, but then she heard his step on the wood-chip path.

"I must see Catherine." Again he took Mother's upper arm, his face lowered, his sharp nose and cheekbones close to her own. He smelled like wool and sweat, with a hint of fresh sage. What she couldn't see in the darkness were his eyes. But she felt his desperation and how much he needed her.

"I'll bring her tomorrow night. At midnight."

"I pray she's well enough."

"You can trust me!"

He looked down, his eyebrows heavy over his eyes, a barely veiled sneer on his face. "Can I?"

CHAPTER 28

⊹ Chores galore ⊹ Catherine's attempted

getaway ⊹ Gretta gets the boot ⊹

The next day Edith had a host of chores for Mother, who straggled down to breakfast around eight, only a handful of hours after she'd returned from the prairie. Gretta was rolling out pie crust, her lips pursed, an expression that usually meant she'd been recently scolded by Edith. Anne-Marie could only imagine why.

"I want the mason jars of blueberry preserves brought up from the basement and wiped clean and stacked in the pantry," Edith said. She poured silver cleaner on chamois cloth and rubbed a barely tarnished teapot.

"Why can't Gretta do it?"

"Don't fight with me, Anne-Marie."

"Where's Dad?"

"He had a business meeting in the city."

"Will he be back tonight?"

"I assume so."

Anne-Marie didn't know it then, but Grandfather Entwhistle was in town to try to ward off foreclosures on several of his properties. He owned dozens of multi-unit buildings on the south and west sides of the city, which were being swiftly vacated by the Irish, Italian, and Greek immigrants as rural blacks moved up from the South. He just couldn't get the same rent, and as property values plummeted, so did his net worth. Grandmother had been after him to unload the properties for years, but he was loyal to his tenants to a fault. They'd abandoned any loyalty to him when they saw their territory shrinking.

Sunlight poured through the window as Mother sipped her coffee. She picked the sleep from her eyes, wondering if her mother could sense the difference in her, that she'd been clutched by a man in the woods at night. She still felt the imprint of his hands on her upper arms, the press of his chin against her head. Everywhere she looked, she thought she saw him: passing by the window above the sink, a silhouette on the other side of the mudroom door. She sat at the table and poured cream and sugar into another cup of coffee. The crows outside seemed to be calling out his location in the woods. She imagined how he would love a cup of Gretta's coffee, a slice of homemade bread. She chewed her toast carefully, as if he were watching.

"The storm last night absolutely destroyed the peonies." Grandmother retied the strings of her apron and secured them with a tight bow. "I want you to cut them all! The petals look like toilet paper when they get stuck in the grass!"

"For bouquets?" Anne-Marie asked.

"God, no. We don't need a million bouquets decaying all around the place. Bring me the healthiest—a good mix of pinks and blues and magentas. The Auxiliary Club ladies are coming for lunch tomorrow. No sense spending a fortune at the florist's! And I want you to wear your suit."

"The Vassar interview suit?"

"Precisely. The pink. You look perfectly darling in it."

"I left it at home."

Her mother snorted in disgust.

"Well, how was I supposed to know I'd need a suit up here? I'm not usually invited to the Lady Luncheons!"

"Well, the time has come for you to become a junior member."

Mother dug her fingernails into the rind of an orange and the juice sprayed into her eyes. "Should we run to Field's to look for something else?"

"No. You can wear something of mine."

Her mother had never offered to share clothes with her before. Anne-Marie pulled the fibrous strings from the orange wedge. Usually her mother never missed a chance to railroad Anne-Marie into buying some fancy, conservative clothes. Hoping that the real reason for her mother's offer wasn't financial problems, she attributed it to the occasional goodwill she'd experienced since being accepted to Vassar. Anne-Marie had lived up to all the expectations: valedictorian (the first girl to earn the title at Lincoln Park High), Ivy League school, and, Grandmother was certain, vestal virgin. With these accomplishments, she'd been allowed to drink wine at dinner and coffee at breakfast, which she certainly needed that morning. After she'd shimmied back up the sheet and into her window the night before, she'd lain in bed for an hour, dreaming of Heathcliff between Catherine's quiet snores. His voice resonated in her memory as she rinsed her plate and coffee cup in the sink, but her mother's constant interruption made it impossible to fully relive the night. She wanted to be out in the garden alone with her thoughts.

"What should I do first, bring up the jars or cut the flowers?" Edith always determined the priority and timetable for Anne-Marie's chores. Hoping the peonies would take precedence, she headed toward the back door.

"Flowers."

Mother opened the back door, ready to rush into the fresh wet garden and let her imagination and memories have full play. She had started to close the door behind her when her mother called again.

"But be particular. Don't bring me any of those half-wilted ones you feel sorry for. And Anne-Marie!"

Mother poked her head back in the door.

"Where's your little English friend?"

"Sleeping. I think she's sick."

"I hope you two didn't stay up all night talking. What's wrong with her?"

"Cold, I think. Fever."

"Gretta, bring her a tray when you're finished with the pies. And after you're done cutting the flowers, put a little cover-up under your eyes, Anne-Marie. You look tired."

Blah, blah, blah, Mother thought. She grabbed the pruning shears off a hook in the shed and walked back to the cutting garden. She was in a sleep-deprived fog, her mind able to manage just one delicious image: Heathcliff. His dark, masculine figure, his commanding grip on her arms, the scent of his spicy tobacco. She'd never felt this way about the respectable, country-club boys handpicked by Edith and her "chums" to escort her to proms and dances. Heathcliff was nothing like those preppy, repressed boys. He was a man, with a whiff of danger about him. When she first met Catherine, Anne-Marie had been dying to raid the library and see if they had a copy of *Wuthering Heights* around. She'd read the book her junior year, so the details were a bit hazy. Now she dreaded reading anyone else's version of Heathcliff; she wanted to relish her own. If anyone in the book said something negative about him, she wouldn't be able to stand it. She had fallen hard, and so she thought nobody could understand him the way she did. They'd met only the night before, of course, but Mother was a romantic, a believer in instant, intuitive attraction. And having watched Heathcliff cry, she'd actually witnessed a crucial aspect of him that nobody in the book ever saw, certainly not Nelly, the narrator of the original tale.

Mother knelt in the wet grass and began cutting the peonies. The drenched blossoms dropped on the wet grass. For every dull, faded pink blossom, a vibrant one emerged. She stacked them in two piles, discards and keepers. The back of her neck itched, and she looked over the hedge at the trees in the distant woods, wondering where Heathcliff might be. It irritated her that she was stuck doing chores while he was out there, lurking and waiting. Where and how did he sleep? What was he eating? And what about Catherine? Was she still sleeping or was she up there tearing out her hair in a feverish frenzy? Anne-Marie dreaded talking to her. She wasn't sure what to tell her about the meeting with Heathcliff. Anne-Marie was beginning to believe that Catherine should be contented with Edgar, who was clearly devoted to her. And wasn't that what Emily Brontë had intended? It wasn't simply that Mother had her own designs on Heathcliff. Her vague romantic notions went no further than hugging and kissing. She honestly believed she was helping by bringing Catherine peace, by not disrupting the narrative. So she found a way to rationalize having lied to Heathcliff about Catherine's decision to marry Edgar and not him. It was inevitable, right? That's how the story went. Still, she had no idea how to manage Catherine, whose cyclical lethargy and mania were sure to irritate Edith. She had to find a way to stabilize her. Mother didn't want her to return to her story yet, as Heathcliff was sure to vanish too.

"Anne-Marie!" Gretta's head popped up above the hedge. "What that crazy girl doing now? You have to stop her!"

Anne-Marie looked up to see Catherine, a cloud of blond hair around her head, lowering the sheet rope out the porch window. She hiked up her yellow dress and extended a pale leg over the window ledge. Anne-Marie dropped her pruning shears and leapt to her feet.

"I'll go around the side. Meet me upstairs!" She walked swiftly across the lawn, arms swinging faster than her legs. After she cruised past the kitchen windows, she took off, heading straight for the wisteria trellis. She heard the kitchen door slam as Gretta reentered the house.

Underneath the porch, Anne-Marie looked up through the vines at the swaying sheet rope. Catherine sat on the window ledge, one leg dangling over, unsure of how to proceed. Mother cried in her loudest whisper, "Catherine, don't come down this way."

"Anne-Marie! You've been gone for hours! What word have you from Heathcliff?"

"I'll tell you everything. Just go back inside! I'll be right up."

She ran like a demon and quietly slipped through the front door. She scampered up the steps on tiptoe, but with every step she fought to regain her composure, to be the young woman who'd met Heathcliff in the woods and not the regressing and resentful rivalrous girl. She loved to imagine that he was watching her every move.

When she got to her room, she found Gretta chasing Catherine back into the wingback chair by flicking at her arms and legs with a dishtowel. "What you thinking, sneaking out the window?"

Anne-Marie slammed the door behind her with one violent flick of her hand.

"Leave me be, old hag!" Catherine darted around Gretta and ran to grasp Anne-Marie's wrists. She fell to her knees and looked up at Anne-Marie with a wretched expression. "Tell me! Before I go mad. Did you see Heathcliff last night?"

"You! You better not see that Gypsy man!" Gretta yelled.

"He's not a Gypsy!" Catherine climbed to her feet, shaking a fist at Gretta.

"Please, Gretta. Leave Catherine and me alone."

"Oh, now you Miss High and Mighty!"

"Do as you're told, hag!" Catherine yelled.

Gretta threw her hands into the air. "I no can take it more! No more!" She stormed toward the door.

Mother felt a pang of guilt, and she shuddered as the door slammed behind Gretta's broad back. Catherine spoke to Gretta more severely than even Edith did. But Mother saw that though the treatment was cruel, it was effective. They were finally alone. She looked around the room; the bedspread had slumped to the floor, the lampshade was tilted, and the English girl was looking at her with the eyes of a wildcat.

"Sit down," Anne-Marie said. "I'll tell you everything that happened."

CHAPTER 29

✦ *Stalking Heathcliff by night* ✦
Lady Luncheon by day ✦ *Intimations*
of financial mortality ✦ *The faulty*
sleeping brew ✦ *Conception* ✦

Another thunderstorm struck that night, and it was well past midnight when the rain finally let up and Catherine and Anne-Marie entered the woods. Mother led Catherine to the spot where she'd met Heathcliff the night before. "Heathcliff!" she called.

Nothing. The wind shook the trees and rained a mini-shower on their heads. Anne-Marie called for Heathcliff again. Nothing. She leaned on a split-rail fence and peered into the darkness between the tree trunks, stunned. Heathcliff had insisted so forcefully the previous night that he must see Catherine, and now where was he?

"Maybe he went deeper into the woods," she said, "for shelter." As they walked a muddy path between arching oaks, Anne-Marie's guilt sharpened into a stomachache. Perhaps her revelation about Catherine's decision had scared Heathcliff away. The wind rustled the trees, loosening twigs and raindrops. Anne-Marie looked back at Catherine, who was calling Heathcliff's name, looking up into the sky as if he might descend on a thunderhead riding an apocalyptic horse. The desperate *0* of Catherine's rounded mouth and her pale, sweaty face unnerved Anne-Marie. Fear crept over her. Maybe Heathcliff was lying in wait to hurt them. She tried to shake off the feeling. Heathcliff wasn't a murderer—exactly. He was passionate, but these were *her* woods. She'd wandered them fearlessly a million times. But still. The sound of Catherine's voice raised the hairs on Mother's arms.

"Heathcliff!" Catherine called, her voice growing hoarse. She lifted her drooping arms toward the sky and called to the trees.

Mother feared that Catherine might lose her voice *and* her mind, might pull an Ophelia and hurl herself into the pond. "I guess he's not here tonight," she said. "Maybe he went to sleep. Because we were late."

"Are you sure he said it was this night he wanted to see me?"

"Of course. I just don't know why he's—"

"What did you say to him? Why isn't he here?"

"I didn't say anything." Mother turned her back on Catherine and started toward the prairie, hoping she'd follow.

"Rubbish!" Catherine grabbed Mother's arm. "I can tell! You're in love with him, are you not? You've schemed against me!"

"I would never do that! You're sick! You need to get back in the house."

"I'll roam these woods till death takes me!" she screamed.

"I can't let that happen!" Mother had a vision of the fresh hell of ambulances and cops and Edith's fury flashing before her. "I swear. I'm sure he'll be here tomorrow!"

"You think you know something about him! You know not how cruel he can be! This is his usual trickery. How dare you try to stop me?" She lunged at Anne-Marie with clawed hands. Her fury was strong, but her body was weak, and Anne-Marie quickly twisted her arms behind her back and grasped her neck in a half nelson. Catherine collapsed, dropping to her knees on the wet ground.

"Forgive me, Anne-Marie. I know you are good."

"Please come back to the house," Mother said. "You need to rest."

"I am doomed," Catherine said. "Why should I go on?"

Mother helped Catherine to her feet and let her lean against her. "You have to go on. I know there are happier days ahead for you," she lied. She had no idea if Catherine would survive this. For now all she could do was get Catherine home and tucked into a warm bed.

The next day Edith stormed into Anne-Marie's bedroom at seven, trailing a plastic bag containing a powder-blue suit. She opened the closet and hung up the suit, then ran over to snap the shades, which spun on their reels. Sunlight flooded the room and pierced Anne-Marie's eyes.

"Rise and shine!" Edith yelled. "I need both of you to help me today! There are a thousand things to do before the luncheon!"

With her back to the girls, Edith pushed open the drapes and tied the satin sashes into fat neat bows. Mother looked at Catherine, who rolled over and draped an arm across her face. She suddenly rose to her elbows and pressed her fist to her mouth. Mother leapt from the bed. She grabbed the pitcher by the bathroom door and ran to Catherine's bedside. Catherine heaved into the vessel and the pot turned warm in Mother's hands.

"What's this?" Edith said. "Sick first thing in the morning?"

"She's had the flu all night," Anne-Marie said.

"Flu in the summer?"

"It's the worst kind, you always say." Anne-Marie ran to the bathroom and poured the stinking vomit into the toilet, gagging at the chunks that splashed onto the toilet seat. She plugged her nose as she wiped the seat and flushed. When she returned to the bedroom, Catherine was lying back on her pillows.

"I was hoping she'd help finish polishing the silver." Edith pressed her hand against Catherine's forehead. "There are a thousand things to do!"

"I can do it. Besides, she'd get everyone else sick," Anne-Marie said.

Catherine moaned and turned on her side, slipping out from under Edith's hand. "I'll die," she said.

"She's a little delirious," Anne-Marie said.

"What a shame! An English girl would have added some color at the luncheon." Edith waved her hand toward the door. "I'll send Gretta up with some aspirin for her. Come have your breakfast, Anne-Marie. Bathe after your chores are finished. My blue suit will work fine. There are a thousand things to do!"

Edith spent the rest of the morning on a rampage of party preparations. She snapped nonstop orders at Gretta and Anne-Marie. Mother polished the silver, a task that required little finesse, while Gretta folded linen napkins into swans, filled water glasses, and decorated the sponge cake with candied orange slices and creamy flowers.

With only four hours of sleep, Anne-Marie stared blankly out the kitchen window, massaging a tarnished spoon with a soft cloth. She was worried. Where could Heathcliff be? How long would this go on? She didn't know how she could possibly make it through the long day. The smell of the polish repelled her, and she looked down at the spoon in her hand. The scoop was brilliant, but the filigreed stem was black. Turning the spoon around, she rubbed the other end, silently repeating, *He'll be there tonight, he'll be there tonight.*

The phone rang and Anne-Marie heard her mother storm across the dining room floor. At first she didn't hear much, but then her mother's voice rose.

"I knew we should have sold two years ago! You never listen to me, Henry!"

Anne-Marie hated when her mother yelled at her father; she'd rather get the brunt of the rage herself. Money had always been the last concern in the Entwhistle household. Using garden peonies as centerpieces shouldn't feel like a big thing, but it did. Usually the florist's truck arrived on Lady Luncheon morning with giant arrangements of roses and exotics. These concessions killed her mother, she knew, and she wondered what other sacrifices would be in order. There was a trust for her education, but she couldn't imagine packing for Vassar while her family's fortunes dwindled.

"Well, what about your own family? We'll be the next ones on the street!"

Mother quickened her pace, rubbing the spoon so hard she felt the filigree beneath the cloth. As if an array of gleaming utensils could rescue her family. She lay the final spoon in its velvet compartment and lifted the mahogany box. As Anne-Marie walked toward the dining room balancing the box on her forearms, her mother's voice chilled her to the bone.

"Useless! Absolutely useless is what you are!"

For a moment, Anne-Marie thought *she* was the useless one. She looked into the crystal chandelier with tear-filled eyes. The pendulum in the Seth Thomas grandfather clock ticked back and forth. She was so tired. Then she realized the insult was directed at her father, and a rage started to boil in her veins. Her fatigue, her frustration with Catherine, her longing for Heathcliff, and most of all her anger at her mother electrified her. She was sick of trying to be good and perfect when chaos was obviously swelling around her. She understood for the first time that the perfection that ruled her home had a name: tyranny. Yes, her mother had always been difficult, but now that her luxurious life was threatened, she'd become abusive. Anne-Marie dropped the box on the dining room table hard, and all the silver rattled.

Her mother turned abruptly and shot her a dirty look. "I have to go, Henry. We'll finish this discussion later." She set the phone in its cradle and turned toward Anne-Marie. "I don't need this right now, Anne-Marie."

"Why are you so mean to him?"

"Mean? Your father and I were having a discussion."

"You talk to him like he's stupid."

"I should be running that business! Your father doesn't have the sense to—"

"Stop saying bad things about him!"

"Lower your voice."

"He's my father!"

Edith clucked. She pulled a cigarette from a silver holder on the buffet and tapped it against her palm. "How sweet. Taking his side. You're the one who should worry. Your trust's in his name till you turn twenty-one."

"What do you mean?"

"I'm looking out for you. Do you think you'll meet the right sort of man if you're stuck at some state school?"

"I don't care about that!"

"You think you don't. But you'll wise up. Reduced circumstances have derailed the dreams of many a girl. I won't let that happen to you. Call me the bad guy, if you must."

"Are you saying I might not be able to go to Vassar?"

"Leave that to me. Just go upstairs, Anne-Marie, and quit being melodramatic. Cool your head in the shower."

"I hate you."

"I suppose you do. But someday you'll understand." She pointed her cigarette at the swinging pendulum of the grandfather clock. "The ladies will be here in forty-two minutes."

Edith turned and walked in the opposite direction, toward the parlor. "Get control of yourself." Her chin was lifted as she walked away, her heels clicking on the hardwood, but Anne-Marie saw that the fingers pinching her cigarette were trembling.

When the doorbell rang and the first guest alighted on the door-step, Edith was all smiles and graciousness. The ladies oohed and aahed over the table setting, the pies, the cucumber and egg-salad finger sandwiches, the punch bowl with foamy sherbet. Anne-Marie, dressed in her mother's linen suit, felt like a fraud as she recited her college plans a dozen times. One gloved and lipsticked matron nodded with approval as Anne-Marie listed her fall class schedule. She had a sinking feeling that she wouldn't attend a single class, especially if her parents were going broke. Another lady said that Vassar girls had their pick of the Ivy League boys. Anne-Marie replaced the image of argyle-vested boys with one of Heathcliff's face. If she was going to be stuck here, nothing could keep her from him. Clean-cut boys didn't interest her; anything that might please her mother didn't interest her. She wouldn't let money rule her decisions. As the women took their seats, Anne-Marie quickly chugged down another glass of the spiked punch.

She picked at her lunch, then found an easy escape by helping Gretta in the kitchen. She had a feeling Gretta had heard the fight with her mother, because as she handed her a scraped plate she said, "Your mother under lot of pressure these days."

"I'm so sick of her!"

"That's normal. All girls want to get away from their parents."

"I think my dad's going broke."

"He smart man. He figure out way to make things right."

"I hope so." Mother scraped another plate of sandwich crusts and smeared mayonnaise into the garbage.

"What about Katerina? How long she planning to stay?"

"I'm sorry she's so mean to you."

"She not scare me."

"I wish she'd just go back to wherever she came from. But I don't even know what to do. I just want her to stay calm."

"Maybe we give her little sleeping potion. Keep her in her room."

"That would be great!" Mother was determined to look for Heathcliff by herself that night. She rushed over and wrapped her arms around Gretta's waist. "Thank you!"

* * *

That night, Mother tried to keep Catherine calm until Gretta finally came into Mother's bedroom with her sleeping potion— hot tea and whiskey. Catherine, still in her nightgown, looked at Gretta scornfully. She'd spent the day in and out of feverish dreams, moaning and perching on the edge of the wingback chair, then collapsing on the bed. Mother had never in her life seen such a pale complexion—bluish and porcelain, but her lips were dark blue-red.

"We have no time for tea!" Catherine cried. "We must go find him!"

"Yes, but you need to drink some tea first, to get your strength up."

Gretta placed the tray on the nightstand without saying a word, though Mother knew she was holding back. She silently left the room, pulling the door gently behind her. Mother poured the tea into a cup and handed it to Catherine.

Catherine took a sip, then drew back, a sour look on her face.

"It's a special brew." Mother didn't mention that it was Gretta's remedy for manic English girls. "It will give you strength to climb out the window."

Catherine swallowed it down, then she began to rave. The usual complaints: Edgar's unfairness, Nelly's insensitivity. Mother was exhausted by it, but she listened, brushed Catherine's hair with long strokes, said soothing words, until finally Catherine fell back on the bed. Mother didn't bother to coax her beneath the sheets. She wanted only to get the hell away from her.

After eleven, Mother headed down the sheet rope, her heart as heavy as the humidity. The woods seemed miles from the house. Tonight she felt like a different girl: a girl whose future looked bleak, a girl who no longer wished to put others' needs before her own. She was tired of being treated like a servant by her mother and Catherine. What was she getting out of any of it? Her mother had planted an evil seed: was her father abandoning her? She had to push away her doubts. She looked up at the sliver of a moon, a golden crescent. Would Catherine be here forever? She couldn't bear the responsibility for anyone else's plot after all. She wanted her own story to begin, one utterly different from what Edith had scripted. As she entered the woods, she looked back to see a faint golden light in her bedroom window. She could have sworn she'd turned it off.

Once her eyes adjusted to the woods, the sky seemed to brighten, the leaves and branches becoming a stark contrast. She headed down the usual paths, calling Heathcliff's name. Her voice sounded pathetic and desperate to her. She entertained the idea of running off with him. She'd been groomed all her life to be quarry, but this time she was the pursuer, seeking something that would make her feel like somebody else. The frogs in the pond croaked unceasingly. Far off she heard the rumble of a truck. There was life out there, roads traveled by cars with people who had direction and purpose. What was she doing out here, chasing down a fictitious hero?

"Are you alone?"

His voice shook her. She held out her arms, looking over each shoulder, stunned to have found what she'd been looking for. Suddenly she realized that all her anxiety stemmed from one fear: not finding him. "Where are you?"

"Here." He stepped out from behind a tree. "Where is Catherine?"

"Ill. Again."

"I don't want to see her again. I hid from you last night. It's useless. Let her marry that half a man! That's what she deserves."

Anne-Marie didn't say anything. Her joy at being near him overwhelmed her. She couldn't believe the electricity she felt in her blood, her body. He wanted nothing to do with Catherine? She was thrilled and terrified. Her weariness evaporated. "What will you do now?"

"I'll find my way."

"I wish you would stay," she heard herself say. The frogs chirped in the silence that fell between them. His boots creaked as he stepped closer to her.

"Why?"

"I'd like to get to know you better."

Laughing, he reached out and took a lock of her hair in his hand. "Certain of that, are you?"

"Not at all." She raised her hand to brush back the hair and saw her fingers tremble. He took hold of them. A train whistle blew. He kissed her fingers. She fell against him. He was so tall. He kissed her lips. His face was thick with stubble. She felt the earth shift. Then she felt wood chips beneath her back. The kiss turned into a touch into a disrobing into a penetration. Before she knew what had hit her.

When it was over, when he'd shuddered, then collapsed on top of her, Mother opened her eyes. There on the path, glowing in a white nightgown, stood Catherine, her mouth wide open. For a moment their eyes met, then Catherine screamed and ran off. Heathcliff leapt to his feet and chased after her. Mother never saw either one again.

PART IV

+

The End

CHAPTER 30

✦ *Back to the present action* ✦ *Hearty carnivores* ✦ *I wonder if I'm a Heroine* ✦ *I question reality itself* ✦

Thirteen years later, in the same woods where I was conceived, I hid with another Hero, a Celtic king. It was late afternoon, and we were waiting for Albie (perhaps the true Hero) to return with word from the Homestead. We had sent him off with a note to my mother, telling her I'd run away. Since then, Conor had gone back to our first camp and brought back the deer, while I hung out in the tent, in a drug-withdrawal fog mollified by periodic tokes on Albie's weed. My paranoia was intensifying. Albie had told me that Nixon was scheduled to resign from office any day now; it seemed like everything was off. Only one day had passed since my escape from the Unit, yet it felt like a week. Thinking about Dr. Keller stimulated a fresh wave of anger toward my mother. How could she have signed me into the Unit? Part of me hoped she was worried sick; another part felt sorry about what Albie had said: that Mother, as much as any other Heroine, needed a break from her story line.

I smelled smoke and crawled out to see Conor by the fire with the deer. My head felt better, and the pot had stimulated my appetite such that I was long past squeamishness about Conor's venison. I was actually craving it. Surviving the Unit and living in the woods had toughened me; fresh air and grass-induced munchies made me ravenous. We sat on a log outside the tent, chunks of greasy meat between our fingers. I'd gotten used to eating without a knife in the Unit. I took a big bite of the meat and licked my fingers. Slobbering over smoked meat felt terrific, and my lack of fussiness made me feel strong.

Conor ate with little enjoyment, chewing slowly as he gazed into the woods without seeing them. He had the blues. It was odd to see this capable and strong king looking vulnerable, and it didn't fit my ideas about ancient heroes, who always had a plan, and groveling underlings to do their bidding. I knew it wounded his pride not to have caught Deirdre yet. The weeks in the woods were wearing on him; his beard was long and scraggly, his hair full of tangled knots.

He picked up some twigs and fed the fire. "It's been too long since I saw the walls of the Twinkling Hoard!" Conor began his rant about axes, skulls, gold-rimmed vessels, etc., which always recharged his self-esteem. Sharp rays of orange light pierced the scrub, the last daggers of sunset, and I picked up long thin branches and cracked them over my knee to add to the fire. Albie had been gone for hours. Something rustled in the leaves, and I imagined billy clubs beating back the brush. I stood frozen, one foot in the air, and looked over my shoulder. The sun seemed to set all at once, and the fire roared, night fell, making the trees suddenly blacker than the sky.

I sat next to the fire and watched the flames. Whether it was the withdrawal or a pot flashback, I couldn't tell, but I started to see evil faces outlined in the flames—wide eye sockets, mouths stretched in terror. We both grew quiet, and I began wondering what was taking Albie so long. My doubts that he would return grew, as did my fear of Conor. When he dragged his hands down his face and I saw the shimmering hair on his knuckles, he looked animal. I didn't want him handed over to law enforcement, but I wracked my brain trying to remember if any Heroine ever could have benefited from the arrival of a Hero. Not Madame Bovary and Rodolphe, not Anna Karenina and Vronsky. Everything about Conor spelled Villain, especially his certainty that he had a *right* to Deirdre. It wasn't a subtle enough conflict for a genuine Hero. But his bold rescue of me at the Unit was kingly—he was a liberator! And that was huge to me. Huge.

It dawned on me, as I studied the blue light at the base of the golden flames, that maybe I was a character in a book. The same way Albie had wondered whether a memory was a dream or real, so it struck me suddenly that my very existence might be nothing more than a string of words along a page, sentences building into paragraphs, paragraphs into chapters, and all of it an invention. If this were the case, did anything I do matter?

I stood up, and my knees buckled. What if I were a Heroine destined for tragedy? Conor ran to my side and helped me back into the tent.

"Rest is what you need."

I nodded, dropped carefully to my knees, and crawled into the tent. I didn't want to think about it anymore. I couldn't get it straight in my head. If this wasn't real, then there was another version of me back home, somebody who could be talking with Albie on the phone, chatting with Gretta, helping Mother with the garden. I wanted this to be the story, the nightmare—and not the reality—so that sleep would lead me back home.

CHAPTER 31

+ The reappearance of a Heroine +
The dreadful trade + The end +

I awoke to the sound of footsteps plodding through the dead leaves. I sat bolt upright; my heart pounded and my thoughts began to race the way they had the day before, as if my brain were on fast-forward, a scrambled, high-speed re-creation of all the events of the past month: Conor, the lawns of the Unit, white hospital gowns, the scent of Jean Naté. The aftertaste of venison soured my mouth. And I wondered, again, was any of this real? Somebody was out there.

I got to my feet. Albie must be back with word from the Homestead. Conor wasn't in the tent. Maybe he didn't really exist. This was it! I was going to find out what was real, real, real. I had no idea what time it was; it felt as if I'd been asleep for hours, and my body was electrified, and words flew through my head—*real, real, real*—but everything felt foggy, groggy, foggy, groggy, foggy. What was real? I would find out what was real. If Albie had seen the real me back at the Homestead, then I would know that this time in the woods was fantasy. The Penny right here wasn't real. The Penny over there was.

"Where's the girl?" a man's voice shouted. "Out of there, now."

I heard the hiss of a walkie-talkie. I couldn't believe it. Albie had brought the cops! That meant that the real me was here, that no other Penny existed at the Homestead. I held my breath. No. This couldn't be real. They couldn't be looking to bring me home; they wanted to take me back to the Unit. I listened for Conor's voice and heard nothing. He was probably gone, he probably had never existed. I'd been holed up with a madman in the woods. I crawled back to the mattress, pressed against the plastic sheeting. I couldn't go back to the Unit! Something clicked inside my head, and my thoughts felt like they were rolling in reverse, and the reversal retriggered my headache. Just before my eyes adjusted to the dark, a spider web swept across my face. I shrank back and crouched on the floor. They were coming with the restraints!

Somebody was swatting at the shelter door. I knew it was Eleanor, summoning me back to the Unit. *It's Eleanor!* my head shouted. *Eleanor, Eleanor, Eleanor!* I crawled on shaky hands toward the door.

"She's in there," somebody said.

"Come on out now, Penny," Eleanor said.

"I'm not going back there!" I shouted. "You can't make me!" I crawled between the mattresses, my legs shaking. I thought of Kristina and Keller and Peggy and, most of all, the hated Eleanor, who'd trooped all the way across the woods in the middle of the night just to get me, to get me! I had to be as strong as Scarlett, staring down the Yankee soldier who held her mother's sewing box. But the shelter was so dark, and the rustle of sounds outside could be anything. I couldn't trust my senses. I didn't really know what was out there, and without a visible enemy as real as a desperate Yankee, my will began to falter.

The flap rustled, and suddenly I found myself looking into the wide eyes and flaring nostrils of Officer Marone, the tall cop who'd come to the house the night I'd first met Conor.

"It's all over now." He reached a hand to me.

"I won't go back there!"

"We're taking you home," he said. "C'mon. It's all right now. Your mother's here."

Ears ringing, my mind deranged, I crawled out of the tent to find Mother standing before me. With the fire backlit behind her, I saw only her silhouette, the long wavy hair, the short-sleeved T-shirt and ankle-length skirt. She grabbed me hard and hugged me, and as I looked over her shoulder, my eyes adjusting to the dark, what I saw next flipped everything around again. Beneath a tree, Albie stood behind one of the wheelbarrows from the Homestead. Inside of it sat Deirdre, bound at the wrists and ankles, duct tape over her mouth. She stared at me with hard, cold eyes, her long curls covering her chest and shoulders. I was frozen in place. Conor stood beside her; the look of triumph on his face struck me as smug.

"Deirdre! At last!"

Marone turned to Conor. "We want to trade, Conor. Penny for Deirdre."

Mother was offering up a Heroine. I couldn't believe my eyes or ears. The thing I'd wished for all along. Mother was putting me before a Heroine, but I was horrified. Seeing Deirdre tied up deepened my paralyzing shock. My brain felt squeezed in a vise, and then it released, and the blood drained from my head and I thought I would pass out. There was no way any of this could be real. It couldn't! I dropped to my knees, unable to believe how Deirdre stood up to Conor, even when bound and gagged. It had taken this brutal abduction to secure her surrender.

Deirdre wiggled and tried to talk from behind the tape. Her long blond curls fell over the metal edge of the wheelbarrow.

Conor drew his sword and pointed it at Marone. "What unmanly way is this to bring her in?"

Marone held up his hands. "Easy there, big fella."

"You dare to threaten the King of Ulster?"

"Conor!" I yelled. "You've got Deirdre. Take her now, just go!" I dropped to my knees and held my mother's arm.

"I'm okay, Penny," Mother said. We held each other tight, both speechless, witnessing a spectacle Mother had always tried to avoid.

Deirdre squirmed against the ropes and mumbled into the tape. Conor ripped the tape from her mouth, and Deirdre spat out a curse. "I'll never spare you much love!"

"You'll spare what I take!" he said. "Unbind her feet!"

Marone obeyed, stooping to loosen the clothesline knotted around her ankles. Deirdre stiffened, pressed her arms to her sides, unyielding as a piece of plywood. I thought she might lash out and kick Marone, but she was stiff with dignity. I couldn't stop watching her. Once she was on her feet, her hands still bound behind her back, she raised her chin and started to chant. "If all of Ulster's warriors were gathered on this plain, Conchobor, I would gladly give them all for Noisiu, son of Uisliu."

Conor said nothing in response, but simply leaned on his sword and drew his horse closer to him. I hardly recognized his manner; Deirdre's presence had transformed him into the regal man I'd met that first night in the woods.

Albie shook his head, muttering, "Holy shit."

I looked up into the trees, into the heavens. The sky was turning a lighter blue between the branches, and I saw through the shrubs a ribbon of pink on the horizon. A male cardinal began to whistle, and a crow cawed right afterward. Another cardinal answered the male's call, and then a catbird did a squeaky imitation. How could they carry on with their morning songs in the middle of all this? I looked at Mother, her face frozen, her mouth ajar; she was witnessing the first return of a Heroine to her story. This was our life, not some distant political tragedy, and much as I would have liked to, I couldn't change the channel. Mother couldn't comment from a cool distance. For a weird moment, I wanted to cover her eyes, so she wouldn't have to see this cold surrender. Betraying a Heroine would kill her, I thought, and vomit rose in my throat. I hunched over and puked venison in the dirt.

I heard the horse, and I rose up to see it lift its knees and clomp in place beside Conor, who tightened the reins. The horse relaxed and allowed him to mount. Conor waved his hand for Marone to lift Deirdre up. Marone grabbed her by the waist and lifted her high. She sat sideways in front of Conor, her chin tilted up, and I remembered how he had pulled me up by my hair and carried me like a bundle of wheat weeks before. Deirdre's dignity and courage surpassed her great beauty, and any envy I had of her melted away. She tucked her long curls beneath the collar of her nightgown and crossed her feet. Conor grasped her around the waist, kicked the horse, and they rode off, in the opposite direction from the prairie.

I closed my eyes as Mother wiped my mouth with her sleeve and caressed my head. It was the most comforting touch I'd felt in weeks. I was unbelievably relieved to be near her again, to feel her cool hands on my hot forehead. I listened to the retreating hoof-beats, not wanting to feel the absence of this king who'd neither said good-bye nor thank you.

Epilogue

When we returned to the Homestead, I was so exhausted I slept late into the next afternoon. My withdrawal dreams were vivid and kaleidoscopic, and though I can't remember any precise sequences, I imagine they were filled with horses and nurses or anxious visions of returning to Prairie Bluff Academy a different girl. Still, the comfort of my duvet, the cross-breezes of my bedroom, soothed me like no medication ever would. I knew then something that I would never forget: meddling with the Heroines was not worth it.

Desperate and looking for someone to turn to, Mother had taken Marone completely into her confidence. After I'd been hospitalized, he'd checked in several times on Mother, and they'd struck up a friendship. With his help they managed to call off the search and ensure that I wouldn't get sent back to the Unit.

Slowly, things returned to normal. After the furious Unit energy and my jittery nights in the woods, just getting up for breakfast seemed a luxury. I cherished the calm Homestead hallways, the hum of locusts on summer nights. Marone came over the night of Nixon's resignation, and we all sat on the couch and watched the sorry spectacle. Mother and he were relieved to see the man get his due, but his stooped shoulders and billowing jowls made me feel sad and sorry for him, in a way that would confuse me for years.

How could I feel sorry for someone so crooked, especially when Mother was so delighted? Distinguishing Villains from Heroes would always be hard for me.

Later that week, Gretta and Mother sat me down in the kitchen and told me about my father. Ever since I was born, Mother had lived in mortal fear that one day I would disappear back into Heathcliff's story, that he might come back for me. That was why she had always warned me against wandering the woods alone. Mother had sent me to the Unit because she thought I would be safe there. That I wouldn't disappear.

"But no Heroine has ever returned," I said.

"Not yet," Mother said.

"These two—Heathcliff and Catherine. They were a lot of trouble!" Gretta said. "Your mother was only young girl. She was no match for them."

"And you're even younger than I was then, Penny," Mother said. "I didn't know how you would fare against a full-fledged king."

"Conor was all right," I said. I didn't want to tell her about his code for sleeping with women. I knew it would only worry her more.

"I want to read the book," I said. "I want to know who my real father is."

"He was a tough character," Gretta said.

"Was he evil?" I asked.

"Maybe just misunderstood," Mother said. "He came from a very different time. But I think maybe you should wait. It's a lot to take in after everything you've been through."

Accepting the news that my father was not a football player from Lincoln Park, but instead a Villain from fiction, didn't come easily. Thirteen was probably the worst age for me to find out. I'd never read *Wuthering Heights,* of course, because Mother had burned her only copy. She still tried to shelter me from it (censorship went against her grain on every other front), but the book wasn't hard to track down in the library. I read it on the sly, tucked the paperback copy under my mattress, and pulled it out to read by flash-light at night. The blurb on the back called Heathcliff a "savage, tormented foundling." We had one thing in common: dicey pater-nity. Yet his was worse, as he'd also been abandoned by his mother. He'd never felt accepted by his adopted family, who harped on his so-called Gypsy looks. Reading his physical description, I knew that I took after my mother, but his character disturbed me. How cruel he was to Isabella, Linton's sister. He'd married Isabella only to get back at Linton for marrying Catherine. Heathcliff and Catherine's passion didn't mean much to me at that age, and I found her fits and fevers annoying. Nelly, the narrator, even implied that Heathcliff might be a changeling—a being with supernatural powers (put to ill use). I started to wonder if there might be some-thing evil in me, that his ugly nature had been transferred through the genes. I became self-conscious about my temper, checking myself when I felt I might be displaying some melodramatic Hero-ine tendencies. I wondered if my need to compete with the Hero-ines for Mother's attention in some way resembled Heathcliff's jealousy of Linton.

Sometimes I wondered if Mother had made the whole thing up, out of some adolescent self-aggrandizement. In public I still continued to say that my father was dead, a former high school football star. But then these feelings of demi-reality would over-come me. At times I felt half real, half illusory, a feeling that con-tinues to bother me to this day. No therapist can coax me out of it, because there is no one I can confess this to who wouldn't want me immediately hospitalized and medicated. I've sometimes wished for children of my own, hoping to dilute the Heathcliff gene pool, but I feared that his genes might dominate, and I'd have children whom I'd eventually fear.

After I read *Wuthering Heights,* I rooted around the Prairie Bluff Library until I finally dug up the story of "Deirdre of the Sorrows." Everything Conor had told me in the woods was there: the druid Cathbad's prophecy that Deirdre, who cried out in her mother's womb ("the weird uproar at your waist"), would be the downfall of many Ulster warriors. Once Conor heard that she would be the most beautiful woman of all time, he wanted her for himself, even though the other Ulstermen wanted her dead.

Reading about Conor, seeing him portrayed in the one-dimensional print, unleashed extremely painful feelings. I suddenly recalled the heft of his body, his voice, his beard—I'd been so close to him; I'd been in love with him in my own childish way.

Deirdre grew up in seclusion with her foster parents, grew into "a woman with twisted yellow tresses, green-irised eyes of great beauty and cheeks flushed like foxglove." The story said that "High queens will ache with envy" and lowly girls did too. Deirdre's dream man would have all the colors of a crow drinking blood in the snow: black hair, red cheeks, fair skin. And along came Noisiu, whose ears Deirdre grabbed as she said, "Two ears of shame and mockery if you don't take me with you!"

Deirdre had such drive, forcing Noisiu and his brothers to escape with her. Then the men of Ulster tricked the sons of Uisliu into thinking they'd be safe if they came home, but when the exiled ones reached Ulster, "Eogan welcomed Noisiu with the hard thrust of a great spear that broke his back." Then all the sons of Uisliu were murdered, and Deirdre was captured. That was when she came to the Homestead. Pages of Deirdre's heartbroken poetry followed, how she refused to eat or sleep and spent a year with her head on her knees.

The final paragraph tore through me like shrapnel. Deirdre was trapped in a chariot, with Eogan and Conor on either side of her, though she'd sworn that two men would never have her. "You're a sheep eying two rams, Deirdre," Conor chided her. Then Deirdre swung her head out of the chariot and smashed it to bits on a rock.

I sat stunned. She'd killed herself. Just like Madame Bovary and Anna Karenina. I couldn't stand it, especially when I recalled her courage when we turned her over to Conor. I pulled a notebook out of my bag and started to write. In my story, Deirdre lived, went on to become a great woman warrior. She had a dozen children who became great leaders of Ulster. But then I stopped and tore up the sheet. The original ending had a purpose. Her suicide was different than Emma Bovary's. It was a kamikaze move to save herself from falling into enemy hands.

I pressed my pen to the next page and wrote about an eighteen-year-old girl who finds true love with a handsome stranger. He takes her away to his house on the moors, and they live together with their darling daughter. The love of the girl Anne-Marie changes the man, softens him. He teaches his daughter to ride horses and hunt. And they all live happily ever after. They live immortally in the pages of *Wuthering Heights,* which had enormous fiscal success in its day, but has no timeless quality to it.

I flip the page and write "Real Ending." I am not the skittish girl in the cold library. Mother forgives me, and I forgive her. Deirdre meets her exact fate. Mother goes on to live in the Homestead; she marries Officer Marone. After Vassar I become the *gardienne* of the Homestead. I welcome Heroines and I never mess with their fates. Franny stops by for holidays. I bury Mother in 2025. And my father never ever returns.

Acknowledgments

For their priceless support during the writing of this book, I thank Cecilia Pinto and Lisa Reardon. I thank my agent, Jennifer Rudolph Walsh, for her enthusiasm and spirited contributions to this book. Hats off to Nan Graham at Scribner for brilliant editing and peerless vision. Many thanks to Anna deVries and Claudia Ballard for their always-kind attentiveness.

I thank the Ragdale Foundation and the wonderful staff who, on many occasions, provided me a break from my narrative line in the lovely home that inspired this work. Thanks to Jim and Purcell Palmer for a glorious residency in the Catwalk tower. For fiscal support during the writing of this work, I thank the Illinois Arts Council and the School of the Art Institute of Chicago. Thanks also to Dr. John Mayer for his precise descriptions of adolescent psychiatric wards in the 1970s.

I thank my parents, Tom and Dolores Favorite, for having only one TV and tons of books around the house. Thanks to my brothers and sisters: Eddie, Reets, Therese, Martha, M.B., Art, Laura, and Phil. *Merci à ma belle-mère,* Françoise Laval, for providing *un petit coin pour écrire à Belle-Ile.*

For their guidance and inspiration, I thank Julia Alvarez, Carol Anshaw, Rosellen Brown, Roderick Coover, Barbara Croft, James McManus, Christine Ney, and Beth Nugent.

Finally, thanks to Martin Perdoux for all his love and faith over the years.

A SCRIBNER
READING GROUP GUIDE

Why I Wrote *The Heroines*

Eileen Favorite

What inspires any author's book is a mixture of the conscious and the unconscious, the imagined and the real, everything the author has read and written. For that reason, I know what precipitated the idea for *The Heroines,* but I cannot say that I completely understand or can name all the influences at work. I can, however, tell the story of how I came to write the book.

Ten months after my brother Eddie's death, I arrived at Ragdale, a writer's residency on a prairie in Lake Forest, Illinois. I had no project planned, but the reality of my brother's death made me yearn for an escape into an imaginary realm. I was also wondering what constitutes a life well lived. I began the book imagining what would happen if a saint returned to contemporary America. But when I put St. Therese of Lisieux in the same room as Penny, the feisty thirteen-year-old girl who had somehow already claimed a place in my story, I found that St. Therese responded flawlessly to Penny's every bad turn. I needed more tension.

At the time I was reading *At Swim-Two-Birds* by Flann O'Brien. O'Brien brings back characters of Irish literature to interact with contemporary characters. So, I thought, let's have Heroines not saints. Flaws are what make characters interesting and create drama. O'Brien also discusses how writers deliberately make life tough for their characters and how unfair that is. Reading O'Brien poking fun at writers gave me the idea of providing great Heroines a refuge, a break from their authors' deliberate tricks. They could go to the Homestead, Penny's mother's bed-and-breakfast on the Illinois prairie. This reprieve was terrific for the Heroines, but what effect would it have on the mother and daughter who housed them?

Visual images also inspired the book. Ragdale's arts-and-crafts main house reminded me of the great manors that are the Heroines' rewards in ninteenth-century English novels. I wanted to twist this romantic and bourgeois notion by introducing magic into this setting. By attracting Heroines from other novels, the Homestead is not Anne-Marie's reward so much as her burden.

I also liked the image of a girl angrily marching through a beautiful prairie landscape, and the nightly expeditions I took in the prairie and woods behind Ragdale inspired the fairy-tale appearance of Conor, the king on horseback. With Conor, I had discovered the plot "twist"—the arrival of a man to retrieve a Heroine—and also several important themes: the conflict of what constitutes a Hero; the power struggles between men and women; and the fallacy of the "knight in shining armor."

Differences in age, experience, and personality pull Penny and Anne-Marie apart. They respond to Conor in different ways, further widening the gap between mother and teenage daughter. How has being raised in a literature-driven household affected Penny? How has keeping secrets changed her? Does believing that fictitious characters are real make her a little crazy? Once these conceits were in place, the book took off of its own accord, leading me in directions I didn't anticipate (the hospital) and toward a conclusion I didn't foresee.

The Heroines

Discussion Questions

1. The book opens with Penny meeting a king on horseback in the woods. How is this situation like a fairy tale and how is it different? What is Penny's relationship to the woods?
2. Do you agree with Penny's desire to prevent Emma Bovary from killing herself? Do you agree with Anne-Marie's rule about not interfering? Have you ever held back from interfering with a friend's or family member's problems? Has interfering ever gotten you in trouble?
3. Why did Anne-Marie agree to commit Penny? Do you agree with her reasons?
4. In the chapter on Franny Glass, what's the philosophical difference between Franny's view of the world and Anne-Marie's? Do you think that Penny is against her mother's brand of feminism? Do you think Penny benefited from it?
5. Why is it so important for Penny to be appreciated by Franny?
6. What are the differing approaches in the hospital and how do they hurt or help the girls? Dr. Keller seems more interested in filling beds than in curing the girls. Do you think that mental health care is driven by insurance policies?

7. Why did Penny open up to Kristina? What does Penny learn from Scarlett O'Hara? How does being in the hospital change Penny?

8. How did Edith Entwhistle's brand of mothering affect Anne-Marie's?

9. Why does Anne-Marie betray Catherine? Is Catherine an appealing guest? How does her character compare to Anne-Marie's?

10. Penny questions reality at the end of the novel, wondering whether she's a fictional character. Have you felt that Penny and Anne-Marie are more "real" than the Heroines who visit? Are there fictional characters that you consider real people?

11. What effect does learning who her real father is have on Penny? Do you think she would have been better off knowing his identity at a younger age?

12. Richard Nixon's demise coincides with the story's conclusion. What effect did his resignation have on Penny?

13. At the end of the book, Penny says that Deirdre's suicide is a feminist act—"a kamikaze move." Do you agree with this? How does it differ from Madame Bovary's eating arsenic?

14. What Heroine of literature would you like to see visit the Prairie Homestead? What characteristics do the Heroines have in common?

About the Author

Eileen Favorite teaches at the School of the Art Institute of Chicago, where she received her MFA in writing in 1999. The Illinois Arts Council has awarded her two fellowships in prose and poetry. She lives in Chicago with her husband and daughter.